FACE
OF THE
ASSASSIN

BILL BREWER

THRILLEX Publishing

Copyright 2020 by Bill Brewer
Cover Design by Jennifer Greef

Dedicated to you, the reader.

Thank you for choosing this book.

The reader's enjoyment is the author's reward.

Praise for Bill Brewer

K. Allen

☆ ☆ ☆ ☆ ☆ **Love this book!**

Love this book! The combination of engaging characters and detailed accounts made it hard to put down. Looking forward to the whole series of David Diegert books.

Lee Anne

☆ ☆ ☆ ☆ ☆ **One heck of a ride!**

This book started out fast and didn't let up. An excellent book of action and suspense. Well written and engaging.

Jarod Farchione

☆ ☆ ☆ ☆ ☆ Made me a fan of fiction again!

Brewer's writing reads like an action movie, while being tactical, well-paced, and realistic in all of the ways I enjoy. I highly recommend this book.

Jimmy Ray

☆ ☆ ☆ ☆ ☆ Assassin on the Run

Characters are well developed, the story is exciting to follow, and it's a fun read. If you like action and adventure, you will love this one. A great story pulls the reader in, and this one had me from the first page.

Jeffrey Miller

☆ ☆ ☆ ☆ ☆ **A Real Page-Turner!**

As soon as I started reading, I couldn't put it down. Bill Brewer delivers a hard-hitting, story that's as much cerebral as visceral. If you like your reading fast and powerful, you don't want to pass this one up!

CHAPTER 1

GUNFIRE ECHOING THROUGH ROOMS he hadn't cleared yet, raised the adrenaline rushing through David Diegert's blood. Tightening his grip on his M4, he pulled the stock into his shoulder as he lowered his gaze just beyond the end of the barrel. Stepping forward in a low crouch, he proceeded to the open doorway. He leaned up against the jamb, flashing a look inside. Two tangoes holding a hostage. In an instant, Diegert assessed the hostage to be exhausted and confused. The tangoes each held an AK, as well as holstered side arms.

Having survived an assassination attempt upon him and his father while on safari in Tanzania, Diegert was undergoing a training exercise within the underground labyrinth of the London Polytechnic University. The enemies he faced, and the hostage he was rescuing, were holographic, yet failure would lead to death for the human image he was attempting to free.

From his utility vest, Diegert selected a distraction grenade--an explosive device designed to give an operator a brief moment to apply deadly force. Diegert's grenade exploded in the far corner of the room, surprising the computer operators, whose holographic tangos reactions were slowed just enough for Diegert to fatally shoot them both. As the tangos' bodies dissolved, a relieved smile appeared on the hostage's face as she too pixelated into the ether.

Over the speakers came the voice of Sebastian Coburn, the computer programmer in charge of holographic technology, "Hey that was a rather dodgy use of a grenade."

"You said I could use anything on my vest."

"Yes, of course, but you could have blown up the hostage."

"That's bullshit. If you bother to look, your own sensors will show no damage."

"Screw you, Diegert."

"Fuck off. You're way too polite. You're just pissed cuz I kicked your ass."

In the changing area, Diegert took off his tactical vest and suit. The clothing had sensors, which recorded his biometrics. Measuring the physiological response of his body provided insight to the psychological state he experienced when facing lethal threat. David Diegert was unnaturally calm when facing violence. His subdued readings when bullets were flying made him the most lethal operator serving Crepusculous. As he got dressed, Diegert thought about what his father had said while flying back from Kenya. Even referring to Klaus Panzer as his father was strange enough, but his perception of the man was changing. Quite uncharacteristically, his father had told him he loved him, and wanted to spend the rest of his life building his empire with him. Fulfilling Diegert's wish for a father overpowered his inherent skepticism. He felt a bond forming between them, which he wanted to believe in, but was hesitant to trust. The buzz of his phone snapped him from his reverie. A text from Carolyn Fuller: *"We need to meet. Highland Park, noon tomorrow."*

Carolyn Fuller was the CIA Agent who helped Diegert return to Europe. Having recovered from her injuries inflicted by Fatima Hussain, she was now assigned to the London CIA office, after being denied permission to return to the United States. Operating in London, Carolyn continued to pursue leads in the assassination of President Peter Carson. She was also concerned with the U.S. locations of a dozen thermobaric bombs. Diegert was her source on that break and her man inside the secret and sinister Crepusculous. She needed intel on those explosives, and Diegert gave her information on Aaron Blevinsky. The wily and determined head of clandestine operations for Crepusculous--the man who orchestrated the placement of the bombs and remained in control of their detonation. The relationship between Carolyn and Diegert was complicated by the fact they'd made love while holed up in a cottage outside London.

Diegert replied to her text, *"Got it, meet you in the park tomorrow."*

AT NOON THE NEXT DAY, DIEGERT arrived at the park well ahead of the appointment to conduct his threat assessment. It surprised him to see that she had come early as well. His stubbly beard, ball cap and sunglasses disguised his looks so he was ignored by the joggers, moms with strollers, as well as the quiet elders observing life from their perches on park benches.

In London, rain is always a possibility but today was warm, and the sun filtered through the trees, creating a dappled mosaic of light. Curiously, Carolyn wore a long beige trench coat. The garment did not have the typical mid waist sash. It just hung from her shoulders to her ankles giving her the fashion appeal of a brown paper bag. Dressing for inclement weather shrouded Carolyn's athletic physique. Her shoulder length brown hair hung loose about her head, leaving it to blow in the mid-day breeze. Carolyn's attractive face and bright smile appeared subdued by an unconscious frown and the formation of diverging wrinkles at the corners of her eyes. Her tense expression was beginning to tell the next phase of her life's story.

As she passed by Diegert's position leaning against a tree, he fell in line with her gait, matching her pace.

"A hoodlum in the park? Is that the best disguise you could come up with?" asked Carolyn.

"A spy in a trench coat, paranoid about rain on a sunny day. You're not one to be casting aspersions. What's with the coat?"

"Shut up. Just keep walking."

Sticking to the footpaths, Carolyn led them out of the park along Kensington Boulevard and unto the London Bridge. She stopped in the middle of the bridge and turned to face Diegert.

"What are you doing?" he demanded. "It's nuts to stop in the middle of the bridge. The CCTV will pick it up and flag us." Diegert stepped around her to continue crossing the bridge. She quickened her pace, closed the gap and grabbed his arm. He yanked his arm away from her and kept walking. She jogged to re-join him.

"You're trying to get me busted. You're drawing them in, on the other side of the bridge aren't you?" said Diegert.

Keeping pace with his intensified walk, Carolyn said, "No I just want to talk where we can't be overheard."

"It won't matter if we're seen as suspicious."

"Well then, listen to me while we walk."

"Start talking."

As they progressed, Diegert watched the eyes of the

uniformed police officers stationed where the bridge met the street. Always vigilant, the officers scanned the crowd of pedestrians, but paid no special attention to Carolyn or Diegert. Off the bridge, Carolyn said, "Are you ready to listen?"

"No," said Diegert.

Turning down a side street, he looked for a sign extended over a door. The Red Rooster Inn was a tourist version of a British Pub. Diegert went inside and took a booth, facing Carolyn who remained in her trench coat. The waitress was quick, and Diegert ordered a pint of Old Speckled Hen while Carolyn requested Perrier.

"I followed up your intel on Blevinsky and the thermobaric bombs," said Carolyn.

Diegert nodded while tapping his fingers on the table.

Carolyn shot a glance around the pub before speaking. "He's a real piece of work. His record of juvenile offenses in Germany is extensive although I am denied the details. I doubt he's earned one single legal dollar his entire life."

Diegert shrugged. "He's rude and selfish as well, but you can't arrest him for any of that, so what."

"His track on the dark net is convoluted," Her tired face was set in a serious expression. "But our counter intel has set some traps for him which he has utilized."

The waitress returned with their drinks. He thanked her and waited until she was out of earshot before speaking. "What are these traps offering?"

"They're underground ordinance companies. They offer to set and manage clandestine explosives."

"But all his bombs are set."

She sipped her Perrier. "Apparently, thermobaric bombs require maintenance and some of the earlier contractors have moved on."

"Or been eliminated."

Nodding to the possibility, Carolyn said, "Yes, that as well. What we've uncovered is the location of one bomb in Cleveland set to go off during the NCAA Final Four basketball tournament."

"A televised attack."

"We're playing Blevinsky, so we can locate the other bombs, but he's skittish. He's limited us to just this one."

"You spook him, and he will turn on you."

"We're worried he'll just go to ground and stop all communication."

"Let him come to you. You solicit him, and he'll drop you like a stone."

"The other thing is, he's not in Romania anymore."

"And you don't know where he is?" asked Diegert.

"Correct."

"But you have contact with him through the net?"

"Correct."

"But you want to know his location?"

"If things go bad quickly, we want to be able to put our hands on him," insisted Carolyn.

"Just cuz you know where he is doesn't mean you'll be able to grab him whenever you want."

"Grabbing him is not my department, but locating him is. Can you gather that Intel?"

Taking a long draft of his Scottish brew, Diegert considered his response. With Panzer now treating him like a son, Diegert had a lot to lose by continuing to help the CIA. Nevertheless, these bombs could devastate the United States, killing millions of people while destroying his homeland. "I don't have direct access to this information. I'll have to ferret this out."

"Well then start ferreting. That's what spies do."

Diegert took another tug on his beer as he contemplated the request. Clandestine betrayal, that's what he was being asked. Seek the truth and share it with those who should never have it. For a man unable to return to the U.S., it seemed a risky proposition.

"Carolyn," Diegert began, "I have something to tell you."

Setting her Perrier back on the table and swallowing her sip, Carolyn said, "Okay, I'm listening."

"I've discovered who my real father is."

Carolyn focused on David's eyes. "Who?" she asked as Diegert avoided her gaze.

"I made this discovery the night you were injured. I went to the Ambassador Hotel. It was where they were holding my mother."

"Okay."

Diegert squirmed in the booth seat, bit his trembling lower lip, while rapping his fist against the table. He stammered, "Mmyy Faa-" Shaking his head as he gathered himself, David spoke in a deadpan tone. "My father is Klaus Panzer."

Carolyn leaned back and looked above David to no fixed point in the distance. She blinked her eyes repeatedly as she processed what she just heard. Diegert looked on, wondering if she believed him.

"Wow, that is a surprise," said the thoughtful CIA Agent.

"It surprised me too. It turns out my mom and Panzer had an affair at a fancy hunting lodge in Minnesota where she worked. Panzer was staying at the lodge and they had sex one night. I was the result, and she never contacted him about me. He never thought about her again, but he recognized her in the suite at the Ambassador. He put two and two together and my mom confirmed it."

Shaking her head with a far off stare Carolyn said, "It's like you two were destined to be brought together."

"Yeah, fucking mystical. I haven't told you 'til now because I wondered if you would stop using me as an asset."

Carolyn looked at him with a fixed gaze. "How does learning this make you feel? How is Panzer treating you?"

"It's amazing. The guy is so focused on himself and his own beliefs, that he just wants me to be his son. He wants me to love him, get along with him, help him build his empire and inherit his legacy."

"That's pretty intoxicating given that this guy really does have a fortune."

"I really don't care about all the money, but I believe I can get in even closer now that I am being treated like his son."

"We'll have to see how this works out, but David, I gotta say that wealth and power are forces of corruption. You're going to have to be mindful that the influence of money will change you."

Diegert heard her words, and when he was with her, he felt the righteousness of her mission and was impressed with her dedication to protecting the U.S. She gave him a sense of patriotism, which now had to compete with Panzer's paternal pull.

"I've been poor all my life. I'm used to living with little. What can all that money really do?"

Carolyn looked at him without responding. Diegert felt she doubted his resolve.

She said, "Resisting the corrupting force of power will be the biggest challenge of your entire life. I'll help you all I can."

Diegert looked at her, feeling as if she knew a lot more than he did about what he faced. "Why are you still here in London?" he asked. "Why haven't you been sent back to the U.S?"

Rolling her eyes while picking at the label on her bottle Carolyn said, "The Assistant Director of the British office has requested that I be assigned to London so I can assist on this case."

"And he got his way?"

"He was suspicious that I was involved in a plot regarding the President's assassination, although that is waning now that I have produced actionable intel."

"But you have to keep feeding the beast."

Pausing to furrow her brow Carolyn went on, "He is a beast."

Diegert picked up on her tension. "What do you mean?"

Rolling her eyes as she turned away, Carolyn said, "It's nothing really."

"I've found that when something is nothing, it's usually something."

Carolyn's narrowed eyelids, intensified her sneer.

Diegert slid his beer to the side and leaned forward across the table. "What?"

Carolyn shifted in the booth seat, peering into her lap.

"Tell me," said Diegert

"The guy's a pig."

She looked up to see Diegert offering eye contact while patiently waiting for her to find her voice. Carolyn's words mixed rage with tears. "He's so conceited and entitled. He's using his position to exert power over me." Wiping her cheek on her sleeve, Carolyn said, "God, I just can't believe my career has come to this." Biting her trembling lip, she snuffed the tears running through her nose.

Diegert slid a paper napkin across the table. She wiped her eyes and blew her nose.

"You mean he's making you work on this case?" asked Diegert.

"Well that, he doesn't have to do. I'm glad to do my job."

"What else then?"

"A few years back we were both at the Farm for training. I remember him as unremarkable and way too conceited for his lackluster performance. He was not in good shape, so he struggled with the physical ordeals we had to accomplish. He was not a team player, and I just wasn't impressed with him. But he kept coming on to me all week long. Finally when the week was over I skipped the goodbye party at the local bar just to avoid him, but he came back to the dormitory, wasted. He starts banging on my door saying all sorts of sexual stuff. I didn't even have to call security, they just showed up and took him away. He was disciplined and demoted. He had to work his way back up the ladder and London is part of his career climb. He's pissed because he thinks I called security on him, yet he's still got a hard on for me."

"Not a great situation, especially in a foreign country."

"Last Friday he asked for an update at 5:00 pm. I arrive at his office and he's got scotch on the rocks sitting on his desk. I tell him, I'm not meeting with him under these conditions. He starts telling me that after 5:00 pm it's okay, and I need to be more flexible. I turned around and left the building. He e-mailed a tirade about disrespect and insubordination, dereliction of duty and inappropriate characterization. I made sure to store that e-mail."

"So who's above him?"

"The director of the London office is a real good friend of Ramsey's father. I'm getting nowhere going up."

"Who would replace him if he left?"

"There's no way Richard will leave. The only way he goes is if he's called back to the States for a promotion."

"If he was called back how would that change things for you?"

Carolyn chuckled. "I don't know what would happen if he returned to Washington."

Tilting her gaze up, she set her elbow on the table and stroked her chin. "I suppose I'm the next highest ranking agent over here. I might have to assume an interim role until his replacement was dispatched."

"How long would that take?'

"I don't know, but it could be a while, especially since they have such a shortage of qualified people."

With head in hand, Diegert tapped his finger on his chin. "And his name is Richard Ramsey?"

Diegert saw Carolyn's eyes widen and her chin drop when he stated her boss's name.

Looking at her for a moment, the intimacy they shared flashed through his mind, and he smiled at her. Carolyn composed herself and smiled back. He hoped she was recalling their time together in the shower as well.

"David," she said, "I gotta go. I appreciate you sharing the information about your father. I'm not sure when we'll be in touch again, but don't let the money go to your head."

She slid to the edge of the booth and gradually stood up. The slow movement caught Diegert's eye, but he didn't mention it. After she left, Diegert sat in the booth finishing his beer. He thought about the corrupting power of money and wealth. He didn't have any experience with wealth.

He'd learned to get along with little because that's the way his life was. By the time he realized how poor his family was, he'd already formed a set of values that didn't see the worth in all sorts of unnecessary possessions. He found enjoyment in nature and realized that happiness came from experiences in the natural world, not wanting things he couldn't afford and really didn't need. Could he keep this perspective when he was now living with the world's richest man? He drained his beer and left the Red Rooster Inn as he searched the name Richard Ramsey on his phone.

CHAPTER 2

FATIMA HUSSAIN, WHOSE STRENGTH, guile and cunning made her the best female operative Crepusculous ever had, sat on the floor of Javier Perez's Sussex town house in London. Across from her sat her nine year old son Hamni, playing with Legos. Hamni's autism made it difficult for him to communicate his thoughts, feelings and needs. He formerly resided in a special service group home, but after Diegert kidnapped him from the facility and delivered him to Fatima, he was now with his mom. The bond between mother and son ran especially deep. Whenever he was with her, his limitations seemed to disappear.

"What are you building?"

"An airplane." Hamni held up his creation.

"Oh, okay. I can see it now. Does it fly in outer space?"

"It can fly around the moon and back."

With a beaming smile Fatima lifted what she had made. "Mine is a house, where a family lives."

"Are we going to live in that house?"

"I will build a house just like this one for you and me."

"Really?"

"Well, we'll see. I might have to build one a little bigger so we fit inside."

Giggling she reached out and tweaked his shoulder.

"I don't want to go back to that place I've been living. I want to stay with you."

Fatima felt the weight of reality descending upon her. Scooching closer, she put her arm around him. "I know. I want that too."

"Then let's do it. I will stay with you."

Hamni moved away and got busy clearing a spot on the floor.

"What are you doing?" asked Fatima.

"I'm going to make the big house you and I can live in."

Fatima smiled at his industrious imagination. Watching him lay out the floor plan and arrange the blocks he would need, she contemplated their tenuous position. Javier Perez was Hamni's father only because of a long ago one night stand of unprotected sex. He had not been aware of Hamni's birth until Fatima, homeless and alone, forced him to acknowledge his paternity and use a tiny piece of his wealth to pay for Hamni's residence in the special needs home. The deal was a tough bargain though, because in exchange she became an operative for Crepusculous. Her duties were directed and controlled by Aaron Blevinsky. She was moved to Romania, trained as an assassin and assigned to carry out lethal sanctions. Her determination and commitment made this stunningly attractive Pakistani Muslim woman an excellent killer of Crepusculous targets.

Now that David Diegert had "helped" free Hamni and deliver him to her, she was left with the responsibility of caring for him and figuring out how they would deal with their eventual discovery and the wrath of Blevinsky for her unexplained absence and the removal of Hamni from his residence. *Fuck it,* she thought, *I am not going back, and I'm keeping my son with me.*

"Hamni you keep working on the house, I'll be right back, okay?"

"Okay, Mommy."

The reply caught her off guard and her reaction to being called Mommy startled her. She was so surprised by the naturalness with which Hamni referred to her. She had missed that title for so long, she had to choke back a sob.

Down the massive staircase, she marched to find Javier stretched out on the couch watching televised futbol. She stood in front of the TV.

"Look, do you mind," said Javier. "This is my team."

"You soccer fans, you get so possessive."

"Yeah, except this is my team. I own it, and I want to see my investment succeed. Now would you please move?"

Stepping to the side and sitting down next to him, Fatima waited until the halftime break. Grabbing the remote, she silenced the TV.

"Hamni and I need another place to live. He's not going back to St. Andrews and I'm not going back to Blevinsky."

Slowly and reluctantly turning his gaze upon her, Javier snorted as he said, "Well then what's your plan?"

"Where else do you have a home?"

A bemused smile crept on to his lips. "You want to live in one of my other residences?"

Leaning in Fatima asked, "How many do you have?"

"What's in it for me?"

"You mean besides having your son raised by his mother. We both know you're no good at managing things. You may own the soccer team, but you don't run the businesses well." Pausing to let her assessment sink in, Fatima continued. "I can. I will be your behind the scenes brain. I will make you look smart and keep you from being manipulated into doing dumb things."

"That's your offer?"

Sliding closer to him, Fatima said in a seductive tone, "I will be the one person in this world with whom you can be honest."

Javier's look went from excited to resigned as her message sunk in.

She smiled. "Don't look so sad. It'll be fun and you won't have to be a phony all the time. Hamni is a great kid. Your father will love his grandson. I won't marry you and you can still screw around. What are the residence locations I have to choose from?"

Smirking Javier said, "Just like that, during the halftime of a futbol game, I'm to let you take over my life?"

"I'm not taking it over, but I am improving it. You will see that my skills and abilities go well beyond being an assassin. Of course, if you choose to be my enemy, I could kill you. It's always an option."

Fatima's glare was lethal, before she let a pleasant smile return. "Look, I'm not going to interrupt your life of leisure, your gambling trips and your sexual escapades. In fact I'm the person who can guarantee that you can keep doing all those things."

Javier's questioning expression gave Fatima the opportunity for which she had hoped.

"You have no one who is invested in your continuing to be an overindulged playboy," observed Fatima. "You need someone for whom your activities produce a mutual benefit. I can run the businesses while raising my son and keeping you enjoying the life to which you are accustomed." She smiled at Javier and gently stroked his chin with the tip of her finger. "If I fail, I lose everything and I'm a homeless assassin with a son. But I will not fail and we will succeed by growing your father's empire and remaining on top of the world."

She filled the pause with direct eye contact during which Fatima knew all she had to do was lean forward and kiss him, and he would turn to putty. She did not though. She realized she need not fuck him in order to control this selfish, immature man. Javier's extended adolescence, gave Fatima the opportunity to elevate her status and that of her son. Pulling back from the brink of sex she asked, "Which residence is the biggest?"

CHAPTER 3

HEARING HIS PHONE BUZZ, DIEGERT reached to his nightstand to pick it up. "Hello."

"Good morning, David. This is Dr. Marie Zeidler."

"Yes."

"I'm calling you with news about your mother."

"Yeah, is she okay?"

"Oh yes, she's fine, but we've gotten some recent test results indicating that she has ovarian cancer."

"What?"

"Ovarian cancer."

"What does that mean?"

"Cancer of her ovaries."

"I mean, what is going to happen to her? How bad is it? Is she going to be OK?"

"The diagnosis has been confirmed. There is no sign of metastasis. She is comfortable and free of pain. A treatment plan is being worked up at this time."

"Holy shit! I can't believe this."

"I'm sorry this news is upsetting to you."

"Yeah, I bet you are," Diegert recalled how Dr. Zeidler was a no nonsense, by the book doctor whose cold hearted bedside manner left him feeling isolated and alone under her care in the medial unit when he was first brought to LPU. "When can I see her?"

"Visitation privileges are under the direction of Herr Panzer."

"Of course they are. Listen, Doc, I want you to make sure she gets the best treatment possible. Everything this place has to fix cancer, I want used on her. Do not let her die from this."

"The treatment plan will be configured when all diagnostic information is acquired. The plan will need to be authorized by Herr Panzer."

Diegert sneered at the phone, realizing that once again Panzer had his mother's life in his hands.

"All right, Dr. Zeidler, just make sure you live up to your oath, and make sure she gets better."

"I will. Goodbye."

Diegert listened to the call go dead. It was a literal rude awakening, to find out his mother had cancer. What a tough life she'd had. All the shit from Tom Diegert and the ostracism she suffered as a young parentless half-breed girl. Now this. Can't this lady catch a break? It dawned on him though that if she were in Broward Minnesota, she might not be getting the kind of treatment she would get here. If you look, you can always find a silver lining.

His phone emitted the text chime.

David, my son, I've heard you are healing well. I would like to meet with you today. We have important business to discuss. Please reply indicating you will be at my office at 10:00 am. K. Panzer

Diegert thought it was weird how Panzer signed his texts, but he replied: *OK.*

Entering Panzer's office, Diegert saw that Avery was already there. Taking a seat next to his mentor and across from his father's position behind the desk, Diegert sensed he had been the topic of conversation. Panzer looked surprisingly well following his surgery. Diegert was of course familiar with Healix, and if all the other enhancements Panzer had mentioned on the flight to Lagos were combined with the rapid repair signals of the Creation Labs genetic modifier, it was no wonder that the gray-haired tyrant did not look like he had just returned from Africa with a gunshot wound to the abdomen.

"David, Avery and I have been discussing our options for responding to what happened to us in Africa."

"And you've come to some conclusions?"

"More or less, but I wanted to discuss them with you." Panzer smiled at Diegert. "In the short term, Mr. Wei will continue to believe that his assassination succeeded. Before that ruse fails, I want to strike. I want to hit him before he realizes a threat exists."

"Wait," said Diegert, "won't this rift destroy Crepusculous?"

"A valid concern, but remember what I told you, that keeping your enemies close gives you the opportunity to know them and control them. I've structured the business of Crepusculous to survive personnel interruptions. We will be okay."

"The Chinese have already called in the U.S. debt. They've played that hand," offered Avery.

"Mr. Wei tried to kill you and me, but he is himself a family man. He's a devoted father especially to his two sons, Qiang and Shing. We are going to strike him where it'll hurt the most."

Panzer paused while he and Avery looked at Diegert.

"How?"

"You are going to kill his son Qiang."

From son to assas-son, thought Diegert as the sting and the surge of being sent on a mission, tingled down his spine.

"How?" he asked again.

Panzer clicked a remote, filling the large screen TV with an image of a handsome young Asian man.

"This is Qiang. He and the family will be celebrating the Chinese New Year during the annual Spring Festival."

The screen changed to show a picture of another good looking Asian guy.

"This is Qiang's friend Jian. He's scheduled to visit Qiang on the second day of the festival. You will become Jian."

Again Panzer paused. He and Avery gazed at Diegert, whose furrowed forehead and lowered eyebrows formed a questioning look.

Avery broke the silence. "Do you remember when you and your father first met… in the medical facility?"

Diegert's raised eyebrows were unaccompanied by a verbal reply.

Panzer interjected, "You remember how you killed me?"

Diegert nodded, recalling how Klaus had an actor undergo a nanocytic face alteration in order to portray him and assess David's feelings toward his father.

"We will use the same technology on your face, giving you the appearance of Jian. He'll take the blame for killing Qiang. When the mission is over, we'll convert your face back again," said Panzer matter of factly.

"Tell me again how the face change works?"

"There is a whole lot of complex protein structure physiology, but the real tech is the genetic manipulation of the cells by nanocytes being directed by an app."

"And I would have to have these nanocytes put in me?"

Through a mischievous grin Panzer said, "They're already there."

Diegert's furrowed brow deepened.

"We introduced them while you were in medical. Remember the nanocytes can do a lot. All your physiological processes can be monitored by the data they send to the medical computers. It's standard procedure in LPU."

With a slight snort, Diegert said, "No positive consent required."

"We're not bound by HIPPA laws."

Diegert looked at the veins in his forearms. "You know I got a wake-up call from Dr. Zeidler this morning."

"About your mother," said Panzer.

"Yes."

"A diagnosis of cancer raises a great deal of uncertainty."

"It certainly does. What I want is a promise that you will make sure she gets the best treatment all your money, technology, and authority can provide. I want you to make sure she does not die."

"You are an amazingly loyal son," said Panzer. "A trait which I highly admire. You successfully complete this mission, and I will make you the promise for which you've asked."

Filling the silence with determined thought, Diegert said, "I want the rest of the diagnostic tests scheduled, and I want to talk to her before I go."

"It will be arranged," came the German accented reply.

"When do I go?"

"Three days from now will be the second day of the Chinese New Year. Qiang will hold a celebration that night to greet his many friends. Avery will prep you with mission details. Your facial transformation will take place in medical."

Eyes moved from face to face as the conversation paused.

"Son, what you will accomplish will not only avenge the attempts that were made on our lives, but your success will tip the balance of global power from Asia back to us. Your success insures ours. Being with you in Africa, I know I can count on you."

Avery stood up. "Come on, David. We've got some things to go over."

Crossing the room with Avery, Diegert stopped at the door, turned to Panzer and said, "When I get back, I get my face back?"

"When you get back, you can have any face you want."

CHAPTER 4

CREPUSCULOUS OPERATORS IN CHINA were able to gather intel on the Wei family's plans for celebrating the New Year with the Spring Festival. In China, the New Year is celebrated from the 15th to the 25th day of the month of February. Each day has specific traditions. On the third day, known as the Spring Festival, it's traditional to receive friends who visit and celebrate. Crepusculous spies discovered that Jian would be visiting Qiang on the second day of the festival. The Wei family was planning a celebration to receive all the friends who would be calling on them. Diegert learned of this from Avery as he was briefed on the schematic of the Wei's home where the party would take place and the critical steps necessary to pull off the extraction plan. Avery also said, "You will be meeting with Ms. Li Wu and Mr. Zhang Yong who will familiarize you with Chinese customs. You cannot learn all there is to know about China in the time we have, but you can at least learn not to make the most obvious mistakes."

"Right. I don't know a single word of Chinese."

"Understood, and it is probably better that you not try to fake it. You will be meeting with Ms. Li and Mr. Zhang after your face change, but they will not know your appearance has been altered, so this will give you some practice portraying someone else."

"Okay."

"Why don't you head over to medical?"

At the LPU Medical facility, Diegert was greeted by Hiram Bellsworth.

"Hello, Mr. Diegert. I don't know if you remember me. I'm the PA who gave you some treatment at the Headquarters facility in Romania."

"I remember. You were the guy who gave me Healix."

"That's right. You were in pretty rough shape at that point, but you're looking a far sight better now."

"Right, but I'm here to end up looking a far sight different aren't I?"

"You sure are. Isn't it amazing what can be done now that we can manipulate genetic information with digital signals?"

"Yeah, it sure is." Diegert brought up the picture of Jian Wong on his phone and showed it to Hiram. "Let's download the app to my phone so we can get on with it."

Hiram hesitated. "Um… I thought you were to provide me with the picture, and I would control the program from my computer."

"Look, you don't want to be the guy who doesn't listen to Klaus Panzer. Didn't you read the e-mail telling you to put the app on my phone so I can do the process in the field if necessary?"

"Was that a recent e-mail?"

"Yeah, I guess so. Look I've got other things I have to do today. Let's go."

Hiram's doubt was evident, but Diegert's insistence was compelling. The uncertain PA sent the program to Diegert's phone. With the app installed, the picture of Jian rendered in 3D, and Diegert sitting comfortably in a reclining chair, they were ready to go.

"Is this going to hurt?" asked a glaring Diegert.

"I don't know. There are no instructions indicating it

will."

"But you've got stuff to give me if it does, right?"

"Oh yes. I'm fully prepared."

"Yeah," said Diegert with a sarcastic smirk. "So fully prepared, I had to ask about the pain. Don't fuck this up. Let's get going."

The structure of the human face is basically the same from person to person. The difference in appearance is in the multitude of subtle variations that exist amongst people. It is these specific structural anomalies that the Creation Labs app instructed the nanocytes to alter in the skin and underlying muscle and bone tissue of Diegert's face. Nerves, blood vessels, sweat glands and tendons are untouched. While the contours and density of the skin, the concentration and color of hair as well as the location of moles, freckles and scars, along with the pigmentation of the face is changed according to the data gleaned from the analysis of Jian's photo.

Diegert was amazed that he felt nothing. No sound, no creepy skin feeling, no pain. The procedure went on for about twenty minutes during which Diegert dozed off and actually snored. Hiram returned when the program on Diegert's phone indicated the process was complete.

Walking in, Hiram was stunned. In spite of being fully aware of the entire process, Hiram Bellsworth was astounded by the completely different looking man sitting in the chair. His astonishment was not hidden, causing Diegert to react with alarm. "Hey, what's wrong? Is everything okay?"

Diegert stepped from the chair, turning to look in the mirror behind him. He too was stunned to see a strange man looking back. The Asian man in the mirror was shocked to see himself and it was even more amazing to see the face expressing such feelings. The novelty made him laugh, and he was so surprised when the reflection laughed as well. His look of consternation in response to the man's mirth was shared, which again surprised him.

Turning to Hiram, he smiled. "I guess it worked. Call me Jian Wong."

"Wow this is the most amazing thing I've ever seen," said the wide-eyed PA.

Diegert shrugged.

Hiram went on, "No pain, no bleeding, no change in function yet you are totally different. I'm amazed, and I was right here the whole time."

"Yeah, it's really something."

"I've got to go tell Avery," said Hiram as he exited the room.

Stepping closer to the mirror, Diegert made funny faces as well as a sad face, angry, happy, goofy and a serious face. He had a new face, and it was his to play with. Feeling like a kid with a new toy, he practiced controlling it. He closed one eye then the other, puckering and twisting his lips to the left and then the right. He ran his tongue over his teeth and stuck his tongue out. It felt no different. After a few minutes he started to pretend he was Jian Wong. He placed his right fist in his left hand and bowed to show respect to an elder as Avery had taught him. He practiced being polite with his eyesight, deferring the western habit of direct eye contact. Leave it to modern technology to change your entire life in twenty minutes without pain or interruption of function.

When Avery walked in, his surprise was more muted since he was practiced in controlling his emotions. He looked at Diegert as he walked around him, seeking the edge of the mask at the border of his face. He stepped forward, reaching out to touch. The skin was soft, warm and pliable. It did not rub off. Taking Diegert's phone he looked at the picture of Jian Wong. He looked back and forth several times until he nodded his head. "You no longer appear like David Diegert. You are Jian Wong."

Hiram glancing up from his computer screen said, "All his nanocyte data is normal. His heart rate is a bit elevated, but I think he's just excited."

Avery gestured with his hand. "Come on, I'll introduce you to your two cultural coaches."

Diegert and Avery entered a conference room, which had a large meeting table with twelve chairs. There was also a kitchenette in the corner, adjacent to several comfortable upholstered chairs around a coffee table. Standing by the kitchenette were a young man dressed in a simple, dark business suit, and a woman wearing a white shirt with dark jacket and matching knee length skirt. They smiled when Avery and Diegert, appearing as Jian Wong, entered.

"Hello," said Avery, shaking hands with the man, "Zhang Yong, this is Jian Wong." Diegert was thrown by being introduced with someone else's name, but he instantly recovered, offering his hand to the man, who smiled broadly as they shook. "And this is Li Wu." Diegert took her hand as she also offered a big friendly smile.

Avery went on, "Jian has never been to China, but he is going there to conduct some important business, so I'm glad you've agreed to help him understand basic customs so his trip will be a success."

Not wanting to let Avery dominate things, Diegert spoke up, "I've always been fascinated by China, so I'm happy to learn how to act so I'm not immediately identified as a foreigner."

Avery gave a wry smile. "Well, I'll leave you folks to it."

Everyone smiled at Avery as he closed the door behind him.

Diegert as Jian said, "I don't speak a single word. Will I be able to get along with English?"

Wu, the young woman, asked, "In what city will you be conducting business?"

"Ah, Shanghai."

"What type of business will you be conducting?" she asked.

"Um, finance and banking."

With a tilt of her head and a coy smile she said, "In Shanghai, the financial sector employs many people who have earned degrees overseas, and most of them are proficient in Chinese."

"In Chinese? What about English?"

Wu giggled and put her face in her hands. "I... I meant English."

Diegert looked at her as her cheeks glowed with embarrassment.

Yong looked askance at Wu as he spoke up. "Only one percent of the population of China are proficient speakers of English; however that is 10 million people. In well-educated, urban populations working in international business, that number rises to 78%. The likelihood that you will be able to successfully complete your mission while only speaking English is quite high."

Trying to pull the embarrassed woman back into the conversation, Diegert asked, "Li, can you tell me about the custom of shaking hands? Do they shake hands in China?"

Her brow furrowed. "First, in Chinese culture, names are used in reverse of English. Therefore, Li is my last name and Wu is my first name. Only close friends and family members would call me by my first name. In a situation like this, you would address me as Ms. Li."

Jian nodded. "Okay, reverse the names and call them Mr. or Ms.. I can do that."

Ms. Li continued, "About shaking hands, it is a common form of greeting, and you will certainly have to do it as part of your business meetings.

"Okay."

"But," interjected Yong, "It is the Chinese custom to shake hands gently. Americans tend to squeeze the hand as a show of strength. They also shake the whole arm and body of the person they're greeting. This is in poor taste for the Chinese. Shake gently and slowly."

Yong extended his hand. Jian took the hand much slower and more carefully than before. He shook just the hand, with no movement at the elbow or shoulder.

"Very good," said Yong, "It's a simple transition."

Once again turning his attention to the woman, Jian asked, "Ms. Li, what about the presentation of gifts?"

"Yes, of course, gift giving is a big part of the Chinese culture. Opening a gift is not done when the gift is presented. This would be awkward."

"What if one insisted, would the receiver of the gift be obligated to comply?"

"Not only obligated, but also embarrassed."

"They would have to open it though," pressed Jain, "if the giver insisted, even in public."

"I do not recommend it, if it is a relationship you hope to build and maintain for a long time. The person will comply with the socially awkward insistence, but they would consider the act to be in very poor taste. It would cause them to lose face."

"Okay, I see. Not a good idea."

Yong added, "If you give a gift, it should not be of too great a value, and it should be done with discretion."

"Well thank you two, you've taught me a lot. Avery gave me your numbers so can I call you if I have any questions?"

The two coaches nodded their heads. Yong said, "Sure." Stepping closer to Jian, he bowed and offered his hand. Jian gently grasped his hand and shook it slowly with very little force.

Wu said, "I'd be happy to help you," as she too lowered and raised her head before extending her hand. Jian was even more careful to be gentle with Wu's delicate hand.

"Great," said Diegert with a winning Jian smile. "I appreciate all your help and look forward to working with you again.".

Back in his quarters, Diegert looked at himself. It was still weird to see a different face in the mirror, but it was also strange how it felt kind of liberating. As if his problems were not his problems anymore. It was a relief to know that his Sino coaches seemed to think that he could conduct his business using only English. This seemed nutty, but the mission perimeters didn't really involve a lot of conversation.

A text from Avery arrived. *You've been authorized to talk with your mom. Audio only, no screen sharing.*

A few minutes later, his phone rang. "Hello, Mom."

"Hey, David. How are you?"

"I'm fine. How are you?"

"I'm doing okay, for a person held in a comfortable apartment who's not allowed to leave."

"You are comfortable though?"

"Yes, but the part about not being able to leave is more my point."

"I know, but I heard some news about your health."

"What did you hear?"

"I heard you've been diagnosed with cancer."

"See, I'm supposed to control who knows this. Health information is confidential. I don't want you worrying about me."

"I'm always concerned about you. I always want to know that you're okay. It's not a worry, it's a concern. Now what have the doctors said?"

"There's only one doctor. That Dr. Zeidler. Have you met her?"

Diegert recalled the coldhearted treatment he received when he first arrived in the medical facility at LPU. "Yeah, she's very clinical."

"I know what that means, but at least she shouldn't make the situation worse."

"Worse? No, they're going to make it better. I'm making sure that Panzer sees to it that you're going to receive the best treatment possible."

"See that, David. There you go again, making me your priority. I always feel like things are going to be okay when you're watching out for me."

"I know you don't like being kept inside your apartment, but if we were in Broward, you would not get the kind of treatment for cancer like you will here."

"I never thought about that, but when the cancer's gone, I'd like to be free."

"All right, I'll work on it." A warning came up on the screen. *Thirty seconds remaining.*

"I love you. I think about and care about you every day."

"I love you too. I hope to see you soon."
"You will, you will. Bye bye."
"Goodbye, David."

CHAPTER 5

THE GULFSTREAM TOUCHED DOWN at the Hongqiao Airport, delivering Diegert, in the appearance of Jian Wong, to the city of Shanghai. His credentials cleared in the Fixed Base of Operations, and a car was waiting to take him to the home of Chin Lee Wei. The ride took forty minutes during which Diegert saw the vast disparity of wealth in China. Passing through the overcrowded urban tenements, where people seemed to eke out a meager living with great difficulty, he moved through middle class homes which were startlingly similar to American suburban subdivisions. As he got closer to his destination, the homes grew bigger, setback farther from the road. There were intricate and ornate gardens, lovely pagodas, golf courses and a serene peace to the area, bought by the huge prices of the homes. Just like America, Europe and South America, money defines housing and here was where the money was.

Throughout the ride, the driver, whose head was covered in a ball cap and eyes were covered with sunglasses, said nothing. Diegert had confirmed the address. The driver nodded and away they went. When the man finally did speak it was with an unmistakable Australian accent. "All right, mate. Your address is coming up here. I understand that you are only going to be here for a short visit and that you'll be leaving in a big hurry."

Leaning to look into the rearview mirror Diegert said, "That's right."

"You'll be leaving that big bag of yours and just taking in your gift."

"Uh ha"

"Very well then, this is your address. I'll be parked over there with the other cars."

Diegert looked to his left at the parking area as he exited the vehicle to the right.

Dressed in a dark wool business suit, Diegert looked like a young man rising to success on a booming aspect of the Chinese economy. A tuxedoed staffer bowed his head slightly and directed Diegert to the section of the house where the family was greeting their friends. Diegert was polite and deferential to the people he passed, but he was certain he was disregarding those who knew Jian Wong and may have been alarmed at his behavior. He pushed forward, always smiling. When he got to the room in which the Wei family was seated, he looked in and identified Chin Lee, his wife Ming Ya, Qiang, Shing and surprisingly Mei Ling. Avery said that Mei Ling would be in London, but here she was for the Spring Festival. Remembering what he had learned for his cultural coaches, Diegert was relieved that well educated, sophisticated people like the Wei family, would all be fluent in English. If he started speaking in English they would reply in kind. Jian graduated from Berkeley and worked for an American firm, hence the English. This would eventually get awkward though, so he knew he had to minimize conversation and move quickly to get the job done.

When Mei Ling saw him, her face beamed, and she walked straight over to him. Her eyes sparkled, and her smile was broad and inviting. She tilted her head, batted her eyelids, and blushed when she got closer to him.

"Hello, how are you?" asked Diegert quickly.

Mei Ling's smile vanished when she heard Jian speak. She replied, with her British accent, "I've been waiting for you. I'm so glad to see you."

She extended her hand, which Diegert knew he could shake, but with a gentle grip.

Reading her signals, Diegert was off guard. He knew that Qiang and he were friends, but he was unprepared for the romance suggested in Mei Ling's coquettish greeting. Often uncomfortable with women, especially in social situations, Diegert had to not be himself and instead be Jian Wong. Diegert had learned that Jian was an outgoing, gregarious and popular guy. Not possessing any of these traits, Diegert had to become a convincing actor. He had the guy's face, but not his talents. He needed to fake it just long enough to kill Qiang and escape.

Taking his arm and escorting him into a side room where warrior armor, swords and other edged weapons were prominently displayed, Mei Ling smiled up at him, asking, "Why are you wearing that business suit? Where are your fun clothes? It's New Years!"

"I just wanted to show respect."

"Yeah right, since when? We look for you to set the trends and bring the new generation to the old. You can't be you, in a business suit. Besides, you're speaking English in our house."

"Everything old is new again."

"What?"

Diegert realized that American saying was of no help. "I have to go greet Qiang."

Grabbing his arm as he turned to leave she asked, "What have you got there?"

"It's a gift for Qiang."

"Why are you giving him a gift on New Years?"

"When I saw this, I knew he would really like it."

"What is it?"

"You'll see."

"Since when is he more important than me? We both know you became his friend just so you could get closer to me."

The look on her face demanded a reply.

"Of course that's true, but I have to keep up appearances."

With a look of astonishment Mei Ling said, "Aha, so now you finally admit it."

Jumping up and down like the little school girl she had just returned to being, Mei Ling said, "Wait 'til I tell him."

"No, you can't tell him that."

"What do you mean? You know how long he has been teasing me."

"I'm going to go see him now."

"Wait." Again she grabbed his arm. "I don't want you to leave."

Diegert was getting confused and running out of time. He grabbed Mei Ling and kissed her. She seemed to accept it for a moment and, after a few seconds, put up a struggle and pushed him away. She looked both mystified and horrified. He hadn't asked anything about Chinese girlfriends, but Diegert knew he'd made a big mistake when Mei Ling wiped her mouth on her sleeve and looked at him through narrow lids with a tightly set jaw.

He said, "I've got to go."

Guests were gathered in the living room. It was enormous with a huge expanse of open space surrounded by three steps built into the floor, creating a sunken living space with fine furnishings, ancient vases and impressive statuary. The Eastern wall was all glass. Diegert was surprised to see that behind the glass was a coral reef. Inside this massive aquarium swam schools of brightly colored fish, a sea turtle, rays gliding by on wings, and all the animals deferred to the eight foot Tiger Shark that pressed its pectoral fin against the glass as it cruised past. He had never seen such an aquarium in a private home, but he had to curtail his curiosity to stay in the role.

Diegert suddenly felt all eyes upon him. Qiang popped up from his chair and strode over with open arms to hug his good friend. With a happy smile and a hearty embrace, Qiang let everybody know that Jian was an important friend.

"Happy New Year," said Diegert

With a slight delay as he shifted to English, "Happy New Year to you too. How are you doing my friend?" asked the amiable host.

"I'm doing well, thank you."

Taking a step back and looking Jian up and down Qiang said, "I never knew you could look so good in a suit."

"I thought I'd give tradition a try," Diegert said with a chuckle. Handing Qiang the gift box he said, "I got you something I think you're going to like."

Qiang looked surprised, but he took the box.

"Open it," said Diegert.

"You haven't even greeted my parents yet."

Smiling nervously as Qiang led the way, Diegert stepped over to Chin Lee and Ming Ha. He gently shook their hands when offered, saying, "Happy New Year" to both of them.

"How are your parents?" asked Chin Lee.

"They're both fine, thank you."

The brevity of his answer created an awkward pause.

Recovering, Diegert continued, "They send their greetings to you and wish you good luck and good health this year."

Wan smiles returned and heads nodded gently.

Ming Ha began in Chinese, "怎么样" then shifted to English, "How is your sister?" Her tone implied there could be a problem but Diegert had no idea.

"She's well."

Ming Ha's surprised expression generated another recovery.

"I mean, she's getting over it and moving forward."

Ming Ha's brow furrowed, and she had that look of maternal concern. As she formulated her next question, Chin Lee touched her forearm, silencing his wife. He said, "We wish your whole family good health and prosperity this year."

Ming Ha's face couldn't let the awkward interchange go. She did not smile as is custom after the New Year greeting is bestowed. Her consternation was captured in the group photo that the family took with Jian.

Diegert pressed forward. "I got Qiang a present."

Now everyone's faces grew uncomfortable. Chinese New Year was a time of celebration, but gifts were for children and the elderly. It was unusual to give a gift as Diegert was doing, but even more unusual to bring direct attention to it.

"I want him to open it."

After putting his request out there, it could not be ignored. The awkwardness flowed through the room and everyone, including the fuming Mei Ling, was watching what was going on.

Qiang untied the ribbon that encircled the long flat box. Setting the ribbon on a side table, he lifted the lid, inverted it and placed the lower tray into the lid. Upon a velvet cushion lay a gleaming Chinese Dagger. The blade was long, at least ten inches. It reflected the light like a mirror with both edges tapering into a needle sharp center point. A substantial hilt of braided gold delineated the handle. The rest of the handle was ivory with a magnificent inlaid golden dragon. Adjacent to the blade was a golden scabbard engraved with the mountain home of the dragon.

Qiang was struck by the gift. It was way too much for this celebration and his gratitude and embarrassment blended into a speechless gap mouthed look around the room. He brought his gaze to the face of his friend pleading for explanation for the presentation of such a tremendous gift. Stepping to Qiang's right. Diegert asked, "Do you like it?"

The room hushed as Qiang bowed his head. "Yes, thank you."

"Feel the balance of the blade," suggested Diegert.

Qiang met the eyes of his friend and then looked at the knife. Shifting the box to his left hand, he lifted the weapon with his right. The knife was expertly designed. The handle's density balanced the blade's length making it feel almost weightless. Qiang rotated his arm, turning the blade left to right and back again. He looked up at Diegert, into the face of his good friend Jian Wong with an awkward smile. Jian smiled back but, in an instant, his face turned grim.

Diegert clamped his right hand over Qiang's, tightening his friend's grip on the dagger. Angling the point, Diegert drove the blade into the chest. The ten inch blade penetrated both ventricles of Qiang's heart. Withdrawing the blade, Diegert ripped it out of Qiang's hand. Lifting his arm above his head while inverting the knife, Diegert let out a primal scream as he plunged the blade into Qiang's neck. The knife sliced the jugular while severing the trachea. Each of Qiang's final breaths sucked blood into his lungs. The attack obliterated his cardiorespiratory system. Qiang was dead before crumpling to the beautifully ornate carpet of the Wei's massive living room.

Diegert's scream had chilled all conversation in the room while the thud of Qiang's body hitting the floor riveted everyone's attention. With the knife in hand Diegert shifted his grasp to the end of the handle. He drew back his arm and threw the knife at the aquarium with all his might. The weapon hit the glass hard and bounced to the floor.

Without further hesitation, Diegert sprinted for the exit. Confusion filled the room as the witnesses questioned one another about what they saw. Some said it was a theatrical prank put on by two friends who were known for being jokesters. Any crazy idea was better than the truth, which made no sense.

Mei Ling witnessed the attack. Trained in martial arts, she knew that her brother's death was no prank. She bolted to the side room, grabbed a pointed pike pole and took a shortcut to the house's front entrance.

The wall of aquarium glass suffered a small divot where the end of the knife's handle hit the pane. The pressure of the water stressed the imperfection, which slowly developed an ever-widening circle of cracks. No one was paying any attention to the state of the aquarium so when the giant pane of glass suddenly gave way, the tsunami inundated the living room sweeping everyone off their feet in a maelstrom of raging water. The force upended everything in the room; priceless vases became waterborne projectiles striking the bodies of guests who were unable to withstand the power of water flooding the opulent home.

Diegert streaked down the hall. He could see the front door and knew that, for a few more minutes, surprise was still in his favor. He didn't see the obstacle, but he felt his foot hit it and he was airborne. His attempt to right himself only made it worse as he twisted and collided with a low table. Upon the table sat a vase, which held a large bouquet of flowers. The crash sent Diegert tumbling to the floor smashing the vase, soaking the carpet and littering the hall with flowers.

Mei Ling retracted her pole after tripping Diegert, entered the hall, charging with her pike pointed at his chest. At the critical moment, Diegert defected the point of the pike and shot his leg up, kicking Mei Ling in the crotch. Diegert's foot stopped her as he yanked the shaft from her hands. She fell against the wall and on to the floor. They both quickly regained their footing, squaring off in defensive stances.

Mei Ling was surprised. The Jian she knew had no martial arts skills at all. She'd beaten him many times in playful sparring. He would never stand up to her, especially in a real fight.

She lashed out with a series of kicks and thrusts to the face. Diegert recognized the attack and fended the strikes instantaneously. Mei ling was shocked. Jian never practiced martial arts. He lacked quickness and coordination while this guy was fast, strong, and experienced.

Diegert was backing toward the door when Mei Ling unleashed another attack with kicks and a spinning chop strike designed to counter the typical defenses for the kicks. Diegert's arm was right there to block the chop strike. He could see that Mei Ling did not expect him to be able to resist her attack.

The door was right behind him now. Frustrated with his skills, Mei Ling screamed,

"为什么" (Why?)

She repeated her scream, "为什么，为什么，为什么！"

Diegert offered no reply. He held the face of Jian in a stern grimace.

Mei Ling, repeated her angry inquisition shouting now in English, "WHY?"

Diegert opened the door and stepped outside. "You will never understand."

Mei Ling launched into a sprint. Diegert timed her arrival at the threshold, swinging the door with all his might. The broad expanse of heavy wood collided with Mei Ling's slim athletic body. The door overpowered her outstretched arms, striking her head and shoulders, sending her to the floor with a resounding thud.

CHAPTER 6

TURNING FROM THE ENTRANCE TO THE Wei's home, Diegert saw his ride lurching forward to pick him up. Climbing into the back seat Diegert said, "Hit it." Looking through the back window he could see people racing out the door, heading towards their vehicles.

"This is where you earn your money, dude. Lose these guys and get me to the airport as fast as you can."

"Roger that, mate."

The black Toyota Camry's acceleration threw Diegert back against the seat as he struggled with his clothing bag. His suit coat, shirt and pants were all splattered with blood. From the bag, he pulled out a pair of khaki pants and a navy blue polo. Stripping off his blood stained clothes; he stuffed them in the bag. Dressing in the back of a car is never easy and the Australian driver did not make it any easier as he zoomed through the boulevards of the wealthy section on his way to the narrower, more modest streets.

Inside the Wei's mansion, the volume of water in the sunken living room allowed the fish to swim amongst the guests, the hors devours, the furniture and the toppled statuary. Several people screamed as they were shocked by the electric eel whose distress had maximized its voltage. Water continued to pour into the room as more of the glass crumbled. The Tiger Shark fell over the edge and into the room. Swimming was difficult for the big fish, but not impossible. The shark was disoriented and aggressive. One man, attempting to cross to a higher point in the room, passed in front of the beast. The shark lunged at the man's leg, crushing the bone within its jaws and flopping the man's body back and forth, as it thrashed between a couch and a coffee table.

Speeding through the suburban section, they were making good time. Diegert pulled on the khaki pants and struggled into the blue polo. Looking behind them, he tried to determine which cars were actually following them.

The driver said, "That white BMW and the gold Mercedes have been with us since we left. I think I'll lose 'em, now that we've got more traffic."

Diegert realized this wasn't his only problem. He scrolled through the photo gallery on his phone looking for a picture that would help him avoid detection. Whatever picture he found would have to be rendered into a 3D file. He had the software, and his phone could handle the required computing power, but the process took at least twenty minutes.

A hard left sent Diegert flopping to the right, causing him to fumble his phone. The device fell to the floor and slid under the front passenger seat.

"Ha ha," laughed the driver in his Aussie accent, "Slipped that bugger in the Beamer!" Checking the rearview, he could see the Mercedes made the turn and was still in pursuit.

Diegert undid his seat belt so he could crawl down and search for the phone. Reaching his hand under the seat, he discovered where all the trash was stored in this car. It was as disgusting as an American minivan on a family vacation.

Orange and banana peels, greasy burger wrappers,

pudding cups with chocolate residue, one glove, a busted old I-pod charger cord, a can of soda from which fluid was still dribbling, and Diegert's phone.

Diegert regained his seat as the driver said, "The buggers are right beside us. Hold on to your skivvies."

The car swerved to the left, bumping the passenger door into the front right corner of the Mercedes. The contact was jolting, but as the two cars separated, the Mercedes stayed right on them. Diegert could see the faces of the chase car's driver and passenger as they angrily gestured through the windows.

"Damn it, those Mercedes are heavier than most," said the driver with determination. "I'll give her a little more this time."

With the cars both driving straight down the road, the Aussie swerved right and then pulled hard and sharp to the left. The Camry bashed the Mercedes on the front corner. Diegert flew across the cabin, colliding with the right door. The Mercedes careened to the left, struck a parked car, and spun out into oncoming traffic. The resulting crash involved four vehicles and the driver from down under whooped it up in celebration.

"Mother of Christ, did you see that? Whoo – Wee, we left them in a jam didn't we?!"

Diegert once again picked himself up off the floor. He set his butt back in the seat as he said, "I can see you were paying attention when they taught offensive driving in school."

"Yes sir, I want to get to the airport with none of them to bother us."

Diegert returned to searching the gallery of his phone for the right photo. As he scrolled through picture after picture, he saw what he needed. He would never have thought of this image, but as soon as he found it, he knew it was right. He copied the file into the app and the 3D rendering commenced.

As he called ahead to the airport to order the Gulfstream prepped and the crew ready for departure, he realized they were driving through congested tenements. Seeing throngs of desperate people clinging to an overcrowded urban existence, Diegert lowered the window and ejected the bag of bloody clothes. Two scrawny women pounced on the bag, fighting like starving cats.

Approaching an intersection, they came to a sudden halt as a Hyundai pickup truck pulled out and blocked their path. The passenger exited the vehicle with his gun drawn. He approached the Camry and yanked open the back door. Diegert slowly slid out of the car. He kept his hands raised as he knelt on the pavement. The man was shouting at him in Chinese, but Diegert did not need an interpreter. He brought his hands together over his head. The man approached and, with the butt of his pistol, he struck Diegert across the face as he stepped behind him. More angry than hurt, Diegert reacted when he felt hands on his wrists. The American spun with surprising quickness, grabbing the man's forearm and pulling him forward as he kicked the man's leg, toppling him head first into the fender of the car. The impact dazed the man allowing Diegert to strip the gun from his hand, stand up and shoot him in the head. Turning to the pickup truck, he fired three rounds, shattering the side window while splattering the interior with the driver's blood.

The crowded street grew eerily quiet as the gunfire ceased. Jian Wong's image had no doubt been captured. The story of the friend gone mad would only be embellished by the video posts of this act of violence.

With Diegert in the back seat, the Aussie swerved around the truck, crashed through a fruit stand on the corner, and continued the trip to the airport.

Within fifteen minutes, they reached Husquiong airport. The Camry, with its dented passenger door and crunched rear quarter panel, boldly proceeded right up to the Gulfstream 650, such was the privilege of the private side of air travel. Checking his phone, Diegert could see the 3D render was 90% complete. Only another two minutes before the image was ready.

Exiting the right side, Diegert rounded the front of the car. "What do I owe you?"

"That's a nasty gash you've got across your cheek," said the man in his down under accent.

Diegert reached up to his right cheek where he'd been hit with the gun. It stung as he pulled his hand back to see the blood on his fingers. "It's no big deal. We've got to settle up, cause I'm out of here. What do I owe you?"

Gesturing with his finger pointing toward the plane he replied, "Just a flight out of here on your jet."

Diegert smiled and gave a nervous chuckle. "Look I appreciate the rough driving, but I'm leaving right now." Holding his phone he said, "Give me your Digival account and I'll transfer ten thousand."

Refraining from offering his account information the Aussie said, "Maybe you haven't been keeping in touch with your superiors, but the deal I made to drive you in and get you out, no questions, was for an airlift out of here."

Diegert sighed. He recalled how it was a similar jam that put him in the grip of Crepusculous. "All right, get on." Diegert followed the Aussie and, at the top of the stairs, he leaned in the cockpit. "Let's get airborne immediately."

"Sir, I'm sorry to tell you this, but our departure is

being delayed," said the flight captain.

"Why?"

"It has to do with a police investigation."

"All right, but as soon as we are cleared I want out of here. You got that?"

"Yes sir."

Turning to his new Australian friend Diegert said, "The delay involves the police. Go ditch that car."

"Roger that, mate."

Diegert went to the rear of the plane, put the Do Not Disturb sign on the knob and closed the door to the sleeping cabin. He brought up the transamination app on his phone, merged the 3D image and activated the program. Anxiety kept him from falling asleep, but he lay on the bed hoping to God for twenty uninterrupted minutes.

Parking the car on the third floor of a garage and returning to the plane by foot took the Aussie ten minutes. Climbing the stairs, entering the plane and not finding his passenger triggered a head swiveling search of the fuselage. The Do Not Disturb sign got his attention and he stepped back, leaning his ear toward the door. Ricardo, the flight attendant said, "Please mind the sign."

Startled, the Aussie said, "I was just… you know… wondering." Addressing Ricardo directly, he asked, "When are we leaving?"

"As soon as we are cleared for departure," said Ricardo. "Can I serve you a beverage?"

"Sure, what kind of beer have you got?"

"I can only serve you alcohol in the air. I have several soft drinks and some juice."

"Nah, I'll just have water."

When Ricardo returned with a bottle the Aussie asked, "How long has it been since we first showed up?"

"About fifteen minutes."

"Is that all?"

"I did not record the time you arrived. I do record the time of our flight from the minute the stairs are brought up and secured. That record is required by law," said the persnickety attendant.

"I see. You been doing this long?"

"I've flown over 1.5 million miles."

"Wow."

"I've been to every continent and almost every country."

"Really?"

"I haven't been to Greenland."

"Is there a flight there?"

"Not one that will hire me," said Ricardo who laughed hysterically at his own joke. The Aussie chuckled a bit, but he was surprised at the hilarity erupting from Ricardo.

Boots pounding up the stairs of the aircraft snapped both of them out their jovial moment.

A Chinese soldier with a military rifle appeared at the top of the stairs, stepped into the plane, and stood at attention. A middle-aged man dressed in a dark, somewhat wrinkled suit appeared next. Behind him, another armed soldier remained on the stairs.

"Greetings, I am Officer Liu. I must inspect the occupants of this plane." He did not ask for any credentials. He simply searched the cockpit, the passenger area, and the lavatory before reaching the sleeping cabin with its Do Not Disturb sign. Before knocking on the door, he looked at Ricardo, who shrugged his shoulders. Striking the door three times he said, "Police, open up."

There was no immediate response. He knocked again, much harder and shouted, "Open up, this is the police!"

The door latch snapped, the knob turned under the Do Not Disturb sign and the wooden panel swung open revealing Javier Perez dressed in pajamas.

Yawning and rubbing his eyes, Javier said, "How can I help you?"

The officer stepped past him to enter the room. He noted the rumpled bedsheets as he searched beneath it. He examined the closet, finding nothing of interest. Eyes gazing around the room one more time, he returned to the front of the passenger area.

"Jian Wong," he said with intentional suddenness. "Do any of you know Jian Wong?"

Ricardo and the Aussie both shook their heads.

Javier tried to stifle another yawn as he shook his head. Appearing more wakeful he said, "Excuse me, Officer, but I do not know that name."

"Where'd you get that cut on your face?" asked Officer Liu.

Gingerly touching his face Javier replied, "I was cut by a branch as I rode on a double decker tour bus."

Liu nodded with a gruff scowl. After one last scan of the faces, he uttered a single terse Chinese word and the two soldiers started marching. He followed them down the stairs and across the tarmac.

Ricardo and the Aussie turned to look at Diegert.

"What the fuck?" said the Aussie. "What do we call you now?"

"Look, I don't even have a name for you yet," said Diegert.

"You can call me Wayne."

"All right, Wayne, I'm Javier Perez."

"What? You're like, Hispanic now? How did this happen? You were Asian when you went in that room."

"Appearances can be deceiving."

"Yeah, but how did you do it? Some kind of super theatrical, special effects makeup?"

"Yes," said Javier.

He then looked at Ricardo, who was staring at him like a love struck puppy.

"Ricardo, so good to see you. How have you been?"

"I'm wonderful, sir. Can I serve you a beverage?"

"Yes, of course. You know what I like. Thank you."

Diegert had to play at being someone else again. Javier used the jet all the time and Ricardo probably traveled with him frequently.

The cockpit received clearance. The stairs came up and the Gulfstream taxied to the runway.

Wayne wouldn't let go. "How do you do it so the stuff doesn't sweat off? That's the biggest problem isn't it?"

"It's a pixelated polymer that acts as hydrophobic ionized particles. They adhere to the skin and avoid the pores of the sweat glands keeping them unblocked. The sweat comes to the surface and evaporates."

"Wow, it sure is convincing."

"Yeah, but I'm glad to be me again."

Ricardo brought him a glass of red wine. "I hope you like it."

Taking the long stemmed glass, Diegert sniffed the aroma and took a test sip. "Yes it's lovely. Thank you."

Ricardo reacted with a hint of surprise and Diegert wondered if Javier was polite enough to thank his servants. He also realized he had no idea how to tell one wine from another.

Ricardo said, "We all have to take our seats and buckle up. The captain is ready to take off."

The acceleration in a Gulfstream is magnificent, and

Diegert really loved the feeling of power that pressed him into the cushions of his extra wide leather seat. Getting out of China, having completed his mission, was a relief. Wearing the face of the asshole Javier Perez kind of sucked.

CHAPTER 7

WHEN A STEADY CRUISING ALTITUDE had been reached, Diegert asked his passenger, "So Wayne, what more can you tell me about yourself?"

"From what I can tell we might be in the same business. You see, sometimes when I've completed a job I have blood splattered clothes and I'm running for my life. It seemed likely to me that when you left that party someone else was lying dead on the floor. Am I right?"

Diegert took a sip of his wine as he nodded his head.

"The bloke who hired me," said the Aussie, "contracts out jobs of a fatal nature. The work pays well, but the risk is enormous."

"You're from Australia, correct?"

"Yes, I am."

"Which city?"

"I was raised in Melbourne but I last lived outside Sydney."

"How did you come to be… stuck in China?"

"Unlike you, I did not have a reliable plan for extraction. The bugger who was supposed to get me out got nervous and left me at the scene of the crime, as it were. I've been living underground seeking a way out of this huge but locked down country."

Ricardo brought Wayne a can of Heineken beer.

"It's hard to hide in China if you aren't Asian." Wayne said as he looked at the label on his can of beer. "An Asian can hide out almost anywhere in the world, but if you're not Asian, the Chinese assume you're up to no good."

Diegert gave him a nod.

Wayne leaned forward in his seat, "The trick is to convince those who will hide you that you are there to make trouble for their enemies. I was able to live in a family's home for two weeks once I convinced them I was going to kill members of their Triad rivals."

Wayne popped the can and took a big swig.

"I used their internet connection to find the posting for this job. I negotiated the flight out and now China never knew I was there or that I left. The only people who knew will never talk. They're the criminals who hired me, or they're dead. Now that's an assassin's success."

Raising his can of beer, Wayne toasted himself and swallowed several gulps.

Diegert looked at the man and saw a guy 45 – 50 years old, who at one time was probably considered handsome, but now looked worn out. The skin on his face was sun beaten with deep wrinkles at the corners of his eyes. His receding hairline of gray and dirty blond was kept covered by a filthy ball cap with an embroidered sailboat on the front. His unshaved face sported gray stubble and flossing was definitely not a daily habit. In unlaundered clothes, he sat in the wide leather chair with the paunch of his abdomen far more prominent than the pectorals of his chest. Well on his way to consuming his first beer, Wayne struck Diegert as both intriguing and cautionary. He looked like a guy whose skills would include fixing old lawn mowers, playing horseshoes and fishing. He did not project; international assassin. Diegert realized that only time can truly tell how life will change a man.

Diegert began, "Can I ask how long you've been an…

an assassin?"

Turning to make eye contact Wayne said, "We're going to speak plainly are we?"

Diegert nodded. "We're 30,000 feet up. I can send Ricardo into the cockpit and it'll be just you and me."

Wayne shifted his gaze to Ricardo and nodded. Diegert pointed to the cockpit and their loyal servant took the jump seat and closed the door behind him.

"Not counting the time I spent as a soldier, I've been contracting for fifteen years now."

"How'd you get started?"

"The Government of Australia got me started. I was just a soldier and then they said I could be part of the Special Forces. I felt so special, and I had much cooler gear than I did as a grunt. We went on night raids in Iraq. We were searching for specific people, targeting them to be killed. We never used the word, assassinate, but rather said things like; 'direct action', 'neutralize' and 'end phase'. No doubt though we were sent into the night to kill guys in their homes."

"Sounds brutal."

"When a government sees itself as its own authority, the rules become self-serving and the sanctity of human life is secondary to the economics of those in power. You must be aware of this?"

"Yeah, Yeah, I know what you mean."

"My commander selected me for a single operator action. I had to infiltrate an estate to kill a Malaysian Army General. We practiced for a couple of weeks in a mansion that was something like his. I learned my assignments, hit my marks in practice, I was stoked and ready to go. In Malaysia I do my recon, finalize my plans and select my time. I make my entry under the cover of darkness. The mansion is different than we practiced, but I improvise. I keep my cool and move to the target site like I'm Sam Fisher himself. I enter the general's quarters and shoot him dead in bed. Well they had some kind of surveillance, either in his bed, or on his body or in the fucking air I still don't know, but the alarms go off and the whole Army floods into the house. Every light is on, the dogs are loose and the guns are drawn. Unlike video games I was caught with no escape."

"A nightmare."

"Worse, you don't wake up and have it all go away. This is where the statement we all hear, but figure will never happen comes true: *This a covert operation. In the event you are discovered your actions will be disavowed and all knowledge of your mission will be denied. No efforts will be made to secure your release from custody foreign or domestic.* No doubt fucking chilling words when they describe your situation."

"You obviously weren't executed."

"Close though. My captors wanted to know who sent me. As far as I knew it was the Aussie SF. These guys wanted to know precisely who, so they pressed me into service as a double agent. They kidnapped my Filipino wife Emilene and held her hostage."

"Holy shit, the government did this?"

"Don't kid yourself, governments fight dirty and consider themselves above reproach. They held her in an undisclosed location and showed me a live video feed."

"What did they want?"

"They wanted to know who in the ASF ordered the strike. So they let me go. When I show up at the ASF station, they're shocked to see me. They cover it well but I could see they did not expect me to return."

"Betrayal."

"Yup. You've been trained to be lethal, and you're highly skilled, but you're still expendable. It took me two weeks until I finally had this captain at knife point for me to learn that the contact for the job came from within the Malaysian Army."

Diegert leaned back in his chair and stroked the chin of Javier Perez. "A double layer of betrayal."

"A high ranking colonel, Nocroe Azera, arranged for the hit so he could ascend. I brought the evidence back to the people who sent me to investigate and they freed my wife. Then they asked me to kill Azera. I did. I left and I will never go back to Malaysia."

"Your wife was saved?"

"Yes she was, but she divorced me immediately. Looking back now, I can't blame her. She raised my daughter, who I have not seen since she was little."

"So you have an ex-wife and a daughter?"

"Well yeah, but really I have no family. I have no contact or relationship with either of them. It's better not to have vulnerabilities."

"You're all alone."

Wayne raised his eyebrows as he nodded. "I have a brother but I squared up with him long ago and told him I would never contact him or my parents again. It's like a damn penance for the sins of the profession." Wayne swigged the last of his beer and walked over to the mini fridge to get another. "What else do you want to know?"

"What are your preferred methods?"

"I like guns, pistols for sure. With a suppressor it is the surest, quickest, most portable method there is."

"Agreed, but sometimes it's not right or available."

"Well then you've got blades. Always a bloody mess

and if you don't know what you're doing, you can stab forever and still not kill the bugger."

"It can be like… surgery though if you understand basic anatomy."

"Yeah, I was never good in school. I always carry a blade for back up but I try not to rely on it. You've got to be careful with explosives too. You can blow yourself up or a whole bunch of people you didn't mean to."

"Right, you have to understand chemistry and the nature of volatile compounds."

"See, more school stuff. I don't usually blow people up unless someone else made the bomb."

"Staged accidents?"

"Yeah, push a bloke off a high building or drown someone, those have worked. I sabotaged a ladder once and this construction supervisor fell and was impaled on a post."

"Bare hands?"

Wayne turned away to look out the window at the night sky. "Using your hands is the most intimate way of killing anyone. To feel the strength and determination in every fiber of their being. To know that there is no way they will give in. You sense their struggle to remain alive and you have to have a greater resolve to kill than they have to survive. It's wrenching, it's dispiriting, and it's painfully desperate. Isn't it?" Wayne turned to look at Javier.

Diegert nodded. "It sure is."

"There are kills you can't forget and never want to discuss. They're shame inducing and hang over you like a curse."

They dissolved into silence and Diegert thought of killing Klaus Panzer, or at least the man he thought was

Panzer. The intensity of the moment and the violence necessary to stop his life was cathartic, but the expelled angst left an emptiness, which reverberated in the cavern of his soul.

"Who are your customers?" asked Diegert, interrupting the mutual moment of contemplation.

Letting out a big sigh, Wayne began, "Governments mostly, corporations, desperate angry people who hate someone, and cowards."

"Not a real reputable bunch."

"I suppose there are elements of good in what we do, but it's all wrapped up in a bloody rag that no one wants to acknowledge. The goodness of your accomplishment is mired by the extrajudicial means in which it is carried out. The law is a hypocrisy that must be skirted by covert actions that are deniable, yet you are subject to prosecution if you're caught. No acknowledgment, no accolades, just a fat envelope or numbered account and a trail that better not be able to be followed. A mystery never to be solved or even investigated."

"I guess you got your sense of satisfaction from somewhere other than your employment."

"If you feel good about killing people, then you need a psych consult."

"How do you cope?" asked Diegert.

"What do you mean?"

"Like emotionally?"

Wayne expressed incredulity at the question, "Well not like you, mate. I never drink wine. Beer, scotch, vodka, even tequila, but never wine."

They smiled at each other while Wayne chuckled. Diegert though remained contemplative. He felt like he could ask a question he would never ask as himself. As

Javier he was less embarrassed and more emboldened.

"Do you ever cry?"

Wayne guzzled his beer and got up to get his third from the fridge. Back in his seat he said, "Boys Down Under don't cry. I won't admit to crying, but in the darkest hour and when the weight of your sins is as heavy as a millstone around your neck, the only way to release that pain is to cry like a baby. Lots of blokes will deny this, even on their deathbeds, but I believe you already know the windows to your soul need to wash out your sins."

Diegert's slow nod was almost imperceptible.

Wayne got up, walked over to Diegert and touched Javier's face. He stroked Javier's chin and traced the cut on his cheek. "Polymer make up is bullshit, This is real skin." Running his fingers into the dark hair, "This is real hair, and it's not chink hair."

With his gaze locked on Diegert, Wayne pressed, "Tell me the truth. I know Crepusculous is pushing the science."

"You know about Crepusculous?"

Wayne nodded. "I know they have enough money and power to do better than sweat proof make-up. Your skin is real, your injury is too, but somehow you switched from chink to spic. Tell me about the science."

"I thought you didn't like 'school stuff."

"I am not asking for all the bio physiology details, but you know how this change took place and I want you to tell me."

"I'm not inclined to tell you."

"Oh, I see. You are okay about asking me about crying, but you fear the intimacy of telling me something I want to know."

"I'm not sure what you'll do with the information."

"Yet you will hold in another secret. Another level of

truth you will not share in order to adhere to rules placed upon you by people I'm not convinced you really respect."

Diegert turned Javier's eyes to the floor as he considered his loyalty to Avery, Panzer and Creation Labs. He wasn't specifically instructed not to discuss the nanocytes, nor was he giving away the secrets by which these things actually worked. Besides this stuff couldn't be kept secret forever. Diegert felt Wayne's gaze pushing down on him as he heard him say, "Unloading secrets is necessary for an assassin's survival. You must have people you can trust to confide in about what you've done. You and I are brothers in the secret guild of assassins."

"I never heard of the guild of assassins."

"Well that's because I just made it up, but the guild exists whenever assassins agree to support one another. I'm here to help you. Does it hurt?"

"What?"

"Does it hurt to change your face?"

"No, not really."

"It seems to take like, ten –fifteen minutes. I'm thinking about how long you were in the back room."

"Yeah, that's about right."

"What's the secret ingredient? What makes it all work?"

Diegert felt the need to answer the question. He did not think about the consequences, just the need to get rid of guilt, regret and recrimination. Telling Wayne about the nanocyte's abilities to alter the genetic code of cells, transforming their proteins to change his appearance would probably confuse him, but it would also weaken Crepusculous's exclusive hold on this unique technology.

Looking at Wayne he said, "Nanocytes."

"Nanissists?"

"Nanocytes are tiny computer chips in my body that change the DNA of my cells, altering their appearance. They can change my face to look like any picture I put in the program."

"Really, a computer program changes your face through the actions of tiny chips in your bloodstream?"

Diegert put a sly smile on Javier's face as he nodded.

"So am I seeing your real face right now?" asked Wayne.

Feeling like he had already done just a little too much truth telling, Diegert replied, "Yeah, this is me. I'm Javier Perez."

CHAPTER 8

ALTHOUGH SHE COULD HAVE EASILY hacked it, Fatima convinced Javier to give her his password. She scrolled through his files until she found the one labeled 'Real Estate.' Inside she perused the list of his holdings. Javier was a wealthy man with many properties. In addition to the London townhouse and a condominium in Miami, he also owned estates in Columbia, Chile, the Isle of Crete and Brazil. After reviewing details of each of the properties, Fatima clicked on the link to the one in Brazil. She was smitten by the beautiful photos of a beach house in Trancoso, north of Rio de Janeiro.

The compound included three living quarters. The main house, which had twelve bedrooms and a state of the art chef's kitchen. A guesthouse with six bedrooms and an elevated screened in sleeping porch. There was also the beach cottage, a four-bedroom structure with a huge veranda opening directly on to a private beach. This region of the Atlantic was warm, crystal clear and home to many species of exotic fish. The beach sand was so fine and soft, it felt like walking on baby powder.

The town was fifteen minutes away and catered to tourists, but it had a school, a farmer's market and a low rate of crime. Two caretakers were in constant residence with kitchen and cleaning staff brought in when Javier came to stay.

Fatima imagined Hamni being there surrounded by

nature with birds, animals, gigantic plants and daily sunshine. No more dreary London, indoors all day avoiding the rain.

"Javier," she shouted. "Come here please."

Leaning back in her chair, she craned her neck as she peered down the hall. "Javier," she shouted a second time. "I've got something to show you."

Fatima saw the scowl on his face as he looked up from his phone. Walking into the room, Javier stood by her side looking at the screen.

"When was the last time you were at this place?" asked Fatima.

Scrunching his nose and scratching his head he said, "Which one is that?"

"It's in Brazil."

"I don't know, maybe a couple of years ago."

"You do still own it?"

"If it's in the file, I guess I still do."

Turning to face him Fatima said, "This is where Hamni and I will live."

Pausing Javier asked, "What about Columbia?"

"Too close to Bogota and there is no beach."

"Crete then?"

"I don't want to live on a tiny Island."

"The one in Chile is by the ocean."

"Yes, but the beach near the house is all rocks and the sand beaches are way too crowded."

"You spoiled bitch," shot Javier.

Fatima held his gaze as she reached into the desk drawer, withdrew a pointed mahogany letter opener and said, "You'd better walk that back."

Javier, aware of the fury that raged in Fatima said, "Okay, okay, you're not a bitch, but you are acting rather entitled. You think you can simply select what you want and it is yours."

Fatima's eyelids narrowed and her grip on the wooden blade did not slacken. "I am doing so from a list of properties you have not visited in years, while you simply select whatever you want from all the available female bodies you see."

Fatima rose from her seat, raising the letter opener between them so the tip of the blade was in clear view. Looking directly into Javier's eyes she continued, "I am the only one who has made you answer for your sexual sins. You are Hamni's father and therefore you have an obligation to provide for him. Living in a house in Brazil, that you forgot you owned, seems to me like a painless way for you to fulfill your parental responsibilities."

She lowered the blade, tilted her head, smiling. "Besides, it's a private beach. When you visit, we can swim naked in the ocean."

Placing the letter opener on the desk, Fatima spun and sat on the desk's surface. "I see the contact information in the file. I will send them an e-mail, from your account, informing them that Hamni and I will be taking up residence in the villa for an indefinite period of time."

Javier sighed and shook his head once.

"I will make travel arrangements and we will leave within the next few days," said Fatima. "Remember that I now have access to all your accounts and financial information. As we discussed, I will be the force behind your success." She rose from the desk and stepped close enough to Javier to press her breasts against his chest. "I will be your best kept secret. You will appear smart, decisive and shrewd, while I will be out of sight as I guide you to profits and power."

Javier looked like a kid whose sister did his homework.

"You provide for Hamni and me, and I will make certain your power and prestige will exceed your father's," said Fatima with an eyelid flutter as she stepped back from the handsome Spaniard as he sought to calm his elevated ventilation.

Pointing a finger at the man Fatima said, "You really ought to go have a shower because you kind of stink."

CHAPTER 9

ACHMAD AMALI, A PALESTINIAN REFUGEE struggling to find work in London, read an ad that appeared in his e-mail;

Young Men of Middle Eastern Decent needed for film work. No previous experience necessary.

Probably looking for terrorists for a movie. The place was called Backlot Studios. It occupied the ground floor of a refurbished industrial site. An up and coming vibe permeated the bare brick walls and thick plank floors. Achmad looked around at the cameras stacked on crates and some pieces of scenery under a set of theatrical lights. He felt like the business was legit. The interview was short and straightforward. He was given the job immediately, provided he could work that day. He was told he fit the type they needed precisely, 6 foot 2 and 200 pounds. He would be paid 3000 Digival for the day. Achmad agreed and was taken deeper into the building for prep work.

First stop was a medical clinic set up in what looked like an old kitchen. The medical people were fast, efficient and painless. To prevent infection, he was given an injection, and to prevent hearing damage from explosives he received a special treatment for his ears.

Moving on to what was called a rehearsal room, Achmad had a scene described to him in which he would help a woman and then be confronted by the police. He was to follow the instructions of the police as they commanded him. The scene would depict violence but it was a fictional portrayal. He did not rehearse the scene but he indicated he understood the role. Achmad was given strong tea and allowed to sit in a recliner. He wouldn't be needed for two hours.

Ten minutes after Achmad finished his tea, a technician entered and found him unconscious in the recliner. Getting right to work, the technician initialized the program which would activate the nanocytes in Achmad's bloodstream that were introduced through his "protection" injection. With a 3D rendered image of David Diegert's face, the program began the process of transamination, restructuring the proteins of Achmad's facial muscles, skin and underlying bone to precisely resemble those of David Diegert. The painless process altered the appearance without scarring or any disfigurement. Upon waking Achmad had no idea that the face he had looked at in the mirror every day of his life was now transformed into one of the most wanted men in the world.

Allowed to use the bathroom before being driven to the place where the scene would be shot, Achmad was surprised there was no mirror above the sink or on the back of the door. He shrugged his shoulders, dried his hands and got in the car. It was late afternoon so traffic was building. Regardless, they made good time. In the car he was told that the action would be captured by concealed cameras and that he should act natural on the street. He was further informed that the scene required him to exit the car, step to the sidewalk and wait for a young woman who would ask him for help. When he begins to help her, actors portraying police would arrive and he would take direction from them.

Pretty simple, he thought. Acting was supposed to take special talent, but maybe he would like the movie business.

Standing on the street in front of the 27 story Altitude

building in the White Chapel district, he was nonchalant and patiently waited for the arrival of the young woman. As the minutes began to add up, a double decker bus stopped in front of him. He noticed in the window of the bus a reflection of a man who was wearing the same blue jeans, dark blue oxford shirt and tweed jacket as he was. He furrowed his brow and cocked his head, but the bus pulled away. What a strange sensation.

While on the street, he was not the only one to be surprised by his appearance. The CCTV system of London was the best in the world. Extracted images were instantly analyzed, producing flagged faces, which were identified for immediate review. Subsequent action could be taken to investigate persons of interest or apprehend wanted criminals. David Diegert's face, when matched with photos in the system, drew instant recognition. The duty commander confirmed what the surveillance system had identified. David Diegert, a high value target, was a confirmed identity on Trafalgar Street in front of address 1442. The sighting triggered an aggressive response from London's SWAT Team, Special Crimes & Operations -19. The force was dispatched for an immediate apprehension.

Achmad felt strange. It was weird to see a man on the bus dressed just as he was. Maybe not so strange, his clothes were actually quite typical. Yet the man was not on the bus, he was reflected in the window glass. Achmad turned to look into a shop window. The sun's glare made his reflection weak, but again there was that same man. Lifting his hand to touch his face, he saw the strange man do the same thing. A shiver percolated up his spine, which turned into a spastic jolt when he heard a young woman's voice saying, "Hey Achmad can you help me carry this bag?"

She was rather thin and almost gaunt, though her baggy clothes concealed a lot about her shape. The dark circles surrounding her pale eyes and her frizzled mop of blonde hair made her look pretty strung out. She was quick to hand him the big bag she had strung over her shoulder while retaining a two-handled tote. "Come on," she said. Achmad threw the strap over his shoulder. The bag was heavy, zippered shut and kind of bulky. It surprised him that such a skinny lady could manage it. As they walked she reached into her bag, Achmad noticed her forearm rotating. She quickly retracted her hand and with startling quickness, used both hands on the tote handles to fling the bag up into the air and into the street traffic.

Upon landing in the middle of the street, the bag exploded. A staggering concussive wave, giant plume of smoke and a deafening roar erupted in the traffic. Cars directly in front of the bomb were instantly disabled, others crashed onto the sidewalks. People in the vehicles were dazed, injured and several looked dead.

But to Achmad it seemed like an effective movie stunt. This was after all, kind of what he was expecting. He heard a reassuring voice telling him, "Be calm. The police are coming. Follow their direction."

Back at the studio, when Achmad was being prepped, a nanocytic tympanic transponder had been implanted on his eardrum. The device was now being activated by a Crepusculous team. He looked around but saw no one who seemed to be speaking to him. He also no longer saw the scraggly girl who gave him the bag.

Maintaining the bag on his shoulder Achmad stood transfixed by the carnage around him. The SCO-19 team arrived in two black SUVs. Officers in battle ready uniforms deployed into forward positions of cover with their Sig Sauer MCX Virtus weapons pointed at David Diegert.

Over a megaphone the officer in charge commanded, "Drop the bag and surrender, now."

The Crepusculous team, watching a pirated CCTV feed, replaced the police commands with alternative phrases timed perfectly to maintain the illusion that Achmad was hearing the police.

So while the police officer said, "Drop the bag and surrender, now."

Achmad heard, "Retain the bag and take a defensive stance."

The SCO-19 officer shouted, "David Diegert, submit to authority or face fatal consequences."

Achmad heard, "The bag is of critical value, defend it for the sake of public safety."

Achmad wrapped his arm around the bag clutching it closer.

The frustrated officer barked one more command, "Drop to your knees and surrender."

Achmad heard, "Unzip the bag and reach inside."

As Achmad's fingers grasped the zipper pull the officer shouted, "Fire."

The bullets pulverized his body, ripping through the cavities of his chest and abdomen, exiting the rib cage while dismantling the spinal column. David Diegert's face was punctured by bullets that pierced Achmad's cranium. The body collapsed with the bag still strapped over the shoulder. Time stood still as gun smoke rose, sending the scent of cordite into the public's nostrils, instilling a sense of foreboding.

The explosion was massive. Much bigger than the first one. The fireball extended the full width of the street and rose up ten floors. Every window within a quarter mile was shattered. Cars were tossed like toys down a staircase. They tumbled end over end and rolled over each other as the blast wave cleared a crater the size of a large amphitheater. People within the blast radius were vaporized by the heat and dispersed as droplets by the propulsive force of the expanding gases. The temperature was so intense that the oxygen in the air ignited, creating a second explosion enlarging the original fireball. The consumption of the oxygen produced a sphere of suffocation in which people were asphyxiated by the lack of life's most precious element.

The twenty seven-story apartment building, in front of which the bomb went off, buckled and shook as the structural supports quivered under the shock of the explosion and the destabilization caused by the mammoth crater in the street. As frantic people struggled to evacuate the doomed dwelling, the entire front of the building sheared off, collapsing into the street. Apartments were ripped open like the foil off a yogurt cup. Falling with the debris were the unfortunate residents who had no time to escape.

When the toll was taken, 511 lives were lost and David Diegert was to blame.

CHAPTER 10

BY THE TIME HE TOUCHED DOWN in London, Diegert had spent over eleven hours with Wayne. In spite of his inebriated state, Wayne walked off the plane under his own power. In the terminal the pair was greeted by Avery, whose surprise could not be hidden as he looked at the face of Javier Perez.

"Hey don't be so surprised," said Wayne. "You knew I was coming."

"Of course," said Avery. "How was the flight?"

"Javier here is quite the disguise artist. At first he looked so Chinese, I thought he was going to fix my computer or deliver egg foo yung. Then he stripped off the high tech make-up and now he's a happy Mexican."

Avery looked at Wayne askance. The salty ethnic insults went down a little easier with Wayne's charming Australian accent, but the rude remarks were not at all appreciated by the man of African descent. Handing him a small electronic card Avery said, "You're in London now. Your contract with me is complete."

An inspection of the card revealed a tiny screen with the number of Digival the Aussie was expecting, Wayne replied, "Yes sir, the fruits of another job are delivered. Do call again. You know I can always provide whatever you need."

"Indeed I will," said Avery as the two men shook hands.

Turning to Diegert, Wayne said, "I really enjoyed talking with you. You gave me a lot to think about."

"Likewise," said Diegert, giving the aging assassin one of Javier Perez's million dollar smiles.

Diegert and Avery watched as Wayne walked away with a slight lean to the left. It looked like he was fighting a gale force wind inside the airport terminal.

"Your car is this way, Mr. Perez," said Avery with that look of consternation he used whenever he was unpleasantly surprised.

Walking with Avery, Diegert said, "I had to change my face, or they would have nabbed me as Jian."

"Yes, but that means you stole a proprietary app."

"So what, I would be dead, unless that was also part of the plan."

Avery's eyebrows descended. "You are much too valuable to be wasted like that."

"Touching, but I want my old face back. This guy is an asshole and I don't want to see how people treat him."

As they climbed into the back of the big black Mercedes SUV Avery said, "There's been an incident."

Pulling out of the terminal Diegert said, "What happened?"

"I'll show you."

On the screen that descended from the ceiling Diegert watched a video of him standing on a London street in front of an unfamiliar building. The audio filled with sirens while flashing lights rotated off the walls behind him.

Looking at Avery with a quizzical glare, he was directed back to the screen.

Commands from police for David Diegert to surrender

could be heard loud and clear over all the background noise. The commands were being ignored while Diegert clutched a big bag he had slung over his shoulder. Watching as his hand went to pull on the zipper, Diegert braced. The images of being shot were stunningly graphic. The clarity of the picture was chilling. Diegert saw himself fall to the ground, his body draped over the big bag.

Diegert's eyes were glued to the screen watching himself being shot. The video of the explosion was in slow motion. The bag under Diegert bulged like a mushroom emerging from the earth. Diegert's lifeless body rose on the crest of the ballooning bag. When the seams of the bag gave way, bright orange flames shot out, consuming the material. Diegert's body seemed to rise into the air as if it was being lifted to heaven, but that only lasted a fraction of a second before the expanding fire engulfed more and more of the image space. Diegert could see his body doing the same thing as the bag, expanding under pressure as his body fluids turned to steam, and his flesh went molten. His skin gave way, bursting into a spray of boiling fluid, which evaporated into the rapidly expanding fireball. The screen suddenly turned totally white.

Without looking at Avery, Diegert asked, "Who was he?"

"Keep watching," said Avery.

The screen now depicted an aerial view of urban carnage. The kind of thing typically seen in the aftermath of the most horrific wars. The street, filled with debris. The building, laid bare, it's naked interior, soaked by fire hoses.

The voice over began, "Currently the death toll from Tuesday's bombing is 511 confirmed fatalities. Cost estimates for the damage range above one billion dollars while authorities say that Abu Jihad is claiming responsibility for the attack. The international assassin, David Diegert was positively identified as the bomber. His bomb ignited after he was shot by the police. Those who feel that shooting the suspect was the wrong thing to do have no one to directly answer for this act, since the entire Special Operation 19 unit was killed in the explosion."

The screen went to a close up of Diegert's face taken from the CCTV minutes before his death.

The announcer said, "Diegert is believed to have participated in the assassination of U.S. President Perter Carson. The fact that he was able to travel to London and operate in the UK is an embarrassment to MI 5 & 6 as well as Scotland Yard."

The screen image morphed into the picture of Diegert from the Security Guard ID tag recovered following the presidential assassination in Detroit. "This troubled and violent man readily killed for reasons unknown, though authorities have evidence that he was well paid. The price of a life bought and sold to the face of death."

The screen went blank as it rose back into the ceiling.

"What the fuck is going on?"

"The plan was to have you die in public so as to free you from your criminal past."

Diegert grew silent as the black Mercedes pulled up to the automatic retracting garage doors, allowing the vehicle to enter the LPU labyrinth.

In the underground parking garage Diegert removed his seatbelt but remained seated, staring forward catatonically.

Avery dismissed the driver and asked Diegert, "Are you okay?"

The lack of response drew Avery closer. Diegert was lost, unable to respond. Avery startled when Diegert popped open the door and bolted from his seat. Avery spun, exiting his side of the vehicle to find Diegert standing there. The young man grabbed Avery by the shirt and flung him to the floor of the garage. On his back, Avery looked up as Diegert roared, "FIVE HUNDRED ELEVEN PEOPLE. You killed over five hundred people just so you could kill me?"

Avery was back crawling, "The plan went awry. Only you were supposed to die." Avery regained his feet. He kept backing up as Diegert deliberately pursued him.

"What gives you the right to do anything in my name?"

"We are helping you."

Avery slowed his pace and began to rotate. Diegert closed the distance beginning to circle his mentor.

"How was this supposed to help me?"

"The whole world will see that David Diegert is dead. You can be whoever you want now. You can start a whole new life."

The two never stopped moving having completed one full circle.

"Just forget I ever existed. My whole life before, just over. I'm now the living dead! What about my mother?" shouted Diegert.

The look on Avery's face told Diegert he hadn't thought of her, or perhaps worse.

"Where the fuck is my mother?" exploded Diegert.

He burst forward, forcing Avery out of his circle as he punched the mystic on the jaw. Avery took the strike, falling back against the wall of the garage.

"She had better be okay," said Diegert as he threw two body blows into Avery's abdomen.

"She's fine," coughed Avery as he blocked the next

series of punches and gained a little distance.

"You fuck'n suck," said Diegert.

Anger and frustration contorted Javier's face as Diegert became unhinged.

Taking a defensive stance Avery shuddered, knowing the ferocious capabilities of David Diegert.

Anger was being channeled into a need for violent catharsis. Diegert jabbed at Avery who dodged the punch, but was not quick enough to avoid the follow up, which connected with the mentor's left eye, snapping his neck and rattling his brain. Stumbling backward, Avery's reflexes took over and he stepped away and around enough to put some space between him and Diegert. Continually moving, the two used no words. Javier's expression revealed the blood lust raging in Diegert. Avery moved toward a corner of the garage. He grabbed a broom and spun off the threaded bristle head. With shaft in hand, he performed a short bo staff kata. Diegert knew the Master's skills, but ignored the risk. He charged the stick wielding man who expertly swung the shaft as he shifted his position. The hardwood struck Diegert on the right cheek and ear. The blow re-opened the split on Javier's face while Diegert winced from the ringing in his ear. Avery's deft moves and rapid re-deployment of the staff began to shift the balance of the battle, yet Diegert would not yield.

"You're just going to have to kill me for real, aren't you Avery?"

"I don't want to hurt you, David, but you're making this difficult."

Diegert softened his facial expression and frowned with a tremble in his lip, before thrusting his hand up and immediately diving forward. Avery hesitated at the change in Diegert's facial expression as well as the high hand, the moment of vulnerability exploited by the younger man who tackled Avery to the cement floor. Proximity brought the advantage back to Diegert who punched Avery with crushing blows to the head and neck. Swinging his legs up over Diegert's head, Avery caught the younger man's neck with his boot and pulled him down to the side. With staff still in hand, Avery climbed on top of Diegert and quickly pressed the shaft across his throat using both hands to exert suffocating force. Diegert grabbed the stick as well and pressed up. Avery's ability to put all his weight on the shaft was a clear advantage, but Diegert kept the stick from completely collapsing his airway.

"Go ahead and kill me, you fucker."

"You're too valuable for that."

"I'm not worth a billion dollars and over five hundred lives," screamed Diegert.

"Actually you're worth way more than that."

Diegert locked Javier's angry eyes on Avery. Gradually Avery slid his hands closer together on the staff until he was able to touch the side of Diegert's neck. With only his first two fingers, Avery probed the side of Diegert's neck behind his carotid artery to press on the vagus nerve. This cranial nerve sends signals that slow and calm the body's physiology. Avery was creating a massive signal response to counter Diegert's agitation, turning the young man unconscious within twenty seconds.

Wasting no time, Avery scrambled to the back of the Mercedes, grabbing flexicuffs from a kit bag. He flipped Diegert on to his front and zip tied his wrists and ankles. With Diegert bound, Avery sat on the garage floor stunned.

He could not, however, indulge his shock. Avery quickly called Medical to have Diegert moved to a secure room. The young man remained unconscious and still had the face of Javier Perez. On his phone Avery selected Klaus Panzer's number. As the call rang, he contemplated how to convey the situation.

"Hallo," came Panzer's greeting. "Avery, has David returned?"

"Yes sir--"

"Excellent," interrupted Panzer. "I will be over shortly."

"But there is something you should know."

"I'm in a bit of a rush right now, Avery. Tell me when I get there."

"But…" Avery heard the call go dead.

CHAPTER 11

REGAINING CONSCIOUSNESS, DIEGERT FOUND himself in the same medical room he occupied when he was first brought to LPU. He rubbed his wrists and swung his legs one at a time off the bed onto the floor. The curtain was drawn over the glass window wall and he was correct when he confirmed that the door was locked. The mirror over the small sink startled Diegert when he saw Javier Perez was in the room with him. Stepping closer to the mirror, Diegert looked closely at Javier's face. He felt kind of weird, like snooping in someone else's medicine cabinet. Yet the face was on his body. He looked at the stubble of beard, much thicker and more coarse than his own. He pulled the lips back to look at the teeth. Perfectly straight and sparkling white. The hair was thick and full with no recession at the brow line. The jet black color absorbed the light and his head quickly grew warm. The guy's skin was without blemish, no zits, no mottled pigment and no rashes. As he was about to stop his intrusive inspection, Diegert noticed a mole on the left temple right next to the hairline. It looked pretty normal but it represented a break from perfection which pleased Diegert enough that he stopped his intimate exploration of the handsome face.

Watching the camera feed, the medic alerted Avery that Mr. Perez was awake. "Shall I begin his physical assessment?" asked the medic.

"No," said Avery. "Leave it to me."

"But it's a required medical record."

"I said, leave it to me," replied Avery sharply. "In fact go on into the office area and wait for me there." The medic sheepishly complied.

Stepping to the wall phone on the opposite side of the hall, Avery pushed the intercom. "David, I hope you're feeling better. We need to talk."

The curtain covering the floor to ceiling glass window flew back, revealing the agitated face of Javier Perez.

"You're full of shit, Avery."

"Now calm down. We've got some serious issues to resolve and we'll get nowhere with that attitude."

"This attitude should have been here to stop you from killing over 500 people."

"I've already told you the plan went a bit awry."

"You can't sweep all this away as a slight mistake. You, and whoever else was involved, royally fucked it up. You destroyed lives well beyond those that died. You pin it on me and expect me to see it as a benefit. That's bullshit."

"David, I can see that you're angry, and I'm trying to understand your emotions but if we don't act quickly and carry out our plan, all that has happened will be for nothing."

"Wait a minute. Who the hell built that bomb? Did you do that, Avery?"

"No. I don't know how to build bombs."

"Who did then? Who had control of the detonation device?"

"I'm pretty sure it was--"

"Don't give me that shit. You know for sure who it was. You're not outside the loop on this one."

The eyes of Javier stared Avery down through the thick glass before Diegert said,

"All right, I believe I already know who built the bomb and controlled the detonation. So it's not a revelation if I already suspect someone and I'm right."

Avery, a master of manipulation said, "Do you have a name in mind?"

"When did he leave Romania?" asked Diegert.

"Who said he left?"

"You mean he did all of this remotely?"

"CCTV and Wi-Fi networks," said Avery in a sullen tone.

"I hated being under that guy. He was sanctimonious and cruel."

"Then it's not too hard for you to believe that Aaron Blevinsky might overcharge a bomb creating a bigger impact than we agreed upon."

"That fucker," said Diegert as a sneer crept across Javier's face and a heavy sigh flowed from his lungs.

An audible buzz sounded and Avery left the area.

In the hallway leading to the medical facility, Avery met Klaus Panzer.

"Sir before you go in, there's something you ought to know."

Panzer's brow furrowed as if he already knew everything there was to know. Avery made his point clear and concise.

"David's upset about all the people who died in the bombing."

Panzer's consternation only deepened. "What do you mean he's upset? Doesn't he realize that he has been freed from all his crimes of the past? I hope he appreciates the effort that went into orchestrating all of this so his life could be given a do over?"

Avery tried for a cautious tone. "I believe he was quite

surprised by the magnitude of the event."

Nodding, Panzer replied, "It does seem as though the bomb was more powerful than was necessary."

"I'm glad you recognize that. David figured out that Blevinsky created and detonated the bomb."

"Aaron often takes things to excess, but that does not alter what we've achieved. The opportunity we sought is now before us. David Diegert is dead and my son can now live a new life. Come on, I want to see him."

Panzer stepped past Avery while pulling his access card from the inside pocket of his jacket.

"Sir there is one more thing."

Panzer looked back at Avery as he slid his card through the reader and leaned into the unlocked door. "What is it?"

Following the tall gray-haired man through the doorway Avery said, "You'll see sir."

Panzer had already turned to see Javier Perez standing behind the glass wall of the medical room. "What's he doing here?" asked the world's richest man.

CHAPTER 12

DENISE DIEGERT SAT IN HER LUXURY PRISON apartment looking at the images on the TV of her son being shot, falling to the ground and then being obliterated by the explosion of the bag he had been carrying on his shoulder. Her tears flowed over her cheeks as she mourned the loss of the little boy she had so much fun with back in Minnesota. She recalled how David loved to go with her on hikes and canoe trips. He had an affinity for the natural world and got so excited when they would find interesting pieces of driftwood, beautiful bird feathers or unusual stones. Once, they found the skeleton of a deer with the skull intact including an eight-point rack of antlers. That skull became a prize possession, which David cleaned up and kept for years in his bedroom. Denise also thought about how David became her protector and confidant while the relationship with Tom Diegert and Jake deteriorated into a domestic feud. Once it was out in the open that Tom was not David's father, the détente, which had allowed David to grow up in the house, degraded into sullen hatred and constant conflict. Denise was stuck in the middle.

She defended David but took a lot of crap for it. David grew tall and strong. Soon Tom and Jake were physically outmatched and their differences with David grew into armed confrontations. Were it not for David, Denise feared that Tom would have seriously hurt or killed her during one of his drunken rages. More than once, it was David who pulled Tom off her and stopped him from beating her to death. Now she had to look at the screen and see her savior as a pariah, committing an act of terrorism, which killed hundreds of people, ruined thousands of lives, and brought down an entire apartment building. How could the boy she loved become such a violent and destructive person? The grief she felt, mixed with the shame of being the mother of a monster, left her with a deep sense of guilt and despair. After watching the looping scenes of David's death several more times, she shut off the TV, dropped her head into her hands and cried out her pain with deep tearful sobs.

RICHARD RAMSEY WATCHED THE VIDEO of David Diegert's death with Carolyn Fuller. The TV in his office was affixed to the wall to the left of his desk. Carolyn sat facing Ramsey's desk, turning her head to see the TV. Ramsey looked over his shoulder to see David Diegert gunned down before his body was eviscerated by a powerful thermobaric explosion.

"You helped him escape and then you lost him and now he has committed one of the world's worst acts of terrorism. What does that make you? An accomplice? A terrorist? An idiot? What the hell are you?"

Carolyn snapped a look at Ramsey, which defied his insolent accusations. She felt the sting of his words, but she knew she was neither a terrorist nor an idiot.

"I did not help him do any of this."

"Oh no? This wasn't part of the plan when you helped him cross the ocean?"

"Instead of wasting our time, let's get to work investigating who was behind this."

"Yeah right, I've seen this before where the perpetrator

is the one actually directing the investigation to make certain they are never found."

"Richard, that's crazy. This isn't some lame TV show. We've got a real crime and we need to pursue and adjudicate the real culprits."

With a shake of his head Ramsey said, "It is a crime on British soil, the London police and MI5 will lead the investigation. We will do nothing unless requested, but I want you to be available for questioning... on background."

Carolyn locked her gaze on Ramsey. "I had nothing to do with this and you have no grounds to consider me a suspect."

As Carolyn leaned forward, her belly protruded with the unyielding solidity of a pregnant abdomen. Ramsey noticed the substantial roundness of her midsection. He had always admired the trim, athletic build of this attractive woman. Richard Ramsey still held a flame for Carolyn Fuller that burned ever since they trained together at the CIA Farm in Virginia. She caught sight of his eyes and drew back into her chair pulling closed her thin cardigan.

Ramsey's lips formed a mischievous smile. "Is there something you're not telling me?"

"I don't have anything to tell you that's not already all over the media."

"No, no," said the man with an, *I got ya* smile. "I mean something personal?" Ramsey widened his eyes and stared at her belly with an exaggerated expression.

"What are you talking about?" said Carolyn crossing her arms over her belly.

"Come on Carolyn, I'm happy for you. How far along are you?"

Carolyn Fuller went red with embarrassment. She

couldn't deny what others were now able to see, but she was not ready to acknowledge her condition and admit that she was going to be a mother. Abortion had crossed her mind and right now, she wished she'd gone through with it. She offered no reply to Ramsey's question.

"Also Carolyn, who is the father?"

"That's none of your business," she shouted. Carolyn surprised herself with the explosive volume with which she just yelled at her boss. She dropped her eyes, bowing her head to Ramsey.

"Given the sensitive nature of the situation in which we find ourselves, it is imperative that I know the paternity of your unborn child so that a determination of the risk of being compromised can be assessed."

"That's bullshit."

"That tone is insubordinate, and given the timing of your pregnancy and your arrival in London, I am curious if the child was conceived in the U.S. or Europe?"

"My body and its functions are not CIA business. If you pursue this I will bring charges against you."

Ramsey leaned his head back, shaking it from side to side before stating, "Now, now Carolyn, you know that personal relationships are open to scrutiny by the Agency, especially those which develop in foreign countries. Your body may be your own, but the obvious situation involving intimacy with another is clearly open to Agency inquiry."

"The only way you're getting any information is through HR."

"HR?" said Ramsey, raising his eyebrows.

"Human Resources," replied Carolyn.

"I know what fucking HR stands for. I don't need to go through them."

"Title IX requires that you do."

"Look we're not talking girls' softball," scoffed Ramsey, "Title IX doesn't apply."

"Oh yes it does, and if you don't abide by it, I'll be glad to see you swing."

Boss and employee stared at each other until Ramsey broke eye contact. "Carolyn, your condition is obvious and I just want to know if the father represents a risk, that's all."

"It's none of your fucking business and I resent the fact that you think I would compromise the Agency with issues in my personal life. Do whatever you must but there is nothing to find. Now if you'll excuse me, I'm feeling a bit nauseous."

Carolyn Fuller exited the office and never looked back. Ramsey watched her leave and thought he saw a waddle in her step.

Passing through the hall of the Embassy, Carolyn felt awful, her pregnancy made her feel nauseous, but the oafish behavior of her annoying boss made everything worse. At her office, she put on her beige trench coat and left the building. Walking along the street, she found her emotions welling up. A sob escaped her lips and tears clouded her vision. She kept up her pace while pulling a Kleenex from her pocket to cover her mouth as another sob erupted from her heart. At London Bridge, she stepped to the side of the walkway, her sadness escaping. She looked out over the water so as not to attract attention. She needn't worry, the pace of everyone's personal lives provided no time for the despair of a young woman. Carolyn's vexing situation made her so disappointed. She always wanted children. It was an immediate yes when asked if she intended to have a family of her own, "Of course," she would answer. The hope she had for starting her family though, was nothing like this. Unwed, with a deep secret about the father being a dead criminal. The video showed David, in the middle of a horrendous act, something she would never imagine the man she got to know ever doing, yet there it was on CCTV. Carolyn couldn't help but question what she'd seen. The David Diegert she knew had an extremely athletic body. His arms were thick and muscular, with broad shoulders and big chest muscles. His midsection was lean, flat and tight. The guy in the video was just the opposite, he was the right height, but his chest was narrow and thin, shoulders sloping and unremarkable while the abdomen had a paunchy layer of fat that was obvious as the body fell back over the bag. How could Diegert get so out of shape so quickly? When she last saw him, there was no indication he had lost his fitness. She could not however deny the face. The close up of Diegert was unmistakable. The photographic images would serve as a positive ID, since the explosion had vaporized the entire body. Any forensic material would be contaminated by the remains of the multiple victims dispersed all over the crime scene. As she continued along the bridge back to her flat, Carolyn remained sad, knowing that David Diegert was dead and her child would never meet its father.

CHAPTER 13

"WHAT'S HE DOING HERE?" ASKED KLAUS Panzer as he looked at Javier Perez through a glass wall in a medical treatment room at LPU.

Avery replied, "I wanted to tell you that David had to change his face to Javier's during his escape from China."

"I'll be damned," said Panzer, with a tilt of his head. "I totally believed that was Javier."

"Yes, but it's David," clarified Avery.

Panzer strode forward and found the door locked.

Avery said, "He was a bit agitated."

"Please unlock the door. I want to speak with my son."

Avery paused as a doubtful look spread over his face. Panzer stoically awaited the door to be opened. An audible buzz and a metallic snap preceded Panzer turning the doorknob.

The tall, distinguished man stepped forward. "Hello David."

From the sneering face of Javier Perez came a chilling question, "Is it really you, or do I get to kill you again?"

"No son, it is I."

"Well look at me and you'll see that your son is not who you think he is."

Thoughtfully Panzer replied, "You seem upset."

"Oh yeah. You must've been reading self-help pamphlets. You're going to engage my emotions? You want to help me with the rage that boils inside when I see hundreds of people killed in my name? You want a piece of that?" Diegert stood toe to toe with his father, an angry snarl scrawled across the face of Javier Perez. Diegert's body vibrated as he held himself back from attacking.

Panzer stepped back as he said, "There is a plan and an outcome that is within our grasp. The loss of life is regrettable and the explosion was disproportionate to our plan."

"Fucking Blevinsky overdid it. I don't know why you even keep that guy around. He's a dangerous idiot."

"Nevertheless." Panzer raised a silencing hand. "The visual death of David Diegert has given us a chance to create a new identity and life for you. Avery can explain."

Avery stood up, eyes rapidly blinking, "The plan is to introduce you as the son of Klaus Panzer. We have manufactured an identity with a backstory explaining where you've been all your life. Who your mother was, what happened to her and what you will bring to the Board of Crepusculous."

"I'll be on the board?" asked Diegert with surprise.

"Yes," said Avery.

Panzer nodded. "Each board member gets to identify an heir. That person participates in the operation of Crepusculous and Omnisphere pursuant to their skills and abilities."

"What am I supposed to do?"

A prideful Panzer said, "I have made you a financier. You are a graduate of the Faculty of Commerce at the University of Victoria in British Columbia, Canada."

"I don't know anything about finance."

"Don't worry, I'll coach you."

"Am I Canadian?"

"Yes," said Panzer. "Your mother was Icelandic. She

lived in British Columbia working as a flight attendant for Air Canada. She and I met on a business trip and you were subsequently born. She refused to leave Canada where she completed medical school and practiced as a physician for twenty years. She recently died from an antibiotic resistant bacterial infection she encountered while treating patients on a medical mission in Paraguay. In her will she revealed that I am your father and so now you are joining me in Europe to take your place on the Board of Crepusculous."

"What was my mom's name?"

"Ayla," replied Panzer.

"Just like that, I get to direct the world's most powerful company?"

"Well," said Panzer, "It's more like an apprenticeship. You will be guided and instructed while being tested to make certain you possess the fortitude, perspective and determination necessary to fulfill the role of a Crepusculous board member." Stepping closer and leaning forward, Panzer said, "Your place on the board will not be simply handed to you, it must be earned."

Diegert held the icy glare of his father's pale blue eyes. Panzer pulled back. "We've got to get you a new face."

"Good. I hate Javier."

Avery said, "You can't go back to David Diegert."

The blunt pronouncement set a bleak look upon Javier's face as Diegert realized his worldwide media death meant his face could never again be the one with which he grew up.

Avery could see the struggle. "We've been working on this for you." With a remote, Avery illuminated a widescreen TV as he typed on a keyboard. The screen appeared but there were no images. Avery said, "There are certain parameters we had to take into account in the creation of a new face."

"Like what?" asked Diegert.

"Age and hereditary factors. The face had to be an original; we do not want you to be a double, like you were on your mission and like you are right now. We had to invent a unique face that was unidentifiable through the world's most powerful facial recognition software. The face had to look real while being created digitally. It also had to be fully functional. The 3D rendering process had to be to the exact specifications we required and the face had to be able to express the full range of human emotions."

Avery stepped in front of the screen facing Diegert and Panzer, who stood a step back, beaming with anticipation. "This face has been researched for authenticity, tested with emotional simulations, digitally remastered for clarity and it is an absolute original."

"All right, bring it on the screen already," groaned Diegert.

The image did a slow resolve, appearing gradually, yet striking Diegert with a sense of shocked amazement as he looked at a picture of what he believed to be a young Klaus Panzer.

Diegert looked from the screen to an anxious Avery Forsythe and back to the screen.

The face was no doubt handsome, with ice blue eyes, chestnut-blond hair, a strong straight nose and high cheekbones. The square jaw tapered into a dimpled chin. The lips were even, with subtle curves and a gentle infundibulum reaching up to meet the nostrils. Ears were well formed, with a tight fit to the head and just the right amount of protrusion.

Fully aware that Panzer was standing right behind him, Diegert asked, "Is this a picture of Klaus when he was twenty five years old?"

Avery replied, "This image includes features of Klaus Panzer that are likely to be passed to his offspring if he were to have had a child with this woman."

The screen switched to reveal an attractive young woman of Scandinavian heritage. She had blonde hair, blue eyes, nice cheekbones along with full lips and a straight but delicate looking nose. Diegert thought she was hot, until Avery said, "This is your mother. We mixed her facial features with your father's to create a mash up which was rendered into the face you just saw. So, now your new face is not simply your father's. The face includes components of hereditary expression that would likely be represented when mixed with the features of your digital mother."

Diegert lifted his left hand to his bowed head, scratching his forehead before running his fingers through Javier Perez's thick hair.

Avery continued, "I want to point out that we were able to give your face a great deal of symmetry. Digital mastering gives us the ability to even out facial proportions, so the two sides of the face are even, and almost identical. Symmetry creates a greater level of attractiveness to the human face."

With a sarcastic tone Diegert said, "A perfectly handsome man. Conjured up out of digital magic to replace the person I really am."

Panzer could hold back no longer. "David, with this face and the rest of the plan, you will be my son and I will proclaim you as the heir to my fortune."

"You will proclaim me, but only if I wear this face?"

"The face is your portal to freedom and a new life with limitless possibilities," extolled Panzer. "Please choose success and become the man everyone wishes they could be."

Avery interjected, "From a practical point of view, you can't stay in Javier's face and every other face in the world is already taken. This is your new face."

Diegert swung his head from one man to the other and back to the screen.

"The image is already 3D rendered," said Avery. "We can activate your nanocytes and begin the transamination immediately. The process will take about twenty minutes and then you'll appear as Vince Kronig."

"My new name is Vince Kronig?"

Avery clarified, "Your mother's name was Ayla Kronig, so you have her last name. Vincent is a powerful name and you have gone your whole life by the name Vince. Some of this history you will have to learn, but some of it will be embedded in your brain through the actions of the nanocytes. It'll make it easier for you to function with basic identity information already implanted in your brain."

"That sounds like digital brainwashing."

Panzer blurted out, "We are nowhere near that sophisticated at this point. What Avery is saying is that the nanocytes can help you with instant recognition of your new name so you don't have to remember it every time someone calls you Vince."

"I will remember who I really am though?" asked Diegert.

"Yes," replied Avery.

Diegert's sense of doubt played across his face.

"Yes." Repeated both men with an absolute sense of assurance.

"I want to change a couple of things on the face."

Avery looked at him with halted disbelief. "What do

you want to change?"

"I want that ridiculous dimple in the chin gone, and I want a mole somewhere on the right cheek. I do not want an absolutely perfect face. Stick a mole on the right side."

Avery got to work on the computer making adjustments to the facial image.

Diegert asked Panzer, "What about my real mother, what does she know?"

"She's seen the video on the media."

"So she thinks I'm dead and that I died a terrorist."

Panzer nodded.

"Is she still getting the cancer care you promised?"

"Yes she is, but you can't see her if this plan is going to work," declared Panzer. "Don't worry about her. We will take care of her for the rest of her life."

Diegert flexed his first two fingers in rapid succession drawing Panzer closer. He grabbed the front of Panzer's shirt and tie pulling him close. "You had better take care of her or I'll kill you!" Diegert flung his father away while maintaining direct eye contact as Panzer rebalanced himself and straightened his shirt and tie.

Avery returned, unaware of the altercation. "Okay, look at the new image." On the screen was the face of Vince Kronig, without the chin dimple and sporting a dark mole halfway between the cheek and jaw on the right side. "Do you approve?"

Diegert looked over the image the way some people inspect a written assignment before handing it in, seeking to make sure everything's right. He wanted to be sure about something over which there would be no certainty.

Avery, with his hands on the keyboard, said, "Ready to commence transamination upon your direction."

Diegert let out a long slow sigh, "Let's get this done."

In spite of the fact that each human face is unique and distinct, the actual differences between two faces are nuances of appearance that our eyes are trained to detect. Analytically the differences are minor but within that subtlety is the key to physical identity. The nanocytes produced changes to Diegert's face adjusting the nostrils, edges of the lips and the shape of the eyelids and eyebrows, creating a face that would be his new image of identity to the world.

When the process was complete, Avery gave Diegert a hand mirror. The eyes went wide as the mouth gaped open when the reflection was perceived. Although the image was exactly as planned, Diegert was surprised at how unsettling it was to look at himself and see this new face. Just like Jian Wong and Javier Perez, Diegert had to again see himself as someone else. This time though he knew this was not someone else's face. It was an original. It was unique to him and unprecedented on the planet. With the others, there were dossiers and experience from which to know the men, but for this one there was no real history. Who was Vince Kronig? It was up to David Diegert to decide and create the persona he wanted to show the world with this new face.

Panzer, Avery and no doubt, Blevinsky had made up the backstory, but it was David who would embody this new person, and he could behave in whatever manner he wanted.

Avery interrupted David's thoughts. "What do you think?"

"I look like a cross between a Ken doll and comic book Aquaman."

Avery chuckled. "Millions of people would kill to look so good."

"In my case, only 511 people had to die for me to look like this."

Panzer stepped forward. "You are a man of whom many will be envious, but many more will look up to with faith, belief and desire. Come my son let's celebrate your arrival."

"Wait!" said Diegert, halting the moment. "I'm not ready to meet people just yet. I want to be alone with the new me." Panzer looked at him quizzically, but Avery directed the tall gray-haired man to the door and together they left Diegert in the room with his new face contemplating his new identity.

Diegert realized he had an opportunity to become the man he'd always wanted to be. Who he was up to now had been someone molded by bad circumstances and worse people. Tom and Jake Diegert never gave him a reason to think well of himself. The duality of his Native and White American blood left him socially adrift in Northern Minnesota. Friendless and ostracized, he looked down on himself as others did. He felt worthless, lonely and despondent. He acted out with rage and turned his violent tendencies into combative sports. When he discovered he was a bastard, the rejection he felt all his life suddenly had validity. He was unwanted and abandoned by a father he never knew. All Tom's anger and abuse made perfect sense. Why would he want the product of his wife's infidelity living in his home? Of course, the kid should be shunned, neglected, and exploited. Were it not for the love of his mother he would have no sense of self-worth at all. Not thinking much of himself left him with little reason to treat others with kindness. Diegert was a product of his dreadful and impoverished upbringing, but he now realized he could break from that. As Vince, he could be kind, gentle, polite, considerate and thoughtful. He would show strength through generosity rather than violence. Respect would be earned, not through fear and intimidation, but through intelligence and the provision of assistance. He would take on the role of a philanthropist, raising and donating money to just and worthy causes. Instead of being a killer of men, he would become a provider, a supporter, a savior.

David lifted the mirror and looked at the new him. He had to admit the face looked like a movie star. The kind of guy who would turn heads and be remembered. He smiled for the first time and the handsome face looked even better. A "Million dollar smile," as they say. His new looks were both captivating and compelling. People would immediately find him attractive and project upon him all sorts of positive attributes. This would be so different than the negative assumptions always made when his old self entered the room. Diegert regretted living down to the old expectations but it was who he was. Now he would be someone new.

Touching his face for the first time, David felt the warm, smooth skin of his cheek. He ran his fingers through the luxurious thick hair and stared back at the ice blue eyes. He lost himself for a moment in the eyes. Peering in, he looked to see if he was really in there. Could he fulfill the potential represented by Vince Kronig? Could who he was, become who he wanted to be, while co-existing in this handsome, but manufactured appearance? Diegert realized that the eyes were definitely Klaus Panzer's. The face was an amalgamation, but Panzer's genetics were directly responsible for the piercing blue eyes. David promised himself he would commit Vince's life to doing good. Although he had his father's eyes, he would see with clarity as he committed himself to a new purpose in life.

Avery knocked softly on the door as he gently opened it. "May I come in?"

"Yeah," replied Diegert.

As he approached Avery said, "It is a bit unsettling to see you looking so different, so I imagine it is taking you a moment to adjust."

Sighing, Diegert replied, "Yeah it is, but I was just thinking about my mom. She must be destroyed thinking I'm dead and believing I was the world's worst criminal. Can't I tell her I'm alive and now I have a new face and I'm going to be someone new and better?"

"Listen to yourself and tell me she's going to be better served with that crazy story."

Diegert hung his new handsome head, sighing more deeply.

Avery spoke up, "Look you can still be in her life. We are going to take care of her forever and you can befriend her and treat her as kindly as you would like. She might be happy to "adopt" you."

"More lies, it's always a lie."

"David the rest of your life is going to be a lie, but that lie can be as good as you want it to be. Not all lies are negative. Your life can be a positive deception, committed to whatever ideals you feel are most important."

Scoffing, Diegert said, "Leave it to you to twist a life of lies into something better than the truth."

THE GRAND HALL CONFERENCE AND banquet center at LPU was selected by Klaus Panzer for the public event at which he would introduce his son, Vince Kronig, to the people who mattered most to Crepusculous and Omnisphere. With the campus CCTV system at full capacity and security personnel on high alert, the venue would be impenetrable to curious media reporters or rivals in the business world. Approximately 200 guests entered the hall to be greeted by Panzer himself before they enjoyed the open bar and the gourmet hors d'oeuvres. In the far corner of the Grand Hall Vince stood with his sisters, Gretchen and Sashi while being introduced to the guests who lined up to shake the hand of the bastard son who would inherit the wealth of Klaus Panzer.

Some of the guests grumbled under their breath, for they found it absolutely disgusting to be celebrating the fact that this incredibly arrogant and narcissistic tyrant would hold a rare, although private, event to introduce a bastard son from an affair he had years ago. Only now, at the peak of his power, was he willing to admit to the deed. How many other poor sods were there out there that would never be acknowledged by the unrepentant philanderer? These thoughts were never given voice as the economic power wielded by Panzer rendered the moral objections mute. The guests adopted the practice of suppressing their displeasure under polite smiles and obligatory handshakes.

Among the corporate executives under the Omnisphere umbrella and foreign dignitaries subservient to the generosity and control of the world's largest company were the board members of Crepusculous and their families. Diegert gave himself over to the role of Vince. Never in his life had he received so much praise and adulation for having done nothing. He thought he might be able to get used to this. He just had to smile and politely shake hands and the men would congratulate him while the woman would flirt with him. His new face was admired, adored and desired. He could see it in their eyes. Diegert realized that with just a little extra expression he could get even the oldest of the women to smile at him with a great deal of mischief in their eyes. Vince took a position next to his father and sisters forming a reception line to greet the people of Crepusculous.

Chin Lee Wei, his wife Ming Ha, son Shing and daughter Mei Ling were the first in line. Diegert could see that the grief from losing Qiang was still fresh on Chin Lee, who had difficulty with eye contact while making his stoic remarks. Ming Ha was also hurting and although polite did not seem comfortable in the big crowd. Shing seemed like a lost boy, who perhaps did not even want to be the man in charge of the Wei Empire's future. Mei Ling however took Diegert's hand with a firm sense of self and purpose for the family. She seemed to realize now was not the time to be filling one's mind with thoughts of loss and grief. She shook the hand of Vince Kronig in a manner that let him know she was someone to remember.

"It's a pleasure to meet you," she said. "I think it's wonderful that the people of Crepusculous finally get to meet."

"Yes, well I'm kind of new to Crepusculous but I'm very happy to make your acquaintance."

Lowering her voice as she stepped closer, Mei Ling said, "The founders can't live forever, it will be up to us to keep the alliance alive."

Vince pulled his head back, casting her a curious gaze.

Mei Ling's dark eyes searched for agreement, but Vince's expression was quite questionable. "We will speak again, when we can focus on business,"

"Certainly," replied Vince, as Mei Ling stepped away to re-join her family.

Next in line were the familiar faces of Javier Perez and

Fatima Hussain. She wore a sleek dress that fell to the floor with just enough slit to allow her long legs the freedom to throw a roundhouse kick. Diegert couldn't help but look at her, and her plunging cleavage, as he shook the hand of Javier Perez. When the grip on his hand increased, Vince turned his eyes to the glare of the dark Spaniard. Javier said, "I apologize. My father Julio is unable to join us. His health is not well. I however am so glad to meet the man with whom I will one day rule the world."

Vince replied, "I wish your father all the best. I believe we will make an excellent team." Turning his attention to Fatima he asked, "And who is this vision of loveliness?"

"I am Fatima Hussain," said the stunning Pakistani woman, not waiting for Javier. "I'm very happy to meet you. I hope that the future of Crepusculous is dedicated to leaving a legacy of generosity and better living conditions all over the planet."

Taken aback by the strength and clarity of her message, Vince replied, "Nobility is not only to be admired but to be acted upon."

With her hand still in his grasp Fatima flinched but re-centered her gaze. A sudden sense of familiarity ran through her nerves, and she shuddered at the feeling. Diegert saw the flinch and a flirtatious smirk rose across his lips. He felt like a kid playing hide and seek. He was looking right at her, but she could not see David Diegert, only the captivating Vince Kronig. She and Javier moved along, but Fatima kept peering over her shoulder at the mysterious new man.

The distinguished bearing of Dean Kellerman always impressed Diegert. The accented English and the chipper sense of keeping a stiff upper lip were the calling cards of the second half of the founding pair of Crepusculous.

Accompanying him were his son Michael and his daughter Colleen.

"Such an honor to meet you," said the man of quiet power, surprising Diegert with the strength of his grip. "I do say your story is quite the tale of a reversal of fortune."

Vince tilted his head as he replied with a questioning tone, "Reversal?"

Holding Diegert's gaze Dean continued, "Well, all right, you were not exactly a pauper, but your mother's resources were certainly less than what lies before you now."

"Are you implying that my current position is somehow inappropriate?" asked Vince.

With a baleful look from under a bushy eyebrow, Dean Kellerman countered, "Oh no, nothing of the sort. I just wanted to point out that your lot in life has changed dramatically, and very much for the better."

Vince's nonstop smile faded as he replied, "Did your children's lives change for the better when their mother died?"

Seeking to lighten the mood Kellerman responded with a return of his classic smile. "Enjoy your evening and welcome to the most powerful alliance on earth. Allow me to introduce my son Michael."

Diegert turned his attention to the one man at the party who was not wearing a tie. The open collar though was the least of the appearance problems for the awkward and unkempt son of Dean Kellerman.

"Dude," came the greeting from the man whose shirttail extruded from his trousers covering the girth of his gut. His pants, unlaundered blue jeans. Upon his feet were scruffy sneakers, the kind with white rubber encasing the toes. The one thing Michael had already clearly accomplished was to have found the bar and enjoyed the free drinks. Trouble with substance abuse was clearly evident in the young man's demeanor. The fact he had a nearly empty highball glass as he met the guest of honor displayed where his priorities were.

Diegert shook the guy's hand which had the feel of a damp kitchen rag. "Pleased to meet you."

"Yeah, welcome aboard. Let's hang out sometime. I can take you someplace a lot cooler than this fuck'n fogey fest."

Cocking his head with a slight nod, Vince said, "Okay, let's do that sometime."

As he walked away, Michael Kellerman replied with a chuck from his lips and teeth while raising his glass and downing the contents.

Diegert watched as he walked away then turned to see the most striking face he had ever laid eyes on. He nearly dropped dead, she was that gorgeous. Colleen Kellerman's smile gleamed across a face of perfect proportions, glowing under smooth soft skin. Her sultry brunette hair framed her face in lustrous waves. Her dark brown eyes sparkled with an effervescent joy which shown like bright beacons of happiness. She was beaming, radiating an appeal that Diegert found irresistibly attractive.

He caught himself staring at her, lost in his impressions. His gleeful smile and wide eyes told everyone that Vince Kronig was immediately and deeply smitten. He was so very pleased to be making the acquaintance of the daughter of Dean Kellerman.

"Hello," said the young lady as she extended her hand. "I'm Colleen Jewel Kellerman."

Pulled from his reverie, Vince took the hand, and gently but firmly accepted the greeting. "It is so nice to meet you. Call me D… Vince."

"D'Vince?"

Chuckling awkwardly, Diegert said, "No, just Vince."

"Well, I go by Julie. I prefer the use of my middle name."

"Excellent, Julie it is then."

"I'm glad you've been reacquainted with your father."

"Yes, it was a long time that I didn't know who my father was."

Julie's furrowed brow showed Diegert that she was listening and found his remark sad.

"One cannot control the circumstances of creation," said Diegert. "But hopefully the consequences have their purpose."

Julie looked at Vince with a quizzical gaze. "I suppose that's true. What purpose do you hope to fulfill now that the consequences have turned out as they are?"

"My purpose will be to serve others with the power and resources of Omnisphere. I only hope I find similar minded colleagues on the Board of Crepusculous."

Her smile was reluctant, not the full beamer from earlier. This smile was hopeful but nuanced. It occurred to Vince that perhaps she already realized that the greatest force of opposition to generosity on the board was his father. How would he influence the direction of an entity with which he did not always agree. She said, "I would like to meet with you at some point and hear some more about your plans for the future."

Vince leaned in with Diegert's reply, "You can count on me reaching out to find time on your calendar."

Julie's smile brightened a few notches and her eyes held more mischief than the old ladies'. As she walked away she simply said, "I look forward to it."

CHAPTER 14

MEI LING STEPPED OVER TO THE BAR for a second drink. While patiently waiting to be served, she looked to her right as a striking dark woman with beautiful black hair, styled in a French braid inlaid with strands of gold, approached. The woman's body filled her figure hugging dress with tantalizing proportions. Mei Ling found herself reacting to the appearance of this woman with thoughts that were surprisingly sexual.

Fatima Hussain extended her hand to Mei Ling as she introduced herself. She was surprised by the firm strength in the grip of the smaller woman who seemed somewhat subservient and demure.

"I'm Fatima Hussain."

"And I am Mei Ling Wei. I was just telling Vince that is so nice to meet the rest of the people of Crepusculous."

"That disgusting corporate name almost sounds pretty when you say it."

Mei Ling smiled as she giggled, "When I first heard the word, Crepusculous I asked my father if it was a fatal disease."

"Believe me, for some people it is. I wanted to meet you because I feel that when the time comes to change the guard, we women should take over."

Mei Ling blinked with astonishment before her attention wavered when the bartender requested her order. "A vodka martini please."

Fatima held her gaze with anticipation.

"I like bold," said Mei Ling. "I too have concerns about the future. My brother is not equipped to rule the world, not even one quarter of it."

Sliding close as she lowered her voice Fatima said, "Javier is only good at one thing, and it is not running the globe's largest corporation."

Mei Ling giggled as her drink arrived. Taking a sip and flicking her eyes to direct Fatima's gaze to the end of the bar she said, "I have grave doubts about the capabilities of the Kellerman family's heir." Together they observed Michael Kellerman, planted on a stool and slumped on the bar as he swallowed his drink in two gulps. Looking at each other, Fatima rolled her eyes and Mei Ling shrugged her shoulders.

"Then there's Vince," said Mei Ling.

"He sure is nice to look at," purred Fatima, "but he's a huge unknown."

Taking charge, Fatima said, "Come on, I want you to meet someone else."

Crossing through the party, the pair turned the heads of those who admired feminine beauty. Fatima led them to a table where two women sat. Mei Ling and Fatima had met Gretchen and Sashi Panzer in the reception line. Fatima continued the role of woman in charge. "Gretchen and Sashi, tonight you met Mei Ling, together we," Fatima circled her hand around them, "are the future of Crepusculous." All four women clinked their drinks, and toasted the proclamation.

Fatima stated, "The board only thinks of themselves, but the whole world is affected by all the decisions they make. We need to think of the future."

Leaning forward Gretchen said, "This party is not the

place, but I agree one hundred percent. Let's meet soon and do some planning."

Fatima shook hands with the handsome blonde woman. Gretchen Panzer was equally self -assured and just as assertive as Fatima, but she realized it was the striking Pakistani who had taken the initiative and she had to respect that.

The evening transitioned into an elegant meal served on fine china. The menu featured braised medallions of veal smothered in apricot nectar glaze upon a rosemary and thyme risotto. The salad, festooned with fresh strawberries and candied pecans, included greens of spinach, arugula, oak leaf lettuce and radicchio. Sangiovese, from a Tuscan vintner, filled the stemware, served at cellar temperature. The meal concluded with a chocolate raspberry mousse molded into the shape of the Omnisphere global logo.

The return of the lost son gave Panzer powerful incentive to spare no expense welcoming the young man he always wanted into the fold of his family, his business and his empire. Tonight was a special occasion for the man and having eaten an excellent meal he was now eager to get to the podium and tell everyone about his joy.

"Ladies and gentlemen, please continue to enjoy your dessert. I just want to thank you for coming to celebrate the arrival of my son. As is widely known I did not know of my son's presence in the world for twenty-five years. His mother and I shared a common passion but not a lifetime together. She was a smart, loving woman with a fierce independent streak and a determination to live according to her own plan. She raised Vince well, and has given him the values and beliefs to which I aspire and hold as the light of the world. Her unfortunate passing led to the reunion of Vince and me. The tragic loss of Ayla Kronig led to the joyful re-connection between me and my son, which we celebrate tonight. I just want to tell you a couple of things about Ayla. She was an incredibly smart young lady. When I met her, she was a graduate student in biochemistry at the University of British Columbia. She was on scholarship from Iceland and had that stoic Icelandic spirit of perseverance. I can tell you that as a single mother, she completed medical school and throughout her career, she both treated patients and studied communicable diseases. It was an investigation into a rare tropical disease that caused her death. Like a sentenced prisoner turning against his captors, the virus she was seeking to control, infected her. Her dedication to science and the relentless pursuit of discovery is the trait for which she would have wanted to be remembered. Please raise your glass in honorable memory of Ayla Kronig."

The whole banquet hall, over two hundred people, raised their glasses to toast a lie. Panzer could see some of the guests sitting near the front tearing up as he told his fabricated story of Vince's mother.

"Now for my son, Vince," said Panzer. "A man, who grew up without a father, now has the best father in the world!" Panzer paused for the laughter but the confused silence quickly grew awkward and he resumed his remarks. "Vince has Canadian citizenship, so he is of course very polite. His heritage however is from Europe which makes him combative." Again no laughter. "In spite of not knowing him, I believe I had some influence since he studied economics at Victoria University. He and I will collaborate on the future of Omnisphere, seeing it grow and prosper. The other day we were discussing Digival and he asked, 'How did you know the world was ready for a global currency?' The question made me realize how important it is to have an heir to whom you can pass on your legacy. Vince is smart, determined and resourceful. He has skills and abilities that go beyond the obvious and I am so happy to have all of you here to share in the celebration of a father's love."

Panzer stopped talking and waited for the applause. It started low at first with just a few brave claps, but it spread and rose into a thunderous roar leading to a standing ovation during which Panzer stood on the podium soaking up all the adoration, never calling up his son, the true man of the hour. When it became obvious, Panzer had overlooked inviting Vince to the stage. The applause slowly broke off and people began sitting down. Panzer resumed speaking, "Thank you all for coming. For your dancing pleasure the band will now begin." With a faux conductor's flourish, he waved his hand and the twelve-piece band got the message and began playing.

Panzer descended the stairs and began speaking with people as he walked over to the dance floor. He did not greet or speak to Vince. Diegert was probably one of the least surprised in the room. He knew Panzer was a self-absorbed narcissist. His speech was a total lie. Diegert had never been to British Columbia. He sat at the table of honor but Gretchen had left with a disgusted look on her face and Sashi just couldn't keep herself from the dance floor.

Diegert looked out over the crowd and watched as people listened to the music and enjoyed their conversations. Games of chance were set up while everyone ate and the Monte Carlo night attracted hopeful gamblers. The chair next to him slid out and Diegert turned to see the wide, short body of Aaron Blevinsky fall into the seat next to him.

In his Russian tinged accent Blevinsky said, "You

know who I am and I know who you really are."

The sky blue eyes of Vince Kronig glared at the man who had turned David Diegert into an assassin. Diegert hated the man and didn't understand why Panzer kept him around. He was suspicious of the dirty secrets Blevinsky must possess. Now the chubby information master was going to have even more incriminating stuff with which he would extract compliance. "Were you actually on the invite list?" Diegert asked sarcastically.

"I created the list."

Diegert wanted to make something plain to this man. "I'm going to take advantage of the opportunity to become a new person."

Blevinsky, still eating sweet chocolate dessert squares out of foil wrappers, scoffed, "No one can become a new person. You have this new identity which is actually a perfect cover so we can keep you around, change your face as necessary and send you on missions that serve Crepusculous."

He licked chocolate from his fingers as he looked into the impossibly blue, but now sad eyes of Vince Kronig. "Don't you go believing your father's lies. You don't have a degree in economics and your mother was not a doctor with Icelandic blood. I'm the one who made up your whole cover story. The bullshit that lets you be someone new, is what I've created to fool the curious."

The foil crinkled as the portly Blevinsky unwrapped another dessert. "Your skills are far more rare and ultimately more valuable. We can hire economists, but Panzer loves the fact that his top assassin is his son. He keeps calling you an NK cell, whatever that is? He will never rescind your operational status. Once a killer, always a killer," Blevinsky said as thick syrupy cherry juice dripped from the corner of his mouth. To Diegert, it was blood on the mouth of a vampire.

"What if I'm done killing? What if I refuse to kill? I'm a public figure now."

"I suggest you don't challenge your father when he requests you to kill. Refusing will only lead to trouble for those you love or an order to execute you. You'll die in a sports car, an airplane, or a snowmobile, something cool and fun. What a tragedy."

"What if I kill you, Blevinsky?" The threat came from deep within Diegert, but it crossed the lips of Vince Kronig in a way that made Blevinsky smile.

"There you go buddy. You see there is a killer inside you. I'm only here five minutes, sharing a sobering perspective and your reaction is to threaten to kill me. That's what I mean, you're a killer at heart."

"I'd only kill you so I could stop killing."

Blevinsky frowned, shrugged his shoulders and said, "An interesting perspective but it still supports my point. Look I remember the guy who blew up Victor Del Fuentes in Miami and shot Gunther Mybuku in Paris. He then used a remote control rifle to kill Constantine Stravopolous in Greece. How about Farogue Arindi in Mogadishu, you used a knife to kill him. Need I go on?"

Blevinsky drew closer as if he were consoling a dear friend. "You've got a lot of great kills, of very bad people, and I'm confident you've got many more to come. So get back in the game and get ready. Look how well the Chinese mission went. Imagine, tonight you stood in the Grand Hall receiving congratulations from the Wei family, when just three weeks ago you stabbed their son right in front of them in their very own living room. How cool is that?"

"It's not cool. I don't want to keep doing it."

"Except for me of course," Blevinsky raised his eyebrows. "Don't worry it's hard to be in full mission mode when you're wearing a tux and every lady in the place wants to suck your dick. But trust me the need, the urge will rise within you and you'll be more than happy to again be assigned a lethal mission."

Vince leaned back in his chair, crossed his arms and looked up at the chandeliered ceiling.

Blevinsky hit him on the knee. "Hey buddy, don't look behind you but someone's coming to talk to you. I gotta go, but I'll always be around, I'll always know what you're doing." The heavy man, with some effort, rose to his feet and waddled away.

Vince looked behind him to see who was coming. He spun out of his seat as he rose to his feet. Denise Diegert was startled by his sudden move.

"I'm sorry I didn't mean to disturb you," she said.

"No, no...That's fine, I...I'm just very glad to see you."

"You are?" she said with surprise.

"Well, I mean, I've met a lot of people tonight and now I'm happy to meet you." He extended his hand to the tall exotic woman dressed in a conservative black dress. Her necklace, a single small pearl. She wore no makeup. Her natural beauty needed no adornment. She seemed nervous so Diegert did his best to help her succeed in this social situation.

"My name is Vince," he said as they shook hands. Her hands still felt rough, with thick calluses in her palms in spite of not doing a lot of work lately.

"I'm Denise," she offered as she withdrew her hand.

"You know there's a big elevated veranda just on the other side of those glass windows; it's supposed to have a beautiful view of the campus." Gesturing with his hand Diegert asked, "Would you like to go outside for a bit?"

Denise smiled, "I like being outside, yes I'd like that."

The veranda was big and broad. Tables and chairs offered seating and a few couples and small groups were enjoying the warm night air. The edge of the structure had a low concrete wall wide enough to sit on. Embedded in the concrete was a metal railing, which rose to the height of an elbow.

Diegert led her to the corner of the veranda where the view was best. Looking out from the 40-foot elevation, the entire campus of LPU stretched out in front of them. The campus lighting highlighted the walking paths and the building entrances. In spite of the hour and the fact that it was a weekend, many people were traversing the paths and entering or exiting the buildings.

"A college campus is always an active place," said Denise.

"Yes, I like them," said Vince. "They're environments designed for people. They are places for people to become their best."

"How was Victoria University?"

"It's actually called University of Victoria, like LPU it goes by UVIC. It's a beautiful place situated on the southern tip of Vancouver Island. One day I was kayaking in the Juan de Fuca and I found myself surrounded by a pod of Gray Whales. It was magical. I paddled with them for about half an hour until just as unexpectedly they disappeared.

"That sounds beautiful."

"I bet you'd really like it." Diegert was uncomfortable with how effectively he was lying to his mother. "You sure are looking well," he said as he thought about how she did not display negative side effects of her treatment for cancer.

The statement seemed to be perceived as awkward, since Denise did not reply and looked at Vince askance, under a raised eyebrow. "I mean you look very well dressed, that outfit is smashing."

"Thank you," said Denise.

"I don't think I caught your last name, Denise." He could see her squirming over having to reveal her association with the world's worst criminal.

"It's Diegert, Denise Diegert."

Their eyes met and Denise held the gaze of the ice blue eyes.

"Is that French?" he asked.

"What?"

"Is your last name French in origin?"

"Oh… I don't know."

"If it were French it would be pronounced De gare, like the guy on TV, Steve Colbert."

"I guess you are Canadian, since you speak French," said Denise

"Well French in western Canada is very different from Quebec. Since you are not French then, what is your background?" asked Vince.

Diegert could see she was uncomfortable with self-disclosure, but she told him, "I am Ojibwa. A tribe of Native people in North America."

"Oh yes, I know of the Ojibwa. They live in Ontario."

"Yes they do. My clan lives in Northern Minnesota. The Ojibwa lived in that region long before the U.S./Canadian border was created."

"It's a matriarchal society isn't it?"

"Women take leadership roles," said Denise nodding, "but it's not just women in charge. It's a cooperative society and the willingness to work with others for the good of all, rather than fighting, has often left us with the raw end of many deals."

"Victims of cheats and swindlers."

"We don't consider ourselves victims, but others do. They try to take advantage of our generosity. If you're going to commit to living by a principle, you have to stick with it even if it means things may be difficult."

Nodding his head and gazing upon her Vince said, "That's beautiful."

"My son David was on a vision quest..." Denise suddenly stopped speaking. She looked at Vince, terrified for having revealed a secret.

Vince smiled with genuine curiosity. "Go on you were going to tell me about your son."

CHAPTER 15

"DAVID WAS ON A VISION QUEST, A journey of self-discovery that guides one to a purpose in life. It turns out David was a troubled man. He got involved in something dark and dangerous and bigger than himself. I believe he was forced to act as everybody now knows he did." Denise's eyes welled up and she wiped the tears with her hands as she fought to hold back from bursting into sobs. Vince stepped close and put his arm around her shoulder. He handed her a paper napkin

"It's okay. Tell me about David when he was younger."

Snuffling, Denise began, "As a young boy David loved the outdoors. He would hike, swim, and paddle. He would collect interesting natural things, like plants, bugs, bones and driftwood. He learned all about the animals that lived near us and far away. African animals fascinated him. He always wanted to go on safari," she said with a chuckle.

"As he got older things changed, as they do for all of us. Being of mixed heritage was difficult for him, we had never discussed it, but the kids at school sure let him know that having a Native mother and white father was not cool. Right about the time that making friends is the most important thing in a kid's life, he was picked on and rejected. He took it hard and became quiet and bitter. I did all I could to help, but I saw that he just looked at me as the problem."

It was Diegert who now had to fight back the tears in Vince's blue eyes.

Denise went on. "I'm going to tell you something that I think is really important for you to know."

Grateful for the soft evening outdoor lighting, Diegert hoped his mom couldn't see the sadness building in Vince's eyes. "Go ahead."

"Your father, Klaus Panzer, was also the father of David Diegert."

"Wow, really?"

Denise nodded her head.

"God, that guy really got around," said Vince.

"He sure did. I hope your mother's encounter with him was consensual and loving, because that was not the case with me."

Diegert swallowed hard as his right hand closed into a fist.

"I probably shouldn't be saying this," said Denise, "but you should know the kind of man he can be."

"What did he do to you?"

She looked around, seeing if others were in earshot. She stepped closer, lowering her voice. "Now a days they call it sexual assault. Even though I didn't want to and I told him no, he forced himself upon me."

Denise got a faraway look in her eyes as she recollected Panzer's violence. Diegert grew angry and felt the familiar rage his father often evoked in him. He wanted to reach out and hug his mother, but he fought to stay in his role as Vince.

"The gossip grapevine at the Deerfield Lodge let it be known that I had sex with this really rich guy. No one cared about my perspective, but the word was out, Denise Diegert was a whore for the ultra-rich. I never set foot on that property again. All the extra money I made catering events just evaporated and my husband was furious. He had to hear all the jokes and then come home and beat the snot out of me."

His mother's eyes dried and her jaw took on a determined set.

"When my pregnancy started to show, I thought he was going to kill me. He wanted me to get an abortion, but I refused. Several times, he punched me in the stomach so hard; hoping to kill the baby, but David was tough and hung in there. Tom kept me around because I brought in more money than he did. He would've had to get two or three jobs to make more than me, so there was no way he was letting me go. But he sure wasn't going to love that child."

"That's terrible."

"Now the boy that was forced upon me, and I fought so hard to bring into the world, is dead. He will always be known as an awful criminal who killed lots of people. And here I am in the clutches of the man who made this all happen. Was I right for not having an abortion?"

Diegert again put his arm around the shoulder of his mom facing the edge of the veranda, looking out over the night lights of the campus. He spoke to her through the eyes of Vince Kronig, telling her, "I think you were incredibly brave, you can never know how things are going to turn out. You did the right thing to give that boy a chance."

Klaus Panzer had been looking all over the inside of the hall for Vince. Stepping out onto the veranda, he saw the blond hair of his newfound son over in the far corner.

Gazing across campus, Denise said, "He was beloved." Turning to Vince's blue eyes she continued, "That's why I named him David." Diegert sniffled as he struggled to hold back the tears welling up in the eyes of Vince Kronig.

Striding across the patio Panzer saw Vince with his arm on the shoulder of a woman who, from the rear, presented a sleek, attractive package. "Oh you rascal you," began Panzer as he approached. "You're a chip off the block aren't you? Cavorting with a beautiful woman on a romantic night."

Denise turned to face the man who was the cause of all her pain. Shocked, Panzer stuttered, "I …, I …, didn't realize who it was." He looked at Denise and then to Diegert shrugging his shoulders, unable to offer any words.

Denise raised her voice as she glared at the impeccably dressed tall gray-haired man. "You don't have to say anything. Your actions long ago have caused enough pain and suffering for a hundred life times." She stepped around Panzer, walking with defiance in her step back to the Grand Hall.

"What were you doing talking to her?" exclaimed Panzer.

"You mean what was I doing talking to my mother?"

"She is no longer your mother."

Diegert wanted Vince to be a really nice, peaceful kind of guy, yet here he was on his debut night ready to strangle his father and throw the fucker off the veranda. How was he ever going to live with this dissonance?

Vince flashed his awesome smile, and he saw his dad's face light up.

"Hey Dad," he said as he reached up and put his hand on the paternal shoulder. Diegert dropped his voice and moved his hand to the back of Panzer's neck. "Don't you ever speak poorly about my real mother," Diegert slid the vice grip of his hand up to the base of Panzer's skull, squeezing so hard that he cut off the blood flow in the vertebral arteries. "Or I'll kill you and gladly go back to having only one parent." A final squeeze for emphasis and a shove forced Panzer to stumble, awkwardly staggering as the blood flow returned to the back of his brain.

"Now why did you come out here?" demanded Vince.

Rubbing the back of his neck, Panzer had to wonder just how dangerous it was to have the world's best assassin for a son. He said, "We're going in to pose for some pictures."

Vince didn't say another word, turning and striding back to the Grand Hall. Panzer hastened his step to catch up with the younger man.

Inside, a photographer had a backdrop and lights set up. First was the Panzer family, Klaus, Gretchen, Sashi and Vince. All attractive people but the lack of family cohesion was evident, especially since Klaus's primary concern was how the lighting would emphasize the wrinkles on his face. Vince motioned with his hand for Denise to join them for a picture. She smiled but shook her head. Panzer shot Diegert, a look of stern rebuke.

Javier and Fatima made a striking couple. They were unable to take a bad picture until the photographer asked them to make crazy faces just for laughs.

The Wei family posed with stoic seriousness, the grief of their loss evident as Chin Lee insisted the space to his left remain vacant in honor of Quiang. Only Mei Ling's expression conveyed a sense of optimism.

The Kellermans were an uneven contrast. Dean struck a regal pose standing between his two children. Michael's posture revealed the state of inebriation to which he had progressed. While Julie exuded energy, vitality, and joy with a smile that dimpled her cute cheeks. Her fit curvy body filled her alluring dress in such a sexy way that everyone ignored the Kellerman men so they would not miss a moment of Julie posing for the camera.

The photographer surprised Diegert by asking that all of the families pose together. Crepusculous maintained its power by being anonymous and unseen. A family picture with all the principles in place along with all the people that are most important to them. It seemed like a tactical mistake. The security for this image had better be damn good because if it got out, personal, operational and corporate security could all be seriously compromised.

No one else seemed to be concerned, and the photographer had that drill sergeant with a flair kind of thing going, so soon everyone was marshaled into place, and the big shot of the Crepusculous family was taken.

As the group split up, Vince found himself approaching Julie; she turned with a smile to see him coming.

"You certainly take a great picture," said Vince.

"I could say the same thing about you," she replied.

"Have you done any modeling?"

Julie choked on her laugh as she cracked up at the question. "No, but thank you for the flattery."

"Well, I'll have to get you an agent and see if we can get you on the cover of a magazine."

She smiled at the jest but responded. "The only magazine upon which I would like to be on the cover is the Economist. It's the only one out there whose editors are addressing serious issues."

"Oh, of course, and they don't bother with any ridiculous celebrity gossip."

She laughed at the teasing; allowing the photographer to see that these two beautiful people would make an excellent picture.

"All right you two, pose pretty for my camera."

Vince and Julie wasted no time wrapping arms around each other, posing as a loving couple. The pictures captured their vitality as well as their curiosity about each other. Before leaving for the night with her dad and drunk brother, Julie promised to meet Vince so they could discuss global economics and the role of Crepusculous. Vince didn't care what the topic was, he just wanted to see Julie again as soon as possible.

When all the guests had left, and the staff was cleaning and clearing the room, Diegert found himself contemplating the night. As most parties do, this one left him thinking of the surprising and the mundane, the joyful and the sorrowful. Large gatherings, even those that are specifically brought together to celebrate; represent every aspect of the human experience. Diegert would not let himself be blind to the suffering of his mother, or the joy he felt when near Julie Kellerman.

CHAPTER 16

IMMEDIATELY ACROSS THE BOULEVARD from the Grand Hall, Vince and many of the other guests were staying at the Imperial Hotel. A five-star establishment catering to the wealthiest of clients, which tonight, was housing people worth nearly three trillion Digival.

The well to do were being well served with every need and desire fulfilled to the best of the hotel's legal limits. As Vince strode across the motor way toward the Imperial's foyer, loosening his Versace bow tie, he heard, "Hey handsome, you're hard to keep up with."

He turned back to see Fatima Hussain quick stepping in her stiletto heels. She closed the gap between them. "I was really intrigued by what you said earlier and I didn't get a chance to speak with you again."

Diegert was dumbstruck. The woman who had commanded him to kill, and trained him to survive his "incarceration" at Headquarters in Romania was running up to him like a fan girl. This exotically beautiful woman, who filled his dreams with erotic fantasies, but flatly dismissed any possibility of a dalliance, was now calling him handsome.

His extended stare at her and his contemplative look, drew a tilt of Fatima's head.

"I'm sorry," said Diegert, extending Vince's hand to receive the warm, soft skin of Fatima Hussain's mocha-hued fingers and palm. "I appreciate your interest."

"You're most welcome," said Fatima as she let Vince caress her hand for a long moment.

"When we were introduced," said Vince as he freed her hand. "You were with that Perez fellow weren't you?"

"Yes I was Javier's plus one for the party, but don't let official obligations confuse you about the veracity of relationships."

Vince cast a bemused smile, "I won't."

Her smile had a bit of mischief, and Diegert couldn't help but feel that old desire.

"With a degree in economics, I imagine you will be able to accomplish a lot within Omnisphere," stated Fatima.

Diegert kept having to remember who he was, but it was quickly becoming obvious, he was seeing a side of Fatima he could have only imagined before.

With confidence, Vince replied, "I hope to expand the dominance of Omnisphere so we can provide necessities for every person on the planet."

"Ooh, I like that take charge attitude. Provide for the whole planet!"

"There's no reason we can't. We have so much, we must share it to make people's lives better."

"That sounds like altruism. Does your father approve?"

"Klaus is reluctant to give away anything. It is a lifelong limitation I hope to overcome."

"Now you sound brave, hoping to alter the mind of the world's most powerful man."

"All men are human and they have their weaknesses."

"It wasn't too long ago I heard someone else say the same thing."

"I claim no ownership over the realization," said Vince with a sly smile.

"I see. So what is the weakness of Klaus Panzer?"

"In addition to narcissism and vanity, he's desperate to leave a legacy, but one over which he wants absolute control. Instead of allowing his inspiration and influence to guide the future, he wants the next generation to bow down and carry out his wishes with unyielding loyalty."

With wide eyes, raised brows and a slight tilt to her head, Fatima softly said, "Wow, you have been thinking about this."

With an adorable dimple forming at the edge of his devilish smile, Vince said, "The keys to the kingdom will not be given without constraints, but when true power passes, one's vision can be realized."

Nodding her head as she shook her extended finger, Fatima said, "Are you sure we've never met before?"

With his broad smile revealing all of his glistening white teeth, Vince said, "Oh, I wish it were so, but believe me I would never forget having met you before tonight. Tell me is it true that Pakistani women are the world's greatest lovers?"

Blinking repeatedly as a ruby blush colored her mocha cheeks, Fatima stammered a moment. "My goodness, how did you learn of our secret?"

Seeing her impish smile, Vince chuckled as he drew closer, "A genie in a bottle told me. The same genie who made me the son of Klaus Panzer."

"I wondered if there was magic involved."

"Black magic I'm afraid. But once the spell is cast, the cursed are obligated. I will play this role and see what destiny has in store for me."

"Such an intriguing mystery?"

Diegert looked into the recesses of her deep dark pupils; he was being pulled into her undeniable charms. He forgot everything he knew and feared about her, and bathed in the attraction she had for Vince. "I've heard it said that Pakistani men are very controlling in order to keep the secret."

"It's a good thing that modern times allow women to live their own lives."

Through a rakish smirk Vince replied, "It certainly is."

"Oh, there you are," shouted Javier Perez as he crossed the hotel's entrance.

As Javier approached, Vince and Fatima took a step back from the intimate personal space they'd been sharing.

"Hello my dear," said Perez beaming his thousand-watt smile. Extending his hand to Vince, he said as they shook, "Congratulations again. I look forward to working with you as we both move forward."

"Indeed."

Facing Fatima as he reached for her hand, Javier said, "Come on it's late, I'm tired, let's go home."

Retracting her hand before he could grasp it, Fatima said, "I do not yet wish to leave. You are free to go."

Javier's bright smile turned to a petulant frown. "You came here with me. I want to make sure you get home safely."

"That's very thoughtful, but I am perfectly capable of safely getting to my own place tonight."

"A gentleman always concludes the evening as it began."

"An anachronism to which I do not subscribe. Thank you for bringing me here, but I no longer need the services of an escort."

"An escort? How dare you-" Javier cut off his own words as he stepped away two paces and signaled Fatima to follow him by forcefully thrusting his pointed finger at the ground in front of him.

She did not move.

"Get over here," he demanded.

She shook her head.

"You raging bitch, I can't believe you are doing this to me."

"You are overreacting. I don't want to go home yet, and I am not going home with you anyway. You're tired and should go home, so please go and sleep well tonight."

With narrowed eyes, a furrowed brow, and a bulging carotid pulse, Javier stepped one pace forward, "Very well, but you are rude and selfish." Javier looked at Vince as his lips contorted into a derisive sneer. Without another word, the angry Spaniard marched to his limousine. The driver closed the passenger door, scampered behind the wheel and quickly departed.

Fatima turned to Vince and said, "Now, you were asking me about a secret."

CHAPTER 17

ABAYA PATEL HAD ENJOYED PANZER'S party. She presented herself as the successful business woman in charge of Omnisphere. She was skilled at playing the role with confidence and assurance. She reminded herself that it was Panzer who handed her this position seemingly out of nowhere, but it was up to her to make the company better and more profitable. She took the position seriously and was determined to show Panzer and the world that she was the right choice for the job.

In spite of the late hour, she checked her e-mail. The message from Tech Sec was flagged, high priority.

Source of system intrusion identified. IP address traced to Aaron Blevinsky, Assistant to Mr. Panzer, and Director of Clandestine Operations for Crepusculous. I await your instructions.

Abaya's shoulders sank as she raised her head to stare into the reflection of the dark windows. She suspected so many other possible intruders, the Chinese, Anonymous, or other group intent on bringing down the corporate greed mongers. Blevinsky was a Crepusculous man. She did not know him personally, but she had heard of his role in special operations and his computer prowess. Abaya replied, *Thank you, Ken, I will address this directly with Herr Panzer. You will be copied in on all communication.*

Abaya sent a text to Panzer. She doubted he would reply tonight, but she wanted him to see her question first thing in the morning. *Good evening sir, I wanted to inform you that the Omnisphere system intruder has been identified. Before I reveal the intruder, I want to ask if you have any information regarding authorized intrusive attacks.*

To her utter surprise, Panzer responded immediately. *I don't know what you're talking about. I have not authorized anyone to attack our system. Who is the intruder?*

Abaya replied, *Sir, I appreciate your quick response. I'm sorry, but for security reasons, I cannot reveal the identity to you tonight. Rest assured I will inform you as soon as possible. Have faith in Tech Sec as they continue this investigation.*

Panzer's response had a surprising tone of humility. *Very well, I leave it in your hands, but I expect details soon.*

Yes, sir and good night replied Abaya. She would initiate an investigation of Aaron Blevinsky in the morning.

VINCE HELD ACCOMMODATIONS IN THE Presidential Suite of the Imperial Hotel. Beyond the marble of the foyer floor, the suite had a large living room with two sofas and several overstuffed chairs. To the north was a fine dining area to seat eight. A large open kitchen with dark marble countertops was adjacent to the dining area. The kitchen was appointed with everything one could want for the storage, preparation and enjoyment of food. On the southern side of the living room was the sleeping chamber. The king sized bed only took up one tenth of the room's open space. The en suite included a large marble laden two-headed shower and a Jacuzzi tub large enough for ten people. Diegert figured the bedroom alone was larger than the house in which he grew up, but as Vince, he knew to act as if such luxury was a common experience.

"Would you like something to drink?" he asked Fatima.

"No thank you. I've had quite a lot this evening."

"A glass of water perhaps?"

"If you insist."

Diegert entered the kitchen and filled two crystal table glasses with ice and chilled water.

Fatima sat on a stool at the counter-bar that separated the kitchen from the dining area. Diegert slid the glass over to her. He couldn't help but notice the cleavage of her breasts as she sat leaning forward against the marble counter.

Fatima casually sipped her water before asking, "Do you like my breasts?"

Diegert was more than a little surprised by the question, but he thought Vince would be real smooth. "They're hard to ignore, but liking them depends on how they feel, and the reactions they can elicit."

"To what reactions do you refer?"

"I mean does caressing them, kneading them, and twirling the nipples stimulate an erotic response."

Fatima smiled as the blush returned, making her cheeks a slight tone of maroon. "I can't imagine such attention eliciting no response."

Raising his eyebrows, Vince replied, "It happens."

Taking a long sip of water, Fatima said, "I'd like to use the ladies room. I believe the facilities are over there," Flexing her wrist and extending her finger, she pointed in the direction of the bedroom.

"You are correct, please be my guest."

Diegert gulped down his water, set his glass on the counter, and moved to sit on the big white leather couch in the living room. He didn't know what would happen next, but he recalled how Fatima had seduced him in the defensive tactics room at Headquarters, where she kicked his ass, until he fell unconscious. What a conniving bitch. Now, as Vince, he was anticipating a different response from the erotically beautiful and supremely confident woman. He heard her bare feet padding across the carpeting of the immense bedroom. She emerged from the doorway dressed in only a black bra and matching panties.

As their eyes met, Diegert's gaze averted from her face, to inspect her body. She was so beautiful. Muscular, yet so feminine, strong, yet so supple. Confidence projected from her near nakedness, as if she would be even more confident once she was wearing nothing. Sauntering over towards him, she stood in profile, rotated her hips as she asked, "Do you like my ass?"

Again Diegert had to find his Vince voice, "Wonderfully symmetrical, but its value also lies in the reactions it elicits."

Cocking her head she said, "You mean can you turn on a woman through her ass?"

"No, this time I'm interested in the response your hips can elicit in a man."

"The motion of the ocean."

Chuckling, Vince said, "Yes, I suppose that expresses it quite succinctly."

"You like big words don't you?"

"I like the right words; they don't have to be big. Big is not a big word."

She tucked one leg under the other as she sat down beside him. "Do you want to know what really turns on a woman?"

"Now you are going to reveal a secret."

"It's not a real secret, but most men just ignore it."

"Please enlighten me to all that my brethren have overlooked."

Snorting with disdain as she rolled her eyes saying, "Big words."

Vince smiled, casting a luminescence from the shining alabaster of his teeth.

Fatima let the pause grow before saying, "Women are turned on by the kiss. A deep, passionate, encompassing kiss that draws all your sensations and emotions into an intense point of contact, allowing the whole world to slip away. The strong embrace, the entwining of two mouths, two tongues sharing the erotic feeling of closeness, togetherness, oneness that sparks the rest of the body to ache for the pleasure of the libido. Without the kiss, sex is just mechanics. With the kiss, it is a symphony of sensations drawn from the soul and manifest in the body. That's what women want."

"There were a lot of big words in there."

"There was a lot of truth in there."

Sliding a little closer, Vince asked, "May I kiss you?"

"Yes, but it better be good."

He slid his hand along the top of the couch cushion, moving it down so his arm embraced her shoulder. Vince felt Fatima's gaze upon his face. She seemed to be seeking direct eye contact. Connecting with her dark penetrating gaze, he felt her seeking to enter his mind, reach out to touch his soul, creating an emotional embodiment within him. He hesitated, pulled back and smiled at her. Her expression remained unchanged. "Don't be afraid," she said as she moistened and parted her lips. The tantalizing pink of her mouth and the heat rising from her body carried an intoxicating scent, to which Vince succumbed with longing and lust. She turned her face to him as he leaned in and brought his lips to hers.

She pushed into him with desire and urgent pressure. She opened her mouth and herself to him. He dove in, his hot tongue driving into her with unfettered abandon. Their heads rotated, allowing themselves to occupy a common place of oral pleasure and mutual exploration. Through touch alone, they each found in the other a place of immediate and seemingly unquenchable desire to hold and connect. The kiss's intensity built into a near spasm of erotic pleasure. Fatima broke the connection, gasping for breath as Vince released her bra, caressed her breast and brought his lips to her hardened nipple. Fatima gasped again as Vince sucked on the dark brown nubbin. He could feel her pleasure intensify as his tongue flicked the end of her sensitive nipple. She moaned and pulled his head even closer to her ample breast. Gently grazing her nipple with his teeth, he elicited a moan from his lover as she shook with tremors of excitement. Ever so carefully, he continued to place gentle bites against the sensitive peak of her breast. The nipple bites elicited staccato gasps, during which Fatima clasped Vince's head in her hands.

Pulling Vince from her breast, Fatima grabbed the front of his shirt, ripping it apart, sending buttons ricocheting off the couch. Vince stepped off the couch to remove his torn shirt, Fatima pulled off her panties. Vince stripped out of his pants and underwear, standing naked before her. Fatima stopped for a moment. Vince stood before her, penis engorged and growing more erect by the second. Fatima scratched her head as she looked away. She looked back at his erection and looked away again. It seemed to Diegert that she was trying to recall something. He remembered that she'd seen his naked body on more than one occasion at Headquarters. Could she have such an astute visual memory to have recognized his cock? He supposed each cock was unique, but this struck him as strange. "Are you all right?" he asked.

"Yes... yes I am. Just having a moment." Fatima shook her head, clearing the cobwebs. She looked back at Vince, whose lean, muscular, masculine athletic body stood nude in front of her. "You've got a beautiful body," she said.

"Thank you, so do you," said Vince as she rose from the couch, straddled his erection, threw her arms around him, and pulled him into a skin on skin embrace. Once again, they kissed with mutual desire and unbridled passion. As they broke the kiss, each was gasping from the building pleasure of their undulating hips. Vince spun Fatima around, pressed her forward as she bent at the waist. With her arms supporting her torso on the back of the couch, he entered her from behind. Like a champion stallion on a prize mare, he drove himself into her. Across the room, he saw their reflection in a full length mirror. He realized that the only reason this was happening was because he looked like Vince. If she knew who he was, David Diegert, this beautiful woman would never have given herself to him. He pumped into her harder and harder, his hips audibly smacking her ass. Fatima clutched the couch cushion but as Diegert's thrusts grew more forceful, her knees buckled and she fell to the couch, with him on top, and still inserted. Against the stability of the couch, Diegert resumed his thrusting. He recalled her derisive statements and dismissive remarks. He remembered her belittling him and stabbing him with a fork in the cafeteria. Thoughts of love and mutual pleasure were dissipating, as he was overcome by a desire to exact revenge upon her for all the cruelty she had shown him in Romania and London. David Diegert was fucking Fatima Hussain and he was going to make sure she felt it.

When he exploded inside her, he roared like a lion. He wanted people in the street to know that a primal triumph had just taken place in the Presidential Suite of the Imperial Hotel.

Diegert extracted himself from Fatima and went to the bathroom to clean up. Upon return, he wore a bathrobe and brought with him Fatima's dress and shoes. She sat on the couch hugging a large pillow over her body. Raising the dress in his hand, he said, "Do you want to put these on here or in the bedroom?"

"That's it?"

"What?"

"That's it? You thrash me like that and then it's over, no thought of reciprocation?"

"Look I don't know what you're talking about. If that wasn't good for you, that's too bad."

Reaching out and snatching the dress, Fatima rose letting the pillow fall to the floor as she covered herself and stormed into the bedroom slamming the door behind her.

Vince frowned, but Diegert smiled.

When she emerged, she found that Vince had laid her shoes before a dining room chair and her overcoat was on a hanger on a wall hook in the foyer.

With her stilettos buckled, she flung on her coat, looked at Vince, flipped him the bird and tried to slam the door, but the pressure hinge denied her expression of anger.

CHAPTER 18

CAROLYN DREADED THE MEETING SHE was heading to with Richard Ramsey, but she had put in an official request to be returned stateside, and it was Ramsey, the British Station Chief, who reviewed the request.

"Carolyn," began the paunchy bureaucrat, "I'm afraid I'm going to deny your request."

"Why?" exclaimed Carolyn.

"Your role here in London is mission critical."

"I want my child born in the United States."

A broad smile spread over Ramsey's face in reaction to Carolyn acknowledging her pregnancy. "This case requires your presence and besides your child, born here in England, will still be a U.S. citizen."

"Do you intend to keep me here during my maternity leave?"

"You'll be able to spend both weeks off duty."

"Two weeks? No way, I get six minimum."

"Not while on foreign service."

Carolyn's jaw went slack. How could he be so insensitive? Bad enough he wouldn't let her go home for the birth, there was no way she was only having two weeks to bond with her new born child.

"You can't control where I am during my maternity."

"In fact, I can. It is also ill advised to fly a newborn over the ocean."

Ramsey turned the discussion away from maternity.

"Now I've got some questions about the case."

Carolyn said nothing but the peevish look upon her face showed that she was not done thinking about maternity.

"Do the police have any leads on the young woman who handed Diegert the bomb bag?"

"I'm meeting with a..." Carolyn consulted her notes, "Detective Jackson tomorrow, hopefully he can provide an update."

"That's all you've got?"

"Richard, I understand we have to play nice with the local police, but this is an international case and I should be collecting evidence and conducting my own investigation."

"Diegert was acting on behalf of a foreign entity on foreign soil."

"So?"

"So we can't interfere with local law enforcement."

"I'm not going to interfere, I'm going to assist."

"You may look at it that way, but the London Police see us as a foreign power interfering with their work."

Carolyn thought to herself that Ramsey was the one who would interfere. He would probably act like an arrogant, overbearing power pusher who would piss off the local cops.

"Detective Jackson was helpful, cooperative and forthcoming. I'm going to interpret our liaison protocol in a manner that allows me to work with him. Do you understand?"

Ramsey's indecision delayed his reply before he said, "All right I authorize you to liaison with Detective Jackson and report back to me with all the evidence you find."

It was just like this asshole to turn what she had just said into an order. Carolyn frowned upon her ineffectual leader as she leaned forward before standing to minimize the impact of her movements on her pregnant belly. Ramsey's eyes went right to her abdomen. Turning as she left the office Carolyn said, "Great idea sir, I certainly will."

"You know I just have to say there is something about pregnant women that I find incredibly hot."

With a furrowed brow and narrowed eyelids Carolyn replied, "No sir, you just didn't have to say that." *OMG what a creep,* thought Carolyn as she made her way down the hall.

CHAPTER 19

AVERY FORSYTHE LEANED BACK IN HIS chair making certain that his coffee cup was well away from his desk each time he took a sip. Not wanting to spill coffee on his computer, he dutifully drank only when his steaming cup was at least a foot from the keyboard. On the screen, Avery read an intelligence report concerning Jarod Masoni, a former member of Cerberus. Just the mention of him as "former" boiled Avery's blood, who considered inclusion in Cerberus the penultimate honor for operators capable of infiltration, sabotage and assassination, once in, you were in for life. Masoni pissed on the idea and vacated the position leaving Avery flabbergasted and distraught. Avery was reading that Masoni was working in a sex trafficking ring for the benefit of Sebastor Sbrebetskov, the Romanian mobster who took over after Mijka Barovitz was eliminated. Running women from the Balkans, into Italy and distributing them into Europe, was a profitable venture for Sbrebetskov. Masoni was in charge of the logistics of receiving and transporting the women throughout Western Europe.

When an expected knock resounded upon his office door, Avery spoke loudly. "Come in."

Wayne Henry, the Australian who helped Diegert escape China during the Wei family mission, strode in with his broad smile and charming sense of over-confidence. "How you doing mate?" he boomed.

"I am well," replied Avery. "It's good to see you again. I trust you've been well since we last saw one another."

"I'm a guy who's happy wherever I am, so I'm just fine. What is it I can do for you?"

"There's a guy in Italy, a former employee, Jarod Masoni, whose working in a sex trafficking ring, which is despicable, but I'm concerned he may be divulging information about Crepusculous and Cerberus.

"Like what?" asked Wayne

"If the information I was concerned about was such that I would just tell you, then it can't be that important can it?"

Shaking his head, Wayne said, "That's quite a fucking insult."

"Sorry," said Avery shrugging his shoulders as he turned up his palms. "Through his service with Cerberus, Masoni's been privy to certain emerging technologies that are proprietary. It would be problematic if he were to divulge that information."

"Secrets are safe in a dead man's head," said Wayne dryly.

Avery nodded, arcing his gaze over to the Australian, to look Wayne in the eyes.

"I want you to eliminate Jarod Masoni. Can you do it?"

"Are you asking, can I, or will I?"

"Both."

"I sure had a spot of fun getting out of China, I still got it in me. But tell me again why you want this guy dead?"

Avery's gaze darkened, "I don't want to explain myself any more than I have. I'm authorized to issue sanctions that involve Cerberus, and if you want the job, then say so."

"How much?"

"One million," said Avery, folding his arms across his chest. "It'll be your last big payday, Wayne. You can retire after this one."

With a twinkle forming in his eye as a smile curled his lips, Wayne said, "When?"

"I'll give you two weeks to get it done."

"Deal," said Wayne as he stuck his hand across the table.

Avery shook it. "I'll send all the necessary intel to your phone."

"Aye, aye Captain. I'll reply with my Swiss account number. When the job's done, I'll send you video confirmation. "

"Swiss? Honestly, with Digival it doesn't matter."

"I know but I already had the account and the bank is handling Digival just like old dollars."

"All right, upon completion, you'll have the full amount in your account."

Putting his coat on and zipping it up, Wayne said, "It's a lot colder than I thought it would be at this time of year."

"Stay warm, Wayne."

As he heard the door close, Avery sent a text: *He's on his way, be ready to activate your phase of this mission.*

DETECTIVE CONSTABLE THEODORE JACKSON agreed to meet with CIA Special Agent Carolyn Fuller for coffee at 10 am. He chose the Starbucks on Strand near the bend in the River Thames thinking the American coffee would make her feel at home. He stood outside conducting a casual surveillance hoping to spot her as she approached.

Carolyn liked being early for appointments and she sipped her Mocha Latte' as she waited for DC Jackson.

Having Googled his police profile, she knew she was looking for a tall, good-looking guy of African descent. Sitting at the window bar she observed a tall man approaching the shop. She recognized him, took another sip and watched for him to enter the store. She was surprised when he didn't come in. She leaned against the window glass to see DC Jackson standing out front of Starbucks.

With her coffee in hand, Carolyn stepped outside. It was cool with a stiff breeze. Carolyn approached at an angle as she said, "Good morning Detective Jackson." The tall man turned to see the person he was hoping to surveil, standing next to him with a steaming latte'.

"Good morning Agent Fuller." said the handsome man, whose light complexion made an attractive contrast with his dark eyes, brows and pencil thin mustache. Carolyn shivered in the breeze. Jackson said, "Please let's go inside," ushering her in with his left hand. Carolyn returned to her seat at the window bar as DC Jackson ordered his espresso with foamed milk.

Joining her he asked, "Do you find it weird how quickly the world has switched to Digival?"

Carolyn looked at him as she sipped her latte'.

"I mean, not six months ago very few people even knew about Digival," stated Jackson.

"Now I can pay for just about everything with it, and they pay the taxes? It's weird, how quickly this currency has been embraced."

Carolyn nodded. "They've made it so if you're using anything else, you're losing out.

"Omnisphere is so big they can afford to create their own money, even Starbucks accepts it."

"Starbucks is part of Omnisphere," stated Carolyn.

"It is?"

"Yeah, that way they get their coffee cheap and live under the big corporate umbrella."

Jackson nodded as he sipped his piping hot espresso.

Carolyn asked, "Are you aware of Crepusculous?"

"Is that some kind of disease?"

"Maybe. An economic epidemic."

Jackson smiled.

Continuing Carolyn said, "Crepusculous is a board of four men who are the power behind Omnisphere."

"Really, not the Indian woman? Abayuba-"

"Abaya Patel," interjected Carolyn. "She is the CEO and is quite powerful, but behind her is this board which is led by Klaus Panzer."

As the name was spoken, Jackson sputtered on his sip of coffee. He quickly covered his mouth with a paper napkin.

Carolyn asked, "Do you know him?"

"A few weeks ago we got a call about a potential terrorist attack. My partner and I apprehended his vehicle and brought him in for questioning."

Carolyn raised an eyebrow. She was impressed.

DC Jackson continued, "We brought him into the station, but he lawyered up and we had to let him walk. I don't think he was involved in any terrorism, so it was no big deal.

Carolyn's brow dropped as she frowned. "His form of terrorism is economic. How long do you think they will continue to give back 10% of all your purchases? How long will they continue to pay the taxes? How long will they be the benevolent provider, sharing the wealth of Omnisphere?" Carolyn's last statement mocked the Omnisphere slogan, which flooded the world with its sappy dream fulfilling promise.

Jackson shrugged, "I kinda like getting money back, and it's about time they shared the wealth, owning 99% of it."

"Crepusculous currently holds 75% of the world's wealth, but they want 100%. Digival puts them on that path. I think we will really regret it when the only currency in the world is a corporate account owned by the world's biggest company. In the meantime the human flock is being ushered into its pen through free coffee, cheap groceries and having somebody else pay their taxes."

"God, you're a real buzz kill. I was looking forward to having Digival pay all my taxes this year, but you make it sound like I'm a lamb led to slaughter."

"Sorry, but I have been studying this company, the Board, and it's Director Klaus Panzer. I don't like what I see."

"Well you would have liked the huge party they had the other night."

"What was that?" asked Carolyn inquisitively.

"Over at London Polytechnic, they had two hundred people attending a ball put on to welcome Panzer's son."

It was Carolyn's turn to choke on coffee when she heard Jackson's last word. Coughing and sputtering she struggled to compose herself as Jackson asked, "Are you okay?" Before the big guy could perform the Heimlich maneuver, Carolyn got herself under control.

"Did you say son?"

"Yeah, it's kind of weird, but that much money can make the strange seem normal."

"What do you mean?"

"Apparently this son was the product of an affair, but Panzer did not know about the kid until his mother died and it was revealed in her will. Panzer didn't deny it; in fact he celebrated it with a huge party with about two hundred friends at the Grand Hall."

Carolyn looked down at the floor and up out the window as she took in this surprise.

"What's the son's name?"

"Vince, Vince Kronig. His mother was from Iceland, but lived in Canada. Vince grew up in British Columbia."

Confusion rained down on Carolyn just as the sun started to break through the gray clouds over London. Googling the name, Carolyn was taken aback by the handsome face of the hunky, blond haired, blue-eyed stud. Turning her phone to DC Jackson she asked, "Is this him?"

"That's the chap, Klaus Panzer's son Vince Kronig. All the girls seem to love him."

"I can see why," said Carolyn almost dejectedly. Scanning her phone she shared, "So Panzer had an affair with his mother and it was all kept secret until just recently when, upon her death, it was revealed in her will that the world's richest man is his unknown father."

"That's a quick read, but you summed it up right."

"Panzer welcome's him aboard and the son is happy to join the family," concluded Carolyn.

Jackson nodded before drinking the last of his espresso. After swallowing the strong, bitter beverage he said, "Threw him a big party so he could meet all the world's richest people. Kind of like a debutante ball," came Jackson's falsetto voice accompanied by a feminine flourish of his flexed wrist.

Carolyn smiled and asked, "Have you looked into this? Like, does the story of the mother pan out? Have you found a record of her?"

"Whoa, this story is just a curiosity. There is nothing criminal; we're not going to spend any time on this. Panzer has enough money to run his own verification checks."

"I see, but it does strike me as curious."

"And the curious can read all about it in the rag mags at the checkout counter. Now what is it that you really want to discuss with me?"

"I'm interested in information about the young woman that was seen with David Diegert before his bomb went off?"

Jackson nodded slowly as he measured his words. "She's known to us. She's pretty strung out and feeds her drug habit with petty crime. She'll do anything to get money for her next fix."

"Yeah, yeah, I don't want to seem callous, but we've all seen these characters before."

DC Jackson narrowed his lids, eyeing Carolyn over the rim of his cup of espresso.

"Her name is Eleanor Norris. On the street she goes by Terry Bull."

Carolyn rolled her eyes at that one. "So you know her?"

"Probably better than she knows herself, which is to say not very well."

Disappointment flowed over Carolyn's face like the shadow of a passerby.

"What can you tell me?"

"She's mentally ill to the point where she should be hospitalized, but she is uncooperative and dangerous when confined. She is a denizen of the dark, residing in abandoned buildings; she's constantly on the move, extremely elusive. Based on the explosive incident there is a warrant for her arrest. We'll let you know when she's apprehended."

Carolyn's eyes glanced from below her furrowed

brow, "If I find her first, I'll be calling you."

"Officially I cannot condone your actions on British soil—"

Carolyn interrupted, finishing the sentence, "Therefore you will only be informed of results, not methods." After swallowing another gulp of latte Carolyn continued, "That's all I needed. I'm sure you've got a full day ahead of you."

Finishing his last sip of super strong coffee, Jackson responded, "Don't we all?" Setting the glass cup on its saucer he continued as he gathered his things, "You know it's not an official policy that makes for successful cooperation in law enforcement. Its personal relationships based on trust and common goals that succeed. I hope we're developing a successful relationship."

Smiling as she lifted her paper cup in a toast, Carolyn replied, "I'll drink to that." She took a quick swig and said, "Have a good day DC Jackson."

"I'll do that," he said as he cinched the belt around the waist of his long hunter green coat.

CHAPTER 20

WAYNE'S ARRIVAL IN ITALY WAS QUITE subdued. He always liked to travel cheaply, and Avery didn't include travel money. One million to wack this guy was huge, but Wayne stuck to his habit of not spending money he did not have. The 2005 Citroen C4 he rented had 300,000 kilometers on it, rusty fenders and seat fabric, which retained the scent of every ass that had spent hours riding in this nearly classic subcompact. Fortunately the manual window cranks worked.

The smugglers itinerary Avery had shared, took them from Makarska, Croatia to the Italian Province of Chieti, to land at the seaside town of Ortona. The crossing of the Adriatic Sea took eight hours, provided the sea was not stirred up by a saltwater storm.

Although he lived with his girlfriend in Rome, Masoni traveled across the peninsula to the dumpy tourist town of Ortona where he had arranged with the Ortona Boat Service to receive his merchandise. The women were unloaded from the 50-foot cruiser at night into the shore side, hangar sized shop within which they were loaded into vans. The vans would take them to the regions where the women would be put to work. Masoni would stay in Ortona until all the vans had arrived and the merchandise was released. The women were his responsibility from the time they unloaded from the boat until they arrived in their places of service. For this, he was well paid, but it was middleman work that wasn't hard as long as you didn't mind selling sex slaves.

Billboards extolling the beaches and the seafood restaurants of this low budget vacation destination dotted the road into Ortona. During the summer, the place was filled with working class people getting some R&R at the seaside resorts. Now in October, the beach was empty and most of the restaurants were closed for the season. Illegal immigration of women went undetected amongst the dry docked boats wrapped in plastic.

At the dock, twenty-four women had disembarked the yacht in which they had crossed the Adriatic Sea. Preceding the two armed men who accompanied them on the boat, the women shuffled into the boathouse hangar and Masoni pulled down the overhead door. Placing a steel case on the workbench, Masoni opened it and fired up his laptop screen. The shorter of the two men from the boat signed into an account. Masoni typed in a code transferring 200,000 Digival to the man's account. Closing the case, they shook hands. The two men returned to the boat, left the dock, and sailed into the dark Adriatic.

The van parked inside the boat hangar was not big enough for twenty-four passengers; in fact, Masoni was waiting for three more vans. The women were destined for four locations, each van carrying six passengers.

Presently the women were standing in the open area of the hangar, surrounded by greasy engine parts, crumpled propellers, a long oil stained workbench with tools suspended above, and cans of grease, oil, and solvents stored below. Long fluorescent fixtures hanging from the ceiling cast diffuse light without heat. Cold seeped through the concrete floor, chilling the women, who were ill dressed for the temperatures of late fall.

Throwing her hood off her head, a woman with a short shock of bleached blonde hair shouted, "Hey what are we supposed to do? There's nowhere to sit and this place is freezing."

Masoni cautioned, "You shut the fuck up. You won't be here long."

As he crossed the room, he menaced the women with a steely glare. At the far end of the workbench, he grabbed a handle emerging from under the surface and pulled out what looked like a rocket engine on wheels. The cylindrical device had two wheels at one end and a metal footing at the end with the handle. Masoni flipped its switch and the cylinder fired up, heat turned the end above the wheels red-hot. An internal fan blew the heat into the cavernous space. The sound wasn't quite jet engine, but it was enough to make conversation an effort. Masoni shouted as he pointed, "The toilets back there in the corner."

Stepping outside Masoni got on his phone, "Yeah, it's me, where the fuck are the other vans?"

"You said to have them there on the 28th."

"Fucking bullshit Arnie, I said the 26th, damn it. Don't you try to fuck with me, check the text, it says 26th."

"Oh... oh yeah, you're right."

"Damn straight I am you fucknut. Now get the two assholes you've misinformed, put'em in the other vans and start driving right now. I want you here in four hours, you got that?"

"Yeah, yeah I got it, we're on our way."

"I'm texting you the address again. Give it to douche bag and shithead and make sure they have it in their GPS. You fuck this up and I will frag your asses without mercy.

Capeesh?"

"Look it was just an oversight, I'm sorry. We'll be there right away."

"Fuck you, you better be here in three hours." Masoni ended the call and looked out over the harbor, angry over the stupid delay. He realized good help was impossible to find. Incompetent imbeciles were the only ones willing to become criminals these days.

As ARNIE ENDED HIS CALL, HE TURNED and looked into the barrel point of a suppressed Glock 19.

"I did like you said."

"So you did, now give me your phone, you won't be needing it."

The Glock's firing pin struck the center of the bullet, sending a 9mm projectile through the extended barrel at 770 meters per second, piercing Arnie's skull, magnifying the area of force to shatter the left side of his calvarium, spraying bloody brain matter upon his bookshelf as his torso flopped sideways in his chair.

The assassin unscrewed the suppressor, placing it and the pistol into foam cutouts before zipping up the case and placing it in the large inside pocket of her coat.

WAYNE STOOD NOT FAR FROM THE Ortona Boat Service hangar. He'd arrived in town and had been surveilling the service building for the past three hours. When the boat docked and women were escorted in, Wayne moved next to a large panel truck parked across from the Boat Service. From his position, he could watch the building shielded by the truck's large cargo box. He saw two men leave the building, launch the boat and drive away. Shortly thereafter Masoni stepped out the side door and was now looking out over the harbor. With Masoni's focus on the water, his back turned to the building and no one else around, Wayne deemed this an excellent opportunity. From within the pocket of his coat he extracted his compressed sniper rifle. This bullpup design had the firing mechanism at the near end of a long barrel. The grip and trigger were halfway along the barrel length, and the sighting scope was secured above the grip. The compact size carried full-length firepower and accuracy. Wayne placed the reticle between Masoni's shoulder blades. He exhaled one full breath as he concentrated on his target. The impact of a blunt object smacked Wayne's head into the side of the cargo truck, the sound reverberating across the parking lot. Wayne crumpled to the ground as his assailant, with a length of steel plumbing pipe, stood over him.

Masoni, hearing the clang of steel against the truck, turned to see his partner Tony, the driver of the van, standing next to a truck.

Masoni strode over to see blood on Tony's pipe and a human heap at his feet. Their looks of surprise turned into determined glares. Slinging Wayne's rifle strap over his shoulder, Masoni grabbed the feet, Tony grasped the wrists and they carried Wayne into the hangar, placed him in the van and shut the door.

The women had put a plastic sheet on the floor, covered with a dusty canvas tarp. Huddled together in the warm zone of the blast furnace, most diverted their eyes from the van. Masoni and Tony glared, but only the woman with the short blonde hair dared to look back.

"Let me know, when he wakes up," said Masoni, "and thanks for bashing him."

"Yes sir," said Tony as he leaned back against the driver's door of the van.

Wayne woke up with his head feeling as big as a beach ball with giant waves slapping against its interior. As he lifted his head, he felt the whole room, or wherever the hell he was, spinning. Grabbing the armrest, he remembered he was last going to shoot his target. He had no idea how he got where he was, but the throbbing in his head felt like trouble. Touching his temple sent pain firing through his scalp. He could feel what he thought was a tennis ball under his skin. Focusing in the dim light, he realized he was in a van.

The sliding door flew open, flooding the interior with light. Wayne squinted as he shielded his face.

Jarod Masoni growled, "You're going to tell me who the fuck sent you to kill me?"

"Kill you? Oh mate you've got it all wrong, I'm here to protect you."

"What? Protect me, with a bullet in my back?"

"I can see now, how it looks. And your friend there whacked me pretty good, but I was sent to make sure those gents from the boat didn't do you any harm."

"The guys on the boat?"

"Aye."

"The guys I've been working with for over a year? The guys to whom I just paid 200,000 Digival? You're trying to tell me, my business partners were going to kill me, and you, a total fucking stranger, was sent to protect me?"

"The criminal world can be very convoluted."

Masoni grabbed the front of Wayne's shirt, pulling him forward, "Tell me who sent you? Who's my fucking guardian angel?"

Swallowing hard, Wayne replied, "I'm not supposed

to-"

Backhanding Wayne across the face Masoni said, "Of course it's all a big secret, but if you were sent to save me, I deserve to know who's so concerned."

"He's quite discreet and wishes to remain anonymous."

"What fucking horseshit, you were sent to kill me and now you're trying to bullshit your way out of it."

Wayne tried not to tremble as Masoni drew closer. With an open hand, the Italian sex smuggler smacked the swollen goose egg on Wayne's temple, sending a shock of pain exploding through the Australian's head. Masoni's scowl turned to a devious smile, as he again smacked the side of Wayne's inflamed head. Wayne fought the tears but they welled up in his eyes as he cowered against the expectation of another strike. Masoni quickly drew his hand back. Wayne flinched and ducked. Dropping his hand, Masoni stepped back from the van.

"Hey Tony, we've got ourselves a flincher," said Masoni, looking over at his partner. "He can't stand much pain. We're going to have a fun time getting the truth out of this weakling."

Masoni turned to Tony, "Let's start by treating his head wound. You really hit a home run on his noggin, there buddy." The man leaning against the van looked ready to sign autographs.

Wayne watched Masoni survey the workbench, upon which he found a length of inch wide black webbing strap with a plastic buckle on one end. From a rusted coffee can, he pulled a heavy inch and a half hexagonal nut. Out of a bag hanging on a pegboard above the bench, he extracted two 10-inch zip ties. Running the strap through the nut, he approached Wayne.

"Step out of the van," Masoni commanded. "Turn around, hands behind your back."

One zip tie bound his wrists. The other was placed between his hands and around the first zip tie. When the second was pulled tight it further constricted the first, nearly cutting off the blood flow.

Spun around, Wayne was shoved into a seated position in the open door of the van.

"Now about that lump on your head," said Masoni playing doctor.

Hanging from the black nylon strap, Masoni placed the nut against Wayne's bruised temple, encircling the strap around his head. Running the strap through the buckle, he cinched the strap tight, forcing the heavy metal nut into the side of Wayne's head.

The pressure forced the pain deep into Wayne's brain where it amplified into an aggravated mushroom cloud of discomfort. Masoni picked up a ball peen hammer, and struck the nut. The shock wave felt as if the hammer had shattered a ceramic vase. Wayne's skull felt like it had fractured into hundreds of fissures radiating across its surface. The prisoner's head and neck quivered as his eyes popped wide open, tears pouring over his lids.

Looking at him with a self-satisfied smile, Masoni said, "I see I have your attention now. Just the right amount of force in the right place can be so effective."

Wayne struggled to remain oriented as the recurring pulses of pain magnified the throbbing of each heartbeat. Lifted by his collar, Wayne was pulled staggering to the workbench.

"Let's see what else we have here," said Masoni as he searched through the shop until he found the power tools.

"Ah, here we are," he said as he hoisted an impact

driver. This concussive power tool uses oscillation to amplify torque force making it an ideal device for driving screws into any solid material.

Masoni punched Wayne in the guts, bending him forward until he looked like a hunched back little old lady. Wayne felt his head placed on the cold metal of a bench vise. Masoni turned the crank, closing the vise on Wayne's ear, trapping the sensitive cartilage between the serrated jaws of the cast iron behemoth. The screaming began as the blood flowed from Wayne's ear.

Placing the impact driver against the metal nut, Masoni steadied the device, pulled the trigger, and held the tool in place for thirty seconds.

The concussive force of the impact driver made the ball peen hammer seem like a Q-tip. The pulverizing force upon Wayne's skull sent magnanimous waves of violent vibration into his cranium. It's a fact that the brain lacks pain sensors, but Wayne was completely unconvinced as it felt like his brain was being liquefied within the cauldron of agony that was his skull.

When Masoni lifted the driver from the nut, Wayne felt his scalp enlarge. The pain seemed to grow even greater, as his head was expanding with inflammatory fluid. With his ear still firmly in the vise, he couldn't believe how badly this whole mission had gone sideways.

"Now, who sent you?" asked Masoni.

Wayne had no idea what an 'out of body experience' was so he didn't recognize it when his consciousness departed from its physical confines and began speaking for him.

"It was Avery… Avery Forsythe."

"I knew that fucker was behind this," said Masoni. "He's twisted and relentless. What's the problem? Why is he after me?"

"You know secrets about Cerberus and Crepusculous. He doesn't want you talking about the nanocytes that can change a person's appearance."

"What?"

"Like the guy in China, who could change his face. Please, I've told you now let me go."

"What do you mean change his face?"

"I don't know, nanocytes, proteins, genetics all controlled by a computer. You must know about this. I figured you knew and that's why Avery wanted you dead. Now let me go."

"You're not going anywhere. Now shut up and stay right there."

Wayne groaned as he spread his legs farther apart trying to find just an infinitesimal amount of physical comfort.

After checking his phone, Masoni said, "Tony, that fucking Arnie's GPS signal hasn't moved since I called him. He and his dopey friends aren't going to show up. Get the seats out of the van, we're putting all these ladies in there."

With a set of wrenches, Tony began unbolting the bench seat in the back of the van.

The woman with short blonde hair said, "Are you planning on stuffing us all in one van? You can't do that."

Masoni scowled as he released the mechanism on the bottom of a bucket seat and removed it through the sliding door. Tony nodded as he worked on the back seat. By the time Masoni removed the second seat from the other side, Tony was extracting the rear bench. With the passenger seats out of the van, Masoni told the women, "Now get in."

With surprising efficiency and a deference to comfort

and safety, twenty-four unhappy women packed themselves into the van like compressed cargo.

Masoni stepped over to Wayne whose vision was directed away from the van toward the waterfront. "You tell Avery he's on my hit list and I'm going to kill him. I don't want him fucking up my life anymore."

"Okay... okay, I'll tell him."

Masoni turned and walked back toward the van.

"Hey, you gotta let me go. You can't just leave me here. Hey, HEY!"

The van's engine started, Wayne heard the overhead door on the street side of the building pulled open, and then he heard it pulled back down after the van drove outside.

The hangar was quiet. Masoni must have switched off the portable furnace because its sound was gone along with its heat. The cold would become a problem, but first Wayne had to get free. The pain in his ear persisted as his head throbbed like a marching band drum. Every movement he made to get a different look at what was around him, was rewarded with a twisting, tearing pain screaming in his ear. He never knew the ear was so sensitive, but he was sure learning about all the nerves embedded in the thin delicate sound gathering structures. His legs were tired, his back was killing him and his hands were numb. He didn't want to vomit, but the nausea in his stomach threatened to erupt at any moment. In spite of all this, his immediate concern was that he was going to piss his pants. Relaxing his sphincters and emptying his bladder felt so good, for such a short period of time. The hot piss running down his leg, soaking his pants and filling his shoes, smelled and felt like shit. He desperately wanted to be free before he had to deal with actually needing to shit.

Wayne screamed, "HELP – HELP," but his calls went

unanswered. The dark of night intensified, leaving the workshop lit by only a couple of battery charging glow lights. He was alone, in pain, uncomfortable, and completely uncertain as to when he might get some help. He stamped his feet in rage. They were the only things he could move. He feared the night. In desperation, he sobbed like a baby and felt absolutely childish as the tears rolled over his nose, down along his cheek. Adding insult to injury, the saline droplets stung the open wounds on his trapped ear. He realized that if he was still there in the morning he may have to deal with people much more sympathetic to Masoni than to him.

He knew what he had to do, but it took some time for the desperation to surmount the desire to keep oneself whole. Since the ear had been trapped in the steel jaws for several hours the tissue was degrading. The loss of blood, the reduction in neural stimuli were denying the ear of the nutrients and signaling it needed to stay healthy. The ear was ruined anyway. Now he just had to detach himself from the wretched flap.

He twisted clockwise. It hurt like hell. Counterclockwise felt just as bad. He moved his head forward towards the workbench. Only a light movement sent searing pain into his head and along his neck. Realizing he was going to have to pull his head up, twisting from side to side, to separate the skin along the edge of the steel jaws meant there was no way this wasn't going to be the most painful event of his life. He screamed, pulled up, rotated clockwise and twisted his torso. The shredded tissue between the jaws gave way. It was only then that Wayne realized the top quarter of his ear was never in the vise. That section was still attached to his head while the chunk of ear was still trapped between the jaws. His scream became more anguished and desperate. He cried again for HELP, but the dark, indifferent night swallowed the mournful plea. He panted away several minutes, hoping time would produce a change. As before, he realized he was going to have to forcibly separate himself from his ear. The fact that he was now losing more blood increased the imperative while weakening his resolve. No time to waste.

He pulled back away from the workbench, hoping the ear would tear along the far edge of the vise jaws. This happened, but the scalp above the ear tore along the injury, peeling an inch of skin away from his head. With a violent twist of his head and a blood-curdling scream, Wayne tore himself loose, stumbled on wobbly legs, and fell to the floor.

The value of a victory depends on the circumstances. Wayne felt like he had bested Houdini as he slowly rose from the floor. Once standing, he realized he was still a long way from winning. He found a light switch near the side door. He found a jagged edge on a damaged propeller, which he used to cut the zip ties. He removed the black strap and the metal nut pressed into his swollen temple. In the toilet, he used toilet paper as a gauze pad for his wounded ear. A greasy shop towel went over the paper padding, and although it was at first an instrument of torture, Wayne removed the nut and used the black nylon strap to fasten his first aid bandage over his ear.

Outside the building, he returned to his car, started it up and drove away without looking back. After five kilometers, he pulled the car into a rest area, parked and cried. He cried and cried. The loneliness of having no back up, no assistance, no one to help at all. The loss of his ear, which he now realized he had left in the jaws of the vise. The anger, the humiliation, the fury all balled up into a violent, pathetic expression of grief, fear and frustration. After fifteen minutes of expulsion, Wayne re-started the car and got back on the road, thinking; *Avery Forsythe is going to pay for this. Masoni won't get to kill him, because I will.*

CHAPTER 21

MICHAEL KELLERMAN WOKE UP TO find himself in the abandoned retail space in Brixton now occupied by fellow junkies and their greedy dealers. Having already been through two rounds of mainlined heroin, Michael was waiting out his recovery while anticipating his third encounter with opioid euphoria. The building used to be a neighborhood supermarket, but hard times let it become a hangout for addicts of all types. The interior was a sordid mess, but perception-altering drugs could turn it into a beguiling temporary paradise. Michael's dealer, Spencer was a tall dude with long dark hair and a Fu Manchu mustache. Dressed in a black full-length leather trench coat, dark turtleneck, black jeans, and heavy Doc Martin boots, the guy looked like a soldier of Satan. He had a businessman's mind, but the appearance of an executioner, which was pretty accurate given the product he was peddling.

Scrolling on his phone, Spencer checked *Celebrizine*, where he looked at all the hot women in sexy dresses who were photographed as they entered Vince Kronig's debut ball. Seeing Michael in a couple of photos he shouted, "Hey fuckin freak, what are you doing at this party?"

Spencer stepped over to the ratty sofa where Michael lay and shook his shoulder. Michael stirred, opened his eyes, trying to focus them on Spencer who now sat on the edge of the sofa.

"What are you doing at this fancy party?"

Michael looked at the phone's screen as Spencer flipped through pictures from the Gala event at LPU. He saw himself, with his father and sister. *How the hell did these pictures get published*?

"Look that's you," said Spencer pointing at Michael. "Is that your old man? It says here he's one of the richest people in the world."

"You can't believe everything you read on the internet," replied Michael.

"Yeah well I definitely don't believe what fuckin junkies tell me. Who's that hot number, is she your girlfriend?"

With the image zoomed in on Julie's face and cleavage, Spencer stuck the phone in front of Michael.

"Is she your girlfriend?" repeated Spencer.

"No… no she's not. She's my sister."

Pulling the phone away so he could look at it again, Spencer traced his finger over the image of Julie.

"So you're really a rich boy not just a fucking freak. All the debt I been carrying for you was completely unnecessary. You lied to me when you said you didn't have any money."

Michael looked at him with fast sobering eyes now that he started to realize the potential consequences of his true identity being revealed.

"Answer me," shouted Spencer as he smacked Michael on the side of the head.

Raising his hands in defense while ducking his head,

Michael said, "Okay, okay, you're right, that is me."

"Well since that's you, you now owe me the twenty grand in debt I been carrying for your habit."

Michael had no idea how in debt he was.

"You either get me that money or we find something else."

Michael said with a trembling voice, "I can get you the money."

"Right now? You can get me twenty grand right now?"

"Well not right now, but I can get it."

"Bullshit. You've been bullshitting me for years. Always saying you'd pay up in full and always leaving me with an unpaid balance. No, I don't want your bullshit money."

Michael swallowed hard as he looked away from the menacing glare Spencer fixed upon him.

"What are you going to do," he sheepishly asked, breaking the long pause during which Spencer had gone back to looking at his phone?

Turning his gaze back upon Michael, Spencer said, "There's something else I want, and you're going to get it here or else your life will be forfeited for your debt."

Shaking and on the edge of tears, especially since he had not had his third hit of heroin, Michael asked, "What do you want?"

Flipping the phone around to reveal a picture of Julie at the party with her hips in profile and her pretty face casting a sexy look over her shoulder, Spencer said, "I want her, tonight."

"What? What do you mean?" stammered Michael.

"I mean I want you to get her to come here tonight."

"Why? What are you going to do?"

With a look of disgusted disbelief Spencer said, "Da,

I'm going to fuck her brains out."

"Oh," said Michael.

"Fucking Oh," said Spencer as he tossed Michael the phone. "Call her, give her the address and get her to come here and I will give you a hit of pure heroin. Uncut, unadulterated, it will make you higher than you've ever been. But not 'til after you make that call."

CHAPTER 22

AT THE BABYLON RESTAURANT JULIE and Vince were seated to dine in the Spanish Roof Garden. Occupying the top of 99 Kensington High Street, this unique eatery, set in a fabulous converted roof garden, evoked the feeling of a holiday in the Mediterranean. The flowers, trees, architecture and flamingoes gave Londoners a break from the English monotony, transporting diners to the Spanish coast to enjoy an exceptional meal. Julie had been anticipating taking Vince to this special place ever since she met him. Tonight the weather cooperated, providing a cool and comfortable evening. The silk dress Julie wore was a deep shade of maroon, its length extending to her knees, while the thin spaghetti straps criss crossed behind her, revealing the smooth muscles of her back. The generous neckline, displaying her cleavage, provided support and coverage of her breasts through a built in underwire with thin padding. She looked stunning and Vince was absolutely gape mouthed when he picked her up. Avery had sent Vince to the Savile Row haberdasher who outfitted Klaus. Dressed in a Desmond Merrion suit of dark worsted wool, Vince projected the image of success and confidence that went with a red power tie, folded handkerchief in the breast pocket, and a pair of Salvatore Ferragamo shoes. Amazed with the décor and ambience of the restaurant, Vince felt privileged to be having dinner with this lovely woman in a uniquely beautiful environment. He looked forward to getting to know her on this fabulous first date.

Having just ordered drinks, they were discussing the menu when Julie's phone chimed. She quickly looked at the screen, and it suddenly drew her full attention. She tapped the screen and Vince watched her eyes rapidly scanning a text message. She cast her gaze upon Vince.

"I'm really sorry but I have to go."

Pulling his head back with amazement Vince said, "Really, what's the matter?"

Clutching the phone to her chest she replied, "It's Michael."

"What's wrong?"

"He's in trouble and needs my help."

Julie picked up her purse and began to slide back her chair.

"Whoa, whoa wait a minute," implored Vince. "I'd like to know, what's the big problem?"

Julie responded, "I know this is sudden," she lowered her voice and leaned in, "but I can't explain it to you here. We've got to go."

As they stood up to leave, the headwaiter approached. Vince apologized while settling the bill using his Digival account.

Once inside Vince's Audi A5, Julie began. "I think you know Michael likes to party pretty hard."

Vince nodded.

"Well sometimes he goes a little too deep and often ends up in a bar or party from which he needs to be escorted out. I'm the one who gets that call."

"How often is often?"

"I don't know, every couple of months, maybe more than that."

"Like once a month?"

"The holidays are especially tough. So are the summer months."

"Where's the party tonight?"

"Up in Brixton. It's not a very nice part of town. I've never retrieved him from up there before."

"Should we call the police then?"

"No, no police. They just bring publicity, which is something we definitely want to avoid."

"But if it's not a nice neighborhood and as you say it's dangerous-"

"I never said it was dangerous."

Stuttering Vince restated, "I mean it could be dangerous and we should ask the police to help us in case there's trouble. We can't handle any trouble."

"Speak for yourself. I've pulled him out of many parties and never had any trouble."

"But you said Brixton is a bad part of town."

"I didn't call it bad, and even if it is, I'm not going to call the police so that Michael can be arrested and charged with public intoxication. That's just not happening."

Julie cast the address to the A5's navigation system while Vince tried to ignore the tension permeating the cabin of the sleek black sedan.

Brixton was a working class neighborhood with no more work. Poverty, blight, crime and despair were on display for even the casual observer. With the evening turning dark and the address approaching, Vince felt like they were making a huge mistake. "Look when we get there, if it looks unsafe, I say we call the police and let them handle it. If Michael is in real danger then the police should be the ones to help him."

Julie's disappointment came across crystal clear as she shot Vince a hostile glare.

132 Trumble Street was an abandoned shopping center with a weed festooned parking lot, smashed glass storefronts and unlocked entrance doors. As they approached, a paunchy middle aged man quickly exited the building, doing up his pants. He was followed by an angry young woman, dressed in a ragged negligee, screaming at him, waving a few bills of currency in her hand. Vince parked the glistening automobile among the chest high weeds in the neglected lot. Being there at all seemed to Vince like a bad idea, but Julie was unperturbed.

"This is not a smart move," he said.

"He needs me, I'm going to help him."

"Is this the kind of place where you've helped him before?"

Turning to look out the window on the dilapidated storefronts Julie replied, "No, it's usually a bar or a house party with lots of normal people around."

"See, we don't even know what we could be getting into. Let's call the police."

Indecision lurked in Julie's eyes but disappeared when her phone rang. The tone was Michael's. Vince listened to Julie's side of the conversation.

"Michael?"

"Yes, I'm on my way."

"Yes I'm going to help you."

"I can see where you are on my phone."

"Keep the GPS signal on and I will come right to you."

"Alone? Yes I can come alone, but why does that matter?" Vince shook his head when she looked at him while speaking.

"What kind of trouble are you in?"

"Now don't panic. I'm on my way, I'll be there shortly. Keep the GPS on."

Julie opened the car door and began to climb out. Vince grabbed her arm. "What are you doing?"

"Let me go," she commanded, burning Vince with a direct glare.

"Hey tell me what he said. Why does he want you to go in there alone?"

"When he has a panic attack, I alone can calm him. Anyone else makes it worse."

"That sounds manipulative. You could end up in a dangerous situation."

While Vince spoke Julie looked right at him, but he noticed three guys enter the building through the same door that the John and the prostitute used earlier.

"Well excuse me, but this is my brother. He's someone I love and trust, He feels the same for me. He would not lead me into danger."

"I don't like it. We should call the police."

"We already discussed that. If you call the cops, I will never have anything more to do with you. Now you stay here, I'll bring him back and we'll go."

Vince watched her make her way through the weeds, which snagged at her knee length dress. She was going into a bombed out drug house wearing a sexy evening dress. Being Vince was hard. As Diegert, he would never have argued with her. He would have simply exited the car, stormed the building and laid waste to whomever got in his way as he searched for Michael. As Vince, he was being thoughtful and deferential, cooperative and supportive in spite of the fact that what she was doing was stupidly ill informed.

She walked through the same entrance as the others, and disappeared from view. Disappeared, is exactly how it felt. Vince had no information, nothing to know if she was okay. He just looked at the open doorway and could see only darkness. What could be happening to her? Where the hell was Michael? How far had he gone off the rails to end up strung out while having a panic attack in a shithole like this?

The next thing Vince saw caused him to question everything. Exiting the building was Michael Kellerman. He passed through the same doorway as everyone else, shook out a cigarette, lit it up and walked away. Vince scratched his temples anticipating Julie's immediate exit. What the fuck was going on? Michael just walked away. He never even looked at the car or acknowledged his ride. Where was Julie?

SPENCER HELD MICHAEL'S PHONE. HE had moved into the back part of the old store. He was no longer alone. With him were three guys that made up his drug running crew. Harold was the tech guy, good with apps and operating communications. He was skinny, not too tall, someone for whom brains meant a lot more than brawn. He had a tattoo that looked like a microchip board creeping out of his shirt and crawling along his neck. Ian was a big dude, heavy set with thick arms and hands like bear paws. His buzz cut hair was the same length as his trimmed beard. Tomas was African. He wore dark sunglasses inside as well as out, and always wore a leather cap. He had a scar on the right side of this lower lip. An unfortunate mark left by a former associate who believed Tomas had not kept a secret.

The three thugs joined Spencer up on the second floor

in the rear of the store where there was an old break room. The door could be locked which was necessary for what they had planned.

Julie followed the signal from Michael's phone. This place definitely gave her the creeps but Michael must be so scared and confused in a place like this. Right now, he really needed her and when they were out of here, she would get him the professional help he needed. She followed the signal to the back of the abandoned store. She walked past empty shelving units, some of which had been tipped over and converted into sleeping spaces by the vagrant denizens. The signal brought her to a staircase. Looking up she saw a door with a window beside it. The window had a shade drawn over it, but light emitted through the thin pale fabric. Julie scampered up the stairs, eager to retrieve Michael and get him home.

VINCE CALLED JULIE'S PHONE, WHICH went to voicemail. "This is Julie's phone; I'll get back to you as soon as I can, Bye." Vince said, "Hey what's going on? Michael just left the building. Where are you? Call me back."

After several minutes during which his tension boiled inside him, Vince waited no longer. He bolted out of the car and moved to the doorway. Inside he could see that the store looked like it had been looted and then reconfigured into a flea market of drugs and cheap sex. Slipshod arrangements of beaten up furniture served as the pleasure emporiums of a variety of illicit drug dealers and pushy prostitutes.

"Blow jobs, twenty quid," called out a scrappy lady with a gravel pit voice. When Vince turned in response, she slipped her hand inside her bra and lifted out her pendulous breast.

Knowing it was useless, Vince had to ask. "Did you see a young lady go by wearing a really nice dress?"

With a flutter of her eyelids, the woman responded, "I'm the only lady for you tonight honey."

Turning away with equal measures of revulsion and pity, Vince noticed a heap of garbage shake and shutter. From the pile materialized a middle-aged woman. She was dressed head to toe in what looked to Vince like six or seven layers of clothing.

"Hey mister," she began. "I saw the lady."

"Yeah, well where did she go?"

"Ten quid and I'll tell ya."

Taking the money from his pocket, Vince replied with a David Diegert tone, "And if I don't find her, I'll come back and take a lot more than ten quid outta you."

JULIE KNOCKED SOFTLY WHILE TURNING the knob and opening the door. Inside she saw three tough looking dudes. With her heart leaping into her throat she asked, "Have you seen a guy named Michael?"

From behind the door, a hand grabbed her arm, pulling her forward as the door slammed shut.

"Michael, your brother, yeah he was here, but he left," said Spencer as he now leaned against the door.

"I... I don't understand," stammered Julie. "I was going to meet him here." Raising her phone, she continued. "I was following the signal from his phone."

Spencer, with a lascivious smile, lifted Michael's phone from his pocket. "You were following the right signal."

"Where's Michael? Why do you have his phone? What

did you do to him?" demanded Julie.

"Whoah, we didn't do anything to him. He left on his own accord. He left his phone with me so you would find your way here."

THE SHABBY, OVERDRESSED INFORMANT led Vince into the back area of the large retail cavern. "I saw her go back here. People who go back here are the high rolling drug users. You want a nickel or a dime bag, you get it right here, but the more expensive stuff is in the back."

None of this impressed Vince. The space was dimly lit by widespread rectangular ceiling panels on way less than half power. The abandoned infrastructure of the old store lay dispersed and disorganized into a haphazard labyrinth covered in dust.

"I don't see why high rollers are going to come back here."

With her scrawny digit extending from her fingerless glove, the heavily bundled tour guide pointed to the rear of the space. "There's an office in the back on the second floor."

Vince ducked down to her height. He could see below and beyond the ceiling that the back of the building rose to a second floor. There was a stairway and an illuminated, curtained window.

"LOOK DARL'N," SAID SPENCER. "YOUR brother owes us a lot of money and we saw your sexy picture, so he offered you to us for relief of his debt."

Julie backed away wishing she was wearing something more substantial than her spaghetti strap dress. Her plunging neckline, which had the exact effect on Vince she intended, left her feeling dangerously exposed. "If you guys touch me you will be committing a crime."

Spencer smiled and laughed while looking at the amused expressions of his three compatriots. "It won't be our first."

The room was furnished with random cast offs. There were two couches, one floral the other beige. The table had metal legs and a Formica top. It was surrounded by four mismatched chairs. A small kitchenette featured a sink flanked by drawers with cabinets above and beside it. The fridge was normal size, which seemed too big for this kind of space.

All four of the men were standing.

It was Spencer who continued to speak. "Your body is just as beautiful as the pictures. This is going to be great." He shrugged off his long black jacket revealing muscular arms. "Harold, Ian," he said as he nodded his head to the two men. They each moved forward quickly, grabbing Julie's arms. Spencer stepped up to her and pulled down the top of her dress.

Vince picked up the pace as he approached the stairway, but he broke into a sprint when he heard Julie screaming from within the upstairs break room.

Julie struggled against the hands that held her arms, but their combined strength easily surpassed her best effort. The force of the movement made her bare breasts sway and bounce, which further entertained Spencer, whose hideous smile broadened as he stared at her exposed chest.

Bounding up the stairs two at a time Vince crested the walkway and strode toward the solid door. It was locked. A closed curtain covered the adjacent window denying Vince a look inside. He could hear voices and see shadows moving. Farther down the walkway was a metal chair with a torn upholstered seat and backrest. Vince grabbed the rigid metal structure and returned to the window.

Spencer tore the rest of Julie's dress off her. As he stood there glaring at her panties, she kicked out at him with both legs. Using the strength of the two men holding her, she was able to land a kick at his groin and another on his face as he leaned forward. Harold and Ian, surprised by the sudden increase in weight, struggled and stumbled, eventually dropping Julie to the floor.

Vince smashed the chair through the window. Bashing the glass several times and pulling the curtain to the side, he cleared the way for him to vault into the room. Julie sat on the floor wearing only panties. Four dudes were in the room, one of them, with long black hair, was down on his hands and knees, blood oozing from his lips. Julie's eyes locked on Vince as she sprang to her feet, scurrying over to him. Still wearing her two inches heels, her feet were spared from the lacerating shards of broken window glass.

Keeping her behind him, Vince now faced all four men as Spencer slowly rose to his feet.

As Vince Kronig, Diegert wanted to be a nice guy. A thoughtful, gentle person, who was generous, kind and fun loving, but those traits were not going to save Julie in this situation. So Vince's handsome pretty boy face took on the hard edged determination of David Diegert's fight face.

Assessing the enemies, Diegert realized the biggest, strongest guy, Ian, appeared slow. The small, skinny guy, Harold, looked like he'd be quick but wouldn't pack much of a punch. The guy with the sunglasses and cap, Tomas, was between the two in size. The lip scar gave him a battle damaged look, but without seeing his eyes Diegert was unable to assess his lethality. The tall guy with the long hair and muscular arms, Spencer, stood warily recovering from the painful kicks. In spite of bleeding from his mouth and ventilating like a blacksmith's bellows, the guy impressed Diegert as the leader of the group. Diegert assessed him as a substantial adversary who was gratefully, temporarily, at less than full capacity.

"The girl leaves," shouted Diegert.

"Fuck you," replied Spencer through heavy puffs of labored breath.

Diegert's first action was against Ian. The big guy could definitely do some damage, so Diegert attacked with a vicious shin strike and stomp on the guy's left leg and foot. Closing the distance and using a fractional moment of surprise, Diegert clocked the guy's jaw with a palm heel strike that caught him with his mouth open. The strike produced a crushing force on the guy's teeth. Chunks of broken enamel flew out as the pulp of the broken teeth pumped dark blood, upon which the big man gagged.

Diegert went next for the low hanging fruit. Harold seemed unprepared for violence, but he was even quicker than Diegert thought as he stepped to avoid the spinning backhand fist strike Diegert shot at him. Continuing the spin, Diegert lashed out with his left leg connecting with Harold's right knee, kicking it into hyperextension. The ligaments snapped, forcing the thigh forward over the lower leg, the knee bent in the opposite direction from which it was designed and Harold fell to the floor screaming with a leg that was no longer able to bear weight.

Tomas pulled his right hand out of his pocket to reveal a solid cylindrical handle. With his thumb, he pressed a button, releasing a six inch blade which shot out of the front end. From the back end of the handle, a razor sharp spike, shaped like the head of a hunting arrow, protruded two inches. A flick of his wrist made a metallic snap when both the blade and the spike locked into position. With his sunglasses still in place, the man squared off against Diegert.

From his coat, Spencer drew a 9mm Beretta. Diegert saw the weapon in his peripheral vision and reacted immediately. Striking sideways, he surprised Spencer by clamping his wrist and bashing the bony joint against the wall. The gun went off as Spencer dropped it. Diegert punched Spencer in the gut and whipped him around into the bull rush charge of Tomas. The two drug dealers collided, sprawling Spencer to the floor while Tomas stumbled forward over the body of his boss. Diegert kicked Tomas in the hip, toppling him over. As he fell, his knife drove into Spencer's thigh.

The groan from Spencer bellowed throughout the room. Tomas, from his seated position, instinctively withdrew the blade, releasing pulses of arterial blood, which sprayed up into Spencer's face. Diegert side kicked Tomas in the head as he reacted to the fountain of blood erupting from Spencer's thigh. The kick knocked the cap off the black man's head as it laid him out on the floor. The pistol lay between Diegert and Spencer. Through his blood-splattered vision, Spencer made a move for the gun. The distance had Diegert a few seconds behind. Spencer got the grip in his hand and pulled the trigger just as Diegert hit the barrel, redirecting the bullet. The projectile went high and behind striking Ian in the throat. A whoosh of air turned into a frothy bubbling as blood spilled from the wound into the big guy's lungs. Grabbing the length of the barrel Diegert torqued the gun out of Spencer's grasp. With the grip in his hand, Diegert stepped back, pointing the gun at

Spencer. Tomas rose from the floor and groggily made his way to his feet.

"Grab the bitch," ordered Spencer.

Diegert moved to shield her. Tomas held his knife in front of him and moved to a flanking position. Spencer used both hands to put pressure on his hemorrhaging leg.

"Shoot him," screamed Julie.

Diegert pointed the gun at Tomas and then back at Spencer. Harold had scooted into a corner, moaning as he clutched his deformed knee. His lower leg stood straight up in the air, toes pointing at his face. Ian was dead, asphyxiated from the GSW to his throat.

"Which one?"

"The one with the knife."

Diegert spun to face Tomas, pointing the Beretta at the knife wielder. Tomas was not buying it. "Drop the knife or die," said Diegert. Tomas looked at the pretty boy taking direction from his naked girlfriend. His smirk was accompanied by a chuckle of disrespect. Flipping the blade into an underhand position, he was not disarming.

"Or die," said Diegert raising the weapon, placing the forehead of the black man in the iron sights. The 9 mm round, moving at one thousand feet per second, ripped through his cerebral tissue, splattering blood and gray matter like ground beef in tomato sauce across the floral couch. His heavy body fell over the arm of the couch, rotated sideways and flopped face down on the floor.

In spite of asking for it, Julie was shocked as she watched Vince dole out violence as she could never have imagined.

Diegert ripped the curtain from the bar above the window, handing the fabric to Julie. She wrapped it around her naked body, securing it toga style around her shoulder and waist.

Stepping over to Spencer, who was desperately trying to staunch the bleeding from his thigh, Diegert backhanded the guy across the face, knocking him from his seated position, flat on the floor.

"Judas, you fucker," groaned the leader of the dying gang. "You really suck, you know that?"

"Yeah, I know," replied Diegert as he took a knee and drove the barrel of the pistol into the open knife wound.

Spencer hollered at the top of his lungs. He swung his right arm in an attempt to punch Diegert, but that only led to his arm being twisted and placed under Vince's Salvatore Ferragamo shoe. Pinned down and in excruciating pain, Spencer kept up the screaming, cussing and hyperventilating a lot longer than Diegert ever thought he would. Bearing down on the gun barrel, Diegert could feel the rigidity of the femur bone. Spencer felt the pressure as well, which took him to a whole new level of pain. For Diegert, the benefit was that Spencer was now silent. He gasped for breath but no longer had the energy to scream. "Are you ready to listen to me now?" asked Diegert. Spencer nodded wordlessly.

"Did Michael Kellerman have anything to do with this?"

Spencer's face contorted into a look of disbelief. Diegert reduced the pressure on the femur. Spencer closed his eyes, trembling with relief as Diegert eased the gun barrel off his leg bone.

"Tell me what Michael's role was in all of this?" demanded Diegert.

Convulsing, Spencer said, "He owes us a lot of money. He said we could have his hot bitch sister for the night. You know, as payment."

The clenched teeth, furrowed brow and determined eyes of David Diegert were now set in the handsome face of Vince Kronig. The deadly expression spelled trouble for the long-haired man hoping to glean mercy for his admission.

"Hey man, you gotta call me an ambulance," muttered Spencer.

"That won't be necessary."

"I'm bleeding bad here man, I might not make it," Spencer explained as if Diegert needed to be made aware of the obvious. "Call them now, don't fuck'n wait."

"You are never going to hurt another woman," said Diegert as he returned to his feet.

"What? What are you talking about? I need an ambulance like right now, and you're talking about slits?" He groaned again as he rolled to his side and pulled his phone from his pocket. Smeared with bloody fingerprints, he attempted to activate it. Perturbed by the pathetic effort to call for help, Diegert kicked the phone out of his hand.

"What the fuck," exclaimed Spencer. "I need help."

With blood dripping from the end of the barrel, Diegert raised the pistol, firing point blank at the spot where the frontal and nasal bones converge. Splintered shards of calcium along with the bullet, shredded the lizard brain of the cruel and callous man.

Diegert turned to face Julie.

"Oh my God," was all she could say.

CHAPTER 23

DIEGERT HAD TO FIND HIS WAY BACK to Vince. He had to let go of the merciless fighter and re-engage with the kind and sensitive person he was struggling to become. With the iron-tinged stench of hot blood permeating the room, Diegert had to show Julie that he was not just a violent killing machine. Looking down to the blood on his bruised hands, he sought to conjure up the feelings that he thought Vince would have. He tried to imagine what Julie needed right now other than a quick exit. It was bewildering, because he just felt so amped up by kicking ass, but he wondered if she needed something more from him to cope with the intensity of the moment. At the same time, he was burning to understand what she knew about Michael.

He continued to look around the room, taking in the dead bodies and bloody gore splattered and sprayed over the killing field. The torn fabric of her evening dress was saturated in a puddle of Spencer's crimson blood.

The posterior portion of Tomas's head was gone. Light reflected in the pool of blood, gathered in the bowl of his cranium formerly occupied by his brain.

Ian, slumped against the wall, had blood covering his shirt from his chin to his belly. His head was flexed so far forward that the top of his head was where his face should be.

Looking at Harold he saw the leg angled awkwardly at the knee. The guy was motionless until he saw his chest rise and fall. With the pistol gripped firmly in his hand, Diegert stepped to the skinny guy and nudged him with his toe. The guy did not move, Vince watched for another moment and then nudged the deformed right leg. Harold bellowed as the hyperextended knee exploded with pain when simply nudged.

"Please don't shoot me. Please don't kill me," pleaded Harold. Diegert didn't care to hear any begging. He pointed the pistol at Harold and readied himself for the blast of the bullet.

Out of the corner of his eye he saw Julie raising her hands to her face as she called out, "Don't do it."

The thought of not killing this dude never entered Diegert's mind. This was the only guy who knew exactly what happened here. That made him an eternal risk. The only guaranteed way to avoid trouble was to kill him. It made perfect sense and it had to happen now. But what about him? What about fairness? What about mercy? Diegert never bothered to consider these questions, but Vince did. Julie peered through her fingers to see Vince lowering his gun and stepping away from the crippled man.

Diegert was drawn back to the Gulf of Tadjoura just before sailing into the Red Sea with Barney Pinsdale. On board the *Sue Ellen* they had Omar Pascal, NCIS Officer stationed in Djibouti, the city where Barney and David had made a port of call. Omar recognized Diegert as wanted in the United States and pursued him until Diegert kidnapped the officer and sailed out into the gulf, miles from shore. He then shot the man and dumped his body in the ocean, never to be found. Diegert and Barney sailed on to Greece without incident. The young Naval Officer was completely gone without a trace or any witnesses, but Diegert was constantly haunted by the ghost of Omar Pascal.

Pascal was a good guy and Diegert lived by a code which allowed him to kill bad guys. He'd overlooked this, and let the fear of being captured and prosecuted cloud his decision. Now he saw the face of Omar Pascal in large crowds, when riding a bus, or trying to fall asleep. A fellow service man, American citizen, and a decent human being snuffed out for convenience. Diegert wielded the power to kill with misguided judgment that made Omar Pascal's death the most regrettable mistake of his life. As Vince, he did not want to take another action he would live to regret, so a little smile crept across his face as a solution came to his mind.

"We're going to make this easy for the cops," said Vince.

"What, how?" responded Julie.

"Mr. Immobile here is going to be the prime suspect in a deal gone bad amongst thieves."

Diegert checked the magazine of the Beretta. Just as he thought, six bullets left out of a ten round magazine. Releasing the clip, he emptied it of bullets and put them in his pocket. As he stepped over to Harold, he untucked his shirt using it to wipe the grip of the pistol, removing his fingerprints.

"What are you doing? You gotta help me get out of here," pleaded the skinny tech thief.

"Didn't you see what happened to the last guy who begged for my help?"

Harold looked beyond Vince to the dead bodies of his partners in crime.

Diegert pulled the ceremonial handkerchief from the breast pocket of his suit jacket and knelt down next to the sniveling criminal. He stuffed the handkerchief into the guy's mouth, grabbed his dispositioned foot and twisted it farther, rotating the femur against the tibia. The joint strained but Diegert kept twisting as Harold screamed into cotton. An audible snap preceded the moment when the ACL gave way and the joint rotated even further. It was now completely useless for locomotion. Harold was going nowhere under his own power.

Spitting out the handkerchief, Harold protested through labored, painful gasps. "What the fuck are you doing?"

Diegert grabbed Harold's right wrist, splashed his hand into a puddle of Spencer's blood and placed the grip of the pistol in the confused man's hand.

Standing up Vince said to Julie, "There's all the evidence the police will need. This skinny runt will tell a crazy story about how someone else did all this, but a bloody murder weapon and a room full of dead associates is damning enough that the power of our wealthy privilege will make that accusation seem absolutely ridiculous."

Addressing Harold, Diegert said, "Give me your phone." When the incapacitated wuss hesitated, Diegert turned his gaze to the disjointed leg. Harold, tracking Diegert's eyes, extracted his phone and held it aloft to the handsome, but increasingly dangerous man.

"What are you going to do?" blurted the trembling thief.

"I'm going to get you some help. When I hold the phone to your face, you're going to say exactly what I tell you. You got it?"

A sheepish nod, got a furrowed response and Harold added, "Yes, yes I will say whatever you tell me."

"There's been a violent crime, 132 Trumble Street in Brixton. The scene is inside the back of the building. You got that? You can remember that and say it?"

"Yes... yes I can," stammered Harold nodding his head as assuredly as he could.

Diegert dialed 999 and held the phone to Harold's face with his right hand as he placed his left on the ankle of Harold's over-rotated and painfully dysfunctional leg.

"999, what is the nature of your emergency?" said the female voice.

"Ah.. Ah, 132 Trumble Street, Brixton. Upstairs in the back of the building there's been a terrible, violent crime."

"Okay, sir are you all right? Can I get your name?"

Diegert pulled the phone away while gesturing with a hand slash across his throat. Harold's response to the woman's question hung on his lips but the gesture caused him to swallow hard.

Diegert disconnected the call, put the phone on silent, made sure the GPS signal was active and placed the phone twenty feet away from Harold on the floral couch. Turning back to the whimpering wastrel, Vince took a knee and came in close as he said, "I don't ever want to see you again, and you sure as hell don't want to see me." Gesturing with his hand to the carnage behind him, Vince added, "This is all on you. That's what I want you to tell them." As Harold nodded, the lids around Vince's striking blue eyes narrowed. The frightened coward's nodding was accompanied by the reply, "Yeah, Yes, I will tell them and you will never see me ever again."

"Good," said Vince as he stood up

Looking around the room Diegert cautioned Julie not to step in any of the puddles of blood as they moved to the door. Stepping into the hallway, Vince was surprised to see the seven-layer lady scuttling away from the stairs.

"Hey," he shouted. She stopped in her tracks, slowly

turning her dirt stained face towards the young couple.

"For $500 quid, we were never here," said Vince as he pulled a roll of cash from his pocket as they descended.

"With $500 quid I won't be here, when the cops come and I won't ever come back neither," cackled the joyful woman.

Getting a closer look at her as he handed over the money, Vince could see the years of hard living etched in her wrinkled face. This woman, who was probably at one time a kind mother and generous provider, was now trapped in desperate inescapable poverty.

Hustling through the shabby den of iniquity, Vince and Julie exited the building, got in the Audi and drove to the Kellerman townhouse.

CHAPTER 24

VINCE HAD NOT ENTERED THE HOUSE when he picked up Julie for their dinner date. The building was a seven-story structure in Sussex. Using her phone, Julie opened the door to the underground garage. Vince piloted the A5 down the concrete ramp and found a parking spot amongst the dozen cars already stored in the beautiful wood paneled carport.

"Wow, this is nice."

"Daddy really likes cars."

"Yeah," said Vince as he looked through the window at the MG, Jaguar, Rolls Royce, Ferrari, Porsche, and Lamborghini even a '74 Corvette Stingray. He turned to Julie who remained in her seat wrapped in her curtain fabric toga. He held the two phones he'd taken from the scene.

Looking down at them he began, "This phone belonged to the guy with the long hair. The GPS has been deactivated. It can't be tracked." Holding up the other phone, which Julie recognized because of the tiger skin case, Vince said, "This one belongs—"

She interrupted him. "I can't talk about that right now."

She looked sad, but also resolved. She had to come to the realization on her own that Michael had so brazenly betrayed and worthlessly discarded her. The brother she loved and was so committed to helping had given her body to drug dealers in payment for a debt. She couldn't discuss it until she had processed the evidence and absorbed the painful truth. "Let's go upstairs," she said with a wan smile.

As they stepped into the elevator, Julie pressed number four. When the door opened, Vince asked, "Your room is on the fourth floor?"

Julie replied, "The entire floor is mine."

Stepping out of the elevator Vince could see that it was a full apartment. Living room, kitchen, balcony with a view, it was all spectacular. The furnishings were classic yet they looked comfortable. Glass, marble and granite surfaces perched above oak floors and lush carpets. It was the kind of place most people would be lucky to afford for an overnight vacation, yet the family photos, the pieces of art and the socks and shoes on the floor marked this as a personal dwelling.

"We own the whole building," continued Julie. "The first floor is for business and entertaining. Daddy lives on the second floor, Michael has the third. Here we are on the fourth. The fifth is a library and computer center. On the sixth is the sports and activity area as well as the movie theater. The seventh is off limits. Daddy said to us, long ago that we are not to enter the seventh floor. The doors are securely locked. I've never been on the seventh floor. The roof is lovely though with a tennis court, a garden and a pool we use in the summer."

Vince smiled as he looked around. Life on the opposite side of being poor was pretty incredible. Three people living in a seven story building that could comfortably house a hundred was the kind of opulence that drew resentment from him. Now he was inside with this beautiful woman, after this crazy night and his perspective was shifting.

"Who are you Vince?" asked Julie as she leaned against the marble counter of the kitchen's island.

The simple question set off alarm bells in Diegert's head. Did she know? Why was she asking this? Is she a threat? Do I just play it cool and see where this goes? Looking at her, in this lovely apartment, wrapped in her curtain fabric toga, Diegert played it cool.

Cocking his head like a curious puppy Vince replied, "What do you mean?"

"I mean who are you, that you can take down four guys and not have a scratch on you?"

Vince looked to his hands. "My knuckles are quite swollen."

Her rising eyebrows furrowed her forehead. "Were you in the Special Forces or are you an agent of some sort?"

Shaking his head, Vince replied, "I'm an economist. We talked about this."

"Yeah, but you seem to know a lot more about fighting than the economy."

"Remember I said, no one knows the economy. It's the world's biggest mystery. A phenomenon that functions by one simple rule, supply and demand. All the rest is not understood until after the fact. I'm just a guy who's trying to predict the future from what we've learned of the past."

She angled her face to him as she shot a look of disbelief. "Where did you learn to fight like that?"

"Like what?"

"Like a guy trained for close quarters combat?"

Vince chuckled. "I think you're giving me a lot more credit than I deserve. I was just lucky tonight."

"You disarmed a guy, killed three out of four while

setting the last guy up as the perpetrator of the crime. That's not the work of an economist."

"I took self-defense at the Y, when I was younger."

"I've taken self-defense. They don't teach killing. They don't teach you how to handle a gun. You demonstrated a whole 'nother level of capacity."

"Julie," said Vince with a sense of concern as he stepped closer to her. "Are you all right? I think you might be in a state of shock. Do you feel okay? Do you want me to leave?"

They held eye contact comfortably, enjoyably. Slow smiles seductively forming on both pairs of desirable lips.

Julie said, "You saw me naked."

Chuckling, Vince nodded, "It was unavoidable."

"Our first date and you get to see me naked before we even have dinner."

"I can tell you I was quite shocked."

"And?" she said with an expectant smile as she shifted her stance, placing her hand where her narrow waist became a curvaceous hip.

"And… impressed," said Vince reading her body language.

"So if I remove my curtain will you be shocked or impressed?"

With a moment of hesitation Vince replied, "Both."

Reaching to the knot at her shoulder, Julie untied the pale fabric. The wrapping came undone and dropped to the floor. She was still wearing her panties, but that was all. Vince inspected her lovely body with careful eyes, amazed at the beauty she was sharing with him. Her torso was exquisitely proportioned, with breasts, waist, and hips exemplifying a feminine ideal. Her legs were long, strong and athletic. She was smiling with an assured sense of confidence that surprised Vince only because of the dreadful situation she had earlier been in, when forced into the state of undress which she was now clearly enjoying.

She reached out, took his hand and led him down the hall, her bare feet padding across the hardwood. Walking down the hall, Julie pointed out the guest room to the left; they passed by her office, and on the right, a sitting room. At the end of the hall, they reached her bedroom. Entering, Vince could see that the sleeping chamber was the entire width of the fourth floor. To the right was a marble bathroom, to the left an enormous closet. The bed itself was gigantic. It looked like an acre of mattress. It was one massive cushion, well beyond 'King Size.'

"You got to see me naked, so how about I get to see you?" She tilted her head and waited an impatient moment before adding, "If you take your clothes off, you can stay with me tonight."

Diegert was confused. The desired action was obvious, but the deeply personal and intimate situation after just having violently killed people was difficult for Vince. He was just so surprised by how forward Julie was being after such a traumatic event. Was she really okay? Was it right for him to do this? Was he crazy for not getting undressed as quickly as he could?

With a soft purr in her voice Julie said, "Don't be shy, it's just you and me."

Vince untied his shoes and removed his socks. Her lips curved into a cute smile. He unbuttoned his oxford shirt and peeled it back off his shoulders. Julie's smile broadened as she took in the muscles on Vince's chest and the lean rippling abdomen. Her eyes though, grew wide with anticipation. Unbuttoning his pants and sliding them to the floor revealed strong legs, but also exposed the deep scar on his left thigh. Vince saw the painful wince in Julie's face. He shrugged at her as she looked at him with concern. Standing in his dull gray briefs, a lustful smile on his face, reassured her that this man's injury was fully healed.

Vince put his thumb under his waistband. Julie smiled and quickly did the same. Looking at him, she started to giggle. Without realizing it, they synchronized their blinks and they both pulled down their underwear simultaneously. A burst of laughter erupted as they stepped out of their undergarments and rose to standing. They felt silly, they felt sexy and Julie was impressed with the rising erection forming in front of her. Vince's aroused penis engorged as he gazed at Julie's neatly trimmed landing strip.

With a fading smile she stepped over to him, hand extended. He took her hand stepping to the edge of the massive bed. She pulled back the sheets, climbing on to the cool cotton. Vince looked at her as he followed on to the soft sheets. He was surprised that the excitement and effervescence of a moment ago seemed to be waning. Perplexed, he searched her face for a message. She was no longer making eye contact. Sliding onto his back, he laid his head on the pillow next to her. She wrapped a leg across his thighs and an arm across his chest. Vince put his arm around her shoulder and drew her close. Julie tucked her head in tight upon Vince's broad shoulder. The room was still, Vince's hard-on was tent-poling the sheets, but he sensed things were different.

The first sob came from Julie like a bursting bubble. The second escaped an attempt at repression. The third and all the rest fell out of her like floodwater cresting a dam. Julie Kellerman cried uncontrollably. She sobbed and trembled as her emotions shook the massive bed with grief, sadness and pain. She cried with such force that the tears seemed to spray from her eyes. Vince could only imagine the pain of betrayal she was feeling over her brother's treachery. The sense of worthlessness with which he regarded her and the belief that what he was doing was somehow okay. Treating his sister like a sexual commodity to be bartered for a debt he could've easily paid. With all the money in the world, he chose to offer the one woman who loved him as meat for the violent pleasures those four creeps had planned. Vince's face grew stern as his Diegert feelings boiled inside.

After fifteen minutes of mournful crying, Julie wiped her face on the sheet. "I'm sorry," she said.

"Shh," replied Vince. "I'm right here. Why don't you go to sleep."

Julie repositioned her head on Vince's shoulder. Soon her soft rhythmic breathing caressed his chest. Before long they were both dreaming of the good thing they'd found in one another and the retribution for betrayal that awaited Michael.

CHAPTER 25

<small>AFTER DRIVING FOR SIXTEEN STRAIGHT</small> hours, Wayne arrived in London and texted Avery. *I'm on the LPU campus, I have critical intel to share.*

Avery: *Was your mission successfully completed?*

That's what I have to talk with you about. Let me in.

Where's the video?

I must see you in person, let me in.

After a long pause, Wayne received a message.

Wait where you are, I will have an escort team bring you in.

Standing in Avery's office, Wayne's pledge to kill his benefactor had faded. Instead, he arrived with a more hopeful request in mind.

"So Wayne I see a substantial injury to your left ear. In fact that's a pretty nasty looking bandage you have there."

"Ah, yes sir, the ear is gone and I'm hoping your super nanocytes can fix me up with a new one."

"I see, but before we discuss any such arrangement, please explain the outcome of your mission. Is Masoni dead?"

"Aye, I got to tell ya, I could have benefitted from a bit more information about that crafty bastard. You see I went to the boat business you told me about and I stole inside so I could kill em, and when I surprised him, he had a bigger surprise for me."

"Yes, what happened then?"

"The boathouse was a big cavernous space. Masoni was inside, and he seemed to be waiting for something or someone. I thought for sure I had him right where I wanted him. I crept along the shadows on the edge of the room to get a good shot. As I drew closer, I was attacked from the side. A powerful force emerged from the shadows, knocking me to the ground. Falling into the middle of the room alarmed Masoni, who looked at me and shouted, "Kill Him." I looked and saw what had pushed me down. It was a man all dressed in black with a skull mask on his face. He drew a long katana from a sheath--that's a big sword."

"Yes, I know what a katana is."

"This guy was a ninja. I rolled to my side and popped off two shots at Masoni. He ran for cover and I'm not sure if I killed him. The ninja struck my wrists with his sword."

Wayne held out his wrists, and the cuts from the zip ties were significant and looked quite painful, but a sharp katana would have taken his hands right off.

"I lost my pistol as I scrambled to my feet. I found a boathook with a long staff and squared up against the ninja. The hook end of the staff had a tapered metal point and it was long enough that I could jab him. I thrust the staff at him, poking him in the stomach and the thighs. He circled me constantly adjusting his stance and his grip on the sword. During one of his adjustments, I whirled the staff and swung the end of it at his head. I could hear the crack of the metal against his skull. He stumbled a bit trying to regain his footing, but not before I whacked his left knee. He went down, and I set the point of the shaft to pierce his throat. As I drove forward he deflected my shaft, slid himself to the opposite side like a cat and struck me in the side of my head with the butt of his sword."

Wayne turned his head, bringing Avery's attention to his bruised temple where Masoni had strapped the metal nut and tortured him with the impact driver. Out of the corner of his eye, Wayne saw Avery wincing at the site of his bruises.

"We were both standing now, a bit groggy but not giving up the fight. I looked around but I could not see Masoni anywhere. The coward either was dead or had run off. The ninja began whirling his sword, cutting through the air with big swooshes. He was trying to intimidate me. I stood and twirled my boathook, shifting it from side to side and brandishing it so that the bastard knew I was ready for his shit."

Wayne saw a glimmer of doubt turn into a full frown on Avery's face.

"I moved forward, aggressively using the boathook to snag the sword from the fucker's hand. He was forced on to the defensive; I had him backing up toward the waterfront. Crossing the open area of the boathouse, I was getting ready to disarm and skewer him when I stepped into a puddle of motor oil. My foot slipped out from under me and I fell to the floor. The ninja flashed forward. As he passed by, he swung the katana at my face. I had only an instant to react. My evasion kept the blade from splitting my skull like a melon, and instead he sliced off my ear like a piece of deli ham."

Avery's earlier frown remained, but was now joined by a furrowed brow and one raised eyelid. After a moment of silence he said, "Well I'm glad to hear you survived this harrowing battle with such a skilled combatant. The boathook turned out to be a very clever weapon."

"Thank you sir," said Wayne with a bow to his sensei.

"But I gather from the story that Jarod Masoni is not confirmed dead."

"No sir. In fact from across the room the ninja shouted something before he left."

Avery leaned forward, opening his palms as he kept his eyes fixed on Wayne's.

Following a thoughtful pause, Wayne said, "The night will never be too dark for us to find and kill the one who sent you."

Avery leaned back in his chair, folded his arms over his chest and said, "These were the ninja's parting words, and he put no more attack upon you?"

"Yes sir, that's why I drove straight back here so I could deliver the warning as soon as possible. I fear Masoni intends to do you harm."

"How does Masoni know you were sent by me? You never mentioned speaking to him."

"AH... That's true sir, but ninjas have a sixth sense. If even a thought of you entered my head during the fight, the ninja would know it. That's why they are so successful in fights because they can enter the minds of their opponents and know their thoughts before they become actions."

After rubbing his forehead in his hand Avery said, "I see. That's amazingly insightful of you to recognize the ways of the ninja. You're lucky to have survived a confrontation with such a formidable mental warrior."

Another deferential bow and Wayne said, "Again, I thank you sir."

"Previously, you mentioned nanocytes. Tell me what you know of them."

"When I flew back from China with Mr. Perez, he told me that the way in which he changed his face involved tiny little cells which could communicate with an app on his phone. These nanocytes, as he called them, could restructure the DNA of cells, making them appear in a different and specific way, such as an image on a computer. I thought it was pretty amazing and I figured that was the technology you said you were afraid Jarod knew about and would sell the information."

"But you never had the opportunity to speak to Jarod about the issue, correct?"

Stammering for a moment Wayne said, "That is correct."

"Have you spoken to anyone else about nanocyte technology?"

"Well there was this one girl in a bar in Italy on my way to the job. She was a pretty girl, but she was all upset about a mole she had on her chin. I told her about the tech and the nanocytes and that one day she would be able to get rid of something like her mole overnight. She was so excited. This capability will be quite profitable when you release it into the market."

Avery's eyelids narrowed and his jaw muscles bulged as he sternly exhaled like a raging bull. Despite his anger, he spoke calmly saying, "Now, about fixing your ear. I'm going to call over to medical and have them prepare to receive you. They will have to gather your medical history, screen you for any risk factors and prepare you for the procedure. Recreating an external structure without the template upon which to generate changes will be new for us, but if you're willing to undergo an experimental procedure then we'll move forward."

"There is no progress without experimentation," said Wayne the wise sage.

Smiling wanly, Avery replied, "I will have the men

who escorted you here direct you to Medical."

Avery arrived in Medical an hour later to find Wayne sedated on a treatment table in the surgical room. To the surgeon and her assistants, Avery said, "Thank you for all your preparations, but unfortunately this procedure is being cancelled and you are to leave the area now. I'm sorry for the inconvenience. Your time is valuable and you will all be paid for your expertise."

Avery kept smiling as all the medical professionals removed their masks and gloves as they exited. Avery stepped over to the anesthesiologist. "How's he doing?"

"He's fine. We just put him under two minutes ago. I can cut things back and bring him around in about fifteen minutes."

"No, no, that won't be necessary. In fact I want you to follow my orders explicitly."

Although the anesthesiologist was wearing a cap, mask, and glasses, the concern in his eyes could not be hidden.

Avery said, "Show me which valve will deliver anesthetics that cease his ability to breathe."

"Ah... I can't do that."

Through a cold, hard, direct stare, Avery said, "You work for Crepusculous, now show me."

With a trembling hand, the anesthesiologist pointed to the red valve, which was currently set at 2.5.

Avery turned the valve up to 7.5. He directed his gaze upon Wayne, who started taking bigger and bigger breaths, until his rate of breathing started to increase and the depth of his breaths became shallower. Finally, after only three minutes, ventilation ceased entirely. Avery turned to the anesthesiologist to say, "Pronounce him, and see to it that he's delivered to the furnace room. I want his cremains on my desk tomorrow morning. Thank you."

CHAPTER 26

"HONEY I JUST DON'T UNDERSTAND WHY you have to remain in London, and why can't we at least come visit you," asked Carolyn's mother Laurie.

"Mom, I've told you many times that my role here is classified and I can't talk about it. I can't leave London at this point in my mission and I can't entertain guests either."

The truth was Carolyn had not told her parents that she was now in her ninth month. She hadn't posted to Facebook or Instagram for months and was doing her best to avoid all social media.

"Darling, I'm just worried about you. We haven't even seen you on Facebook. Why not?"

"We are restricted from social media."

"You used to post on Facebook all the time."

"This mission is different. I'm not allowed to be active on any social media. I'm only allowed to make this phone call from a secure line in the consulate."

"I know secrecy is what the CIA is all about, but I just don't like it. I can't be sure you're okay."

"Mom, I'm okay. You can be sure because I'm telling you everything is fine. Now how's Dad and the kids?"

Laurie Fuller veered off the topic of Carolyn and spent the rest of the phone call praising her other children, grandchildren, grand-dogs and local charity events. Carolyn kept the conversation focused on the family and all her mom and dad's activities. After listening to as much as she could before bursting into tears, Carolyn told her mom they had to get off the secure line. Laurie asked, "Will you be home for Christmas?"

"I don't know, Mom. If I can make it home, I will let you know. Love you, I gotta go."

"I love you too dear; I'll tell your father you said hi."

"Okay, mom thanks, and please give him a hug."

After disconnecting the call on her cell phone, where she kept several burnable numbers, she felt terrible lying to her mom. Her mission was classified, but she was lying to cover up the fact that she would soon give birth and had not told her parents she was pregnant.

How could she? The father was the assassin of the President of the United States whom she assisted to escape the U.S., and who then died carrying out one of the most horrific acts of terror to ever strike the United Kingdom. This was more than just a lapse of judgment. A wild night gone too far. This was in her mind an act of treason. A betrayal of the trust the Agency had in her. She was going to bring into the world, a child whose father she had feelings for, but was a professional murderer capable of incredible violence. How was she ever going to tell this child about his or her father? In spite of all the technology, Carolyn went old school and did not seek to know the gender. Since so much of this was a surprise to her, she figured she might as well leave the gender unknown like so much of her future.

A text message popped up from Richard Ramsey. *Call me.* At 9:00 pm on a Saturday, she figured, it must be something important for him to be asking her to call. As the phone rang, she prepared for the worst.

"Carolyn, I'm so glad you called."

"I'm returning your call Richard. Now what's up?"

With a slur in his speech, Ramsey replied, "Don't forget, that's Agent Ramsey, but I'll let you call me Rich if you want to. You can even call me Dick!"

"Oh believe me I've already called you that. You sound like you've been drinking and if this is not official business I'm terminating the call."

"Wait! Wait just a minute. It's Saturday night and I know you're home alone. Why don't we get together for some social time?"

"I do not want to spend social time with you."

"Ok, Ok, I get it. We don't have to go out and 'be social.' I can come to your place and we can just hang out."

"You may not come to my place. I have no interest in hanging out with you."

"Are you with your mystery man? The mysterious father of your soon to be born baby?"

"That is none of your business. We've been over this."

"We have been over this and I believe I made it clear that your pregnancy is my business. Your condition is a risk to both you and our mission."

Carolyn felt a pang of guilt when he said this. She had slept with the enemy and now held his progeny in her womb.

"I wanted to tell you something else though, Carolyn, something I have never told anyone."

Rolling her eyes in disgust Carolyn replied, "What?"

"There's no easy way to say this so I'm just going to come out and say it. I get really turned on by pregnant women."

He stopped talking and just let it hang in the air. Carolyn wanted to immediately hang up, but she knew he would just call back.

"I can hear you breathing," said the inebriated boss.

"Ya see, what can happen? You're already pregnant. You can't get pregnant twice, so why not fool around?"

She did not respond, but just tried to keep her breathing normal.

"The fertility of life really turns me on. It makes me hard to be so near and close to new life. Wouldn't you say the rear entry position would be best for your late stage in the third trimester?"

Carolyn nearly retched like when she first had morning sickness hearing this pervert's disgusting suggestion.

"I could be there in twenty minutes."

Carolyn coughed as she choked back a bolus of vomit.

"I know you're thinking about it," intoned Ramsey. "If the mystery man is not around, how about I make your evening one you'll never forget?"

Carolyn gulped down her nausea to say, "Richard you are not welcome at my residence. I have two friends staying with me tonight, so do not present yourself at my door. I find your sexual proposition abhorrent and I do not ever want to hear such a suggestion from you again. Do you understand me?"

"Yeah, I understand. You're turned on and you just can't admit it. Don't worry. My offer extends all the way through the ninth month. Call me back when your friends leave."

Gratefully, he hung up. Carolyn had never considered that pregnancy would put her in the crosshairs of a deviant pervert. Her boss was breaking every rule of appropriate conduct. She, however, was reluctant to call attention to her condition. She was concerned about the ramifications of legal action. What a fucking creep!

CHAPTER 27

SUN STREAMED INTO THE BEDROOM casting a warm soft light across the bed. Julie tickled the hair on Vince's chest with her fingers. She explored his pectorals, letting her fingers do the walking right up to his nipple. Vince was startled and immediately awake when Julie circled his nipple and tugged on its center. He had never had his nipples touched and he was surprised how erotic it felt. Julie giggled when she saw how he reacted. She got a bit more aggressive, increasing the pressure on this sensitive, yet otherwise useless part of the male anatomy.

Vince drove his head back into the pillow as he gave himself over to these new sensations. He had never considered his nipples an erogenous zone, but Julie was showing him how wrong he was and there was nothing better than the first time. She positioned her lips over the tiny dark piece of flesh and blew a gentle breeze across the densely innervated circle. Vince gasped as her blast of breath cooled his hot skin. Julie lowered her lips to kiss the little nipple, enveloping the vestigial portal in warmth and moisture. Vince groaned with pleasure as sensations he had never imagined rocketed through his body, giving rise to an incredibly unexpected level of delight. Her tongue flicked across the tip of the nipple sending waves of stimulus coursing through Vince's sensory cortex. She had never seen such a strong reaction and she timed her ministrations to coincide with Vince's groaning expressions of pleasure.

She lifted her head to see Vince looking down at her. She slid forward bringing her lips to his. She kissed him without hesitation and he returned the kiss with fervent passion. When their lips opened and their tongues touched, a connection seemed to take place that felt so right, so good and so unprecedented. They both felt like they knew each other, yet were so excited and enthralled to be getting to know someone new. The kissing was powerful, intoxicating and illuminating. She felt like she was exploring someone familiar, yet totally new. He reveled in the stimulation and exploration, yet felt the comfort of knowing where he was going. To be both elated by the newness and sedated by the sense of acceptance, gave both of them a feeling of connection for which all people long. To find that feeling in a beautiful sexy person was exhilarating and gratitude inducing. Their tongues continued to dance together as if they were a couple in a ballroom.

Vince's hands explored Julie's body, her abdomen smooth and taut, her skin soft and warm. His fingers felt the edge of her breast. The round soft mound held its shape as he covered it with his fingers and palm. Her nipples protruded upward as Vince gently grasped the right one between his thumb and forefinger. Twirling it gently and squeezing it ever so slightly, Vince could sense that she enjoyed this as much as he had. Julie arched her back, pressing her breast forward, into Vince's hand. He brought his other hand to her left breast, treating both of her nipples to a delightfully sensual fingertip massage. For quite a while they lay there caressing each other's nipples, driving each other crazy with the sensual stimulation which seemed to have no end in its ability to delight them both.

Bringing his lips to her eager left nipple was

immediately reinforced when she grabbed the back of his head and pulled him as close to her as she could. Her inch long nubbin was suckled, tongue flicked and gently nibbled by Vince's teeth. He could feel her rhythm, sense the rising intensity in her enjoyment and felt like he was connecting with her on a physical, sexual, sensual level, which was unprecedented for him.

Vince's penis was fully erect and Julie was hot wet and moist. She grabbed a condom from the nightstand, placed it over the length of Vince's shaft, positioned herself above him and inserted his length into herself. They both succumbed to the intensity of insertion and penetration. Julie sat back on Vince's hips, with her torso perpendicular to his. She rocked her hips, undulating her pelvis, and stimulating Vince in the most erotic way he had ever felt. In this position, she could still play with his nipples, and she watched his eyes and listened to his gasping moans as she pinched, pulled and caressed the little points of pleasure on his chest that Vince had always ignored.

Squeezing her breasts and teasing her nipples, Vince felt their connection deepen as he could share with her what he was learning felt so good. Together, their shared pleasure sent their bodies into simultaneous orgasms, which rocked the big bed, and touched their souls in an unexpected way. The sensations were great, but they both felt surprised by an intimacy that seemed to go beyond bare-naked sex.

Julie lay on top of Vince. She was breathing heavy, yet she was relaxed, enjoying the serene peace of the post orgasmic bliss. Wow, she thought, that was the most intense sexual experience she'd ever had. This guy was awesome and she was smitten with both his cute boyishness and his testosterone driven masculinity, what a combination. She was hesitant though. She didn't want to scare him off with too much, "I love you" too fast. Did she love him or was she just so horny and this guy caught her at the right time? No, she thought he was something special, so she wasn't going to ruin it by telling him how emotional she felt.

Vince too was in a state of absolute comfort and satisfaction. He was so happy and peaceful; he didn't want to move and had no need to do so. The feeling of contentment and connection with Julie was surprisingly joyful. He felt more alive and happy than he had ever felt before. He wanted to be nowhere else, and to his astonishment, he felt like he never wanted to leave Julie's side. She was incredible. Together they seemed to know what buttons to push, how hard and how often. The sex was great, but Vince felt like it was a prelude to the real connection that could exist between them. He realized now that he had always hoped to get to know and love someone, and what he hoped for, was what he was experiencing right now with this beautiful woman. He kept these feelings to himself except for the ear to ear grin that was plastered across his sleepy face.

After twenty more minutes of silent snoozing, Julie asked, "Are you hungry?"

"Yeah, I'd love something to eat."

"First, I'll show you to the shower."

Rolling to the opposite edge of the bed, Julie stood and looked back at Vince. He followed her as she disappeared around the corner of a wall. Vince found there was another wall to step around. Beyond this was the most luxurious bathroom he had ever seen. The dark marble floors must have radiant heat because they were so warm on the toes. The countertops were contrasting white marble with three separate sink and mirror stations. The shower however was incredible. Fashioned out of the dark marble it had live plants growing over and around it so it felt just like being in a fantasy jungle. At the center of the structure was a waterfall, on each side there were two separate showerheads featuring infinite temperature adjustments.

The only thing more beautiful than this Fantasy Island setting was Julie' gorgeous body stepping under the showerhead to the right of the waterfall. Vince stepped into the shower on the left. The water was just the right temperature and it felt good to soap up and clean himself off.

Julie had stepped out of the jungle and was drying herself with a thick soft towel. Vince exited the tropical shower and, as he passed the last of the hanging plants, all the water, including the falls, turned off.

He was startled by the sudden cessation of all that water. Julie giggled as she took in his reaction.

"It wouldn't be very green if we left it running all the time."

"I suppose not," said Vince as he picked up the most luxurious towel he had ever touched. Unfolding to a length of six feet, it felt like a soft cloud of cotton that seemed to suck the droplets of water off his skin. He was dry in no time, but he did not want to unwrap from within his comfortable cotton cocoon.

Julie was dressed in a short black silk robe. She approached Vince. "Here, put this on."

She handed him a full-length dark black silk robe. Vince slipped his arms in the sleeves, wrapped the sides across the front and tied the sash tight. He had never felt silk against his skin. It was so smooth and soft, and the fabric seemed to flow. It was almost as if the luxury cloth seemed to exude an energy that radiated from the garment to his skin.

Julie smiled, as Vince could not hide his reaction. "You like it?" she asked.

Vince invoked his million-dollar smile while nodding his head.

"Come on let's go eat," said Julie as she led the way through the privacy maze back to the bedroom out into the hall and down to the kitchen.

"Breakfast is my favorite meal and that's what I cook best," she told him.

"I like breakfast too. Do you do French toast here in England?"

"You mean egg toast?"

"Yeah, I guess I must."

In no time, Julie had cooked bacon and sausage as well as half a loaf of egg dipped fried bread. Vince had cut up the fresh fruit and tossed it all together in a big glass bowl. Coffee was brewed, juice was poured and they sat at the kitchen counter on high stools as they tucked away almost all the food while exchanging more smiles than words.

"That was delicious," said Vince.

"I'm glad to see you like egg toast. It's all gone!"

Vince just smiled as he popped the last of a sausage link into his mouth.

After chewing, but just before swallowing, Vince asked "What are you going to do today?"

Julie suddenly looked pensive. "You know there is something I have to do before anything else. Would you mind cleaning up the kitchen?"

Vince was concerned with the quick change in her demeanor, but he was a guest in her house. "Sure, I'm happy to clean up after a fine meal like that."

Julie forced a smile and retreated to the bedroom.

While cleaning up and putting away dishes, Vince looked at all the family photos. The ones from when she was young included her mother. Elizabeth Kellerman was beautiful and looked like a happy, loving mother in every picture with her children. She seemed proud of them and joyful to be in their presence. In pictures depicting Julie's teenage years, and great moments from college her mother was conspicuously absent. Vince was surprised when he came across a small framed photo on a bookshelf. It was a picture of her mother's grave. On a wall in the living room was a framed composite of photos with her brother Michael. The shots had been taken at many different locations, beaches, mountaintops, fancy parties, cruise ships, college campuses, holidays. Studying the pictures, Vince thought Julie looked beautiful in every shot, even the ones where she was obviously mugging for the camera. Michael, however, looked wasted in every picture. Maybe that was just the way he was, but in every picture he looked drugged out, stoned, plastered, drunk, or totally crocked. He was almost always holding a drink and in many he was either dragging on a cigarette or had it lit in hand. Growing up as he had, Vince was able to easily spot a drunk and Michael qualified as a committed alcoholic.

Returning to the kitchen, Julie smiled, nodding her approval to see the place cleaned up and tidy.

"Thank you, Vince. I have to go pay someone a visit. I hope you will still be here when I return."

Caught by this abrupt statement Vince looked at her pleadingly, but no further information came forth. She held his gaze while projecting a strong stance. She was dressed in a black form fitting combat suit. There were knee pads and shin guards built into the pants. The top had reinforced elbows and there was composite armor in the chest plate and the shoulder cape. She was wearing sturdy black boots and, as she stood talking to Vince, she was pulling on strategically padded combat gloves.

"Are you going down one floor?"

"Yes."

"You want me to come with you?"

"No, but I would like it if you were still here when I get back."

"Yeah…, okay, of course. I'll be here. Is it okay if I stay in this robe?"

Smiling Julie replied, "I like you dressed for easy access."

When the elevator doors opened, Julie gave him a little wave with her dark black gloves, smiled and stepped into the cabin.

He immediately missed her. He felt a longing to be with her. He wanted to protect her and help her; he wanted to reassure himself she was real. He was afraid he would wake up and find all of this to be a dream. A fantasy he was playing out that would dissolve and leave him feeling like a fool. Never had he felt this way. This woman brought out in him emotions that confused, confounded, and delighted him. His smile was genuine and spontaneous. It was there before he knew it, it was there to tell the world, I am so happy and I love this beautiful person. He loved his mother, but that felt nothing like this.

He looked at himself in a full-length mirror, startled for a moment. He remembered he was Vince, not David. The feelings he had were felt as David. No matter his face, and the way it allowed him to act, deep down he was still who he was. That man had baggage, that man had doubts, fears, deprivation, and anger. Being loved caused the negative emotions to dissipate, replaced with acceptance, reassurance, hope and joy. Were these the emotions of David Diegert, or false feelings that accompanied being the imposter, Vince Kronig? Would Julie ever even talk to him if she knew in fact it was David Diegert, the deadly assassin, with whom she shared her bed and body?

He stroked the silk robe and could see why people often described other fabrics as "silky." It felt so smooth, almost like liquid cloth. This robe was the real thing, true silk, not a polyester synthetic. Was he the real thing? A true man, this woman could love, or was he a cheap imitation, that over time would reveal its false fibers and artificial mimicry? Was he synthetic?

CHAPTER 28

MICHAEL KELLERMAN SAT IN HIS THIRD floor apartment. Like Julie's it was an entire floor. Unlike Julie's it was a pig sty. It was hard to believe one could live with so much trash and make such a mess of his dwelling, especially since he had staff who regularly cleaned the place.

Michael hated the morning. People talk about hangovers, but for Michael the whole day was drudgery as he struggled to overcome the discomfort from the drugged up, drunken state he achieved each night. He sat with his Glenfiddich single malt and a bottle of opioids hoping the combination would relieve the splitting headache throbbing in his brain. What Michael didn't realize was that his drug and alcohol habits left him in a permanent state of dehydration. The drugs interfered with kidney function, lowering fluid volume. Insufficient fluid reduced the effectiveness of his blood, his intercellular communication and his muscles' ability to generate force. A big drink of water would do him more good than anything he was considering consuming, but such is the state of the addicted mind.

The opening of the elevator startled him. He blinked hard when he saw his sister stride into his apartment decked out in a tight ass black ninja suit. She tightened the Velcro tab on her glove as she approached.

Michael remained on the couch in a drab green oversized t-shirt, which clashed with his blue plaid boxer shorts.

"Get up," she demanded.

"What?"

"Stand up. Get your ass off that couch and stand up."

"Why, what's wrong?" asked Michael as he slowly set his bottle of scotch on the floor while attempting to place the cap back on his container of pills.

Julie lost patience with him. She slapped the container of pills out of his hand sending caplets of OxyContin scattering across his trash-filled living room. He looked up at her with bewilderment, just in time to see the back of her padded glove streaking towards his face. The impact was immense, twisting his head, wrenching his neck and nearly dislocating his jaw. He flopped to the side of the couch, blood dripping from his lower lip. Looking up he saw her open palm plummeting down to slap the other side of his face. The contact stung his cheek and battered his nose while making it feel as if all his teeth had been dislodged. He raised his arms in defense.

"What the fuck are you doing?"

"You bastard. How dare you treat me like some kind of a whore you can pimp out whenever you want?"

Michael was open mouthed and speechless until Julie hauled off and kicked him in the shin with her steel-toed boots. He yowled reaching for his lower leg. As he leaned forward, she punched him in the side of the head with enough force that he fell to the floor in front of the couch. Laying in an open pizza box with chip bags pinned under his legs, Michael knocked over his bottle of scotch. The prized liquid spread across the floor, soaking into the greasy cardboard of the pizza box. Michael squealed, "Is this about last night?"

Kicking his legs apart, she placed her boot on his balls. "You're damn right, it's about last night."

Struggling to scooch backward, trying to escape her boot, Michael smeared pizza sauce and cheese on his forearms and back.

"Don't move," said Julie as she increased the pressure of her foot on his tender flesh.

"Okay, okay," said Michael

"After all I've done for you and all the places from which I've rescued you, and all the times I've found you and brought you back from near death, you have the audacity to set me up to be sexually assaulted to pay back your debts."

Michael stammered as the pressure on his testicles increased. "I... I... don't know what you're talking about."

"Bullshit," screamed Julie. The full weight of her body descended on her boot as she stepped over his body.

Michael hollered from his soul. The pain was the most excruciating a male human can sustain. He rolled into a fetal position and rocked slowly as the nausea passed through his abdomen and creeped up to his throat.

Julie strode around his place, disgusted at the unkempt state of her brother's life. The kitchen and living room were a mess but the bedroom was untouched. It seemed to her that he spent all his time on the living room couch, ignoring the other four thousand square feet of space on his floor.

Walking over to his huddled mass, she kicked him in the ass. "You know what pisses me off the most, Michael? The lack of trust I now have for you. You betrayed me. You took advantage of the fact that you can rely on me going anywhere and doing anything to help you. You knew I would go there and even as decrepit as that place was, I marched in there to help Michael."

She grabbed his shoulder, rolling him onto his back and looked into his eyes. "You are an untrustworthy ingrate, who I still can't believe led me to a place to be raped."

Michael's eyes clouded over with tears as he gasped, "I... I..."

"SHUT UP, I don't want to hear anything you have to say. You will lie to me and try to make up a story that makes no sense. You are selfish and incapable of caring about anyone but yourself."

Taking a knee and drawing her face closer to his she said, "Trading your sister to be raped for drugs shows me you have no love in your heart, no conscience in your soul."

Standing back up she looked down on the pathetic man, holding his genitals while lying in a scotched soaked pizza box. "You make me so ashamed to be your sister. To have you be from the same family as me is a damn, pitiful shame. The next time you overdose, you will die. I will not come to save you."

With a guttural snort, Julie drew a glob of phlegm from her lungs. She rolled the respiratory mucus into a gooey ball and spat it out on to Michael's face.

She never looked back as she stepped to the elevator, opened the door and pressed the button for the fourth floor.

CHAPTER 29

VINCE STOOD AT THE WINDOW LOOKING out onto the street below. Rolls Royces, chauffeurs and doormen were the most common sights on this exclusive boulevard. Homeless bagmen were discouraged at the intersection and directed to make their way down an adjacent street. Wealth insured a rosy view of the world.

The elevator door opened, surprising Vince. It had not yet been ten minutes. Julie entered, looking formidable in her battle ready body suit. The pace with which she exited the elevator cabin slowed as she entered the living room. Still dressed in the dark silk robe, Vince faced her, searching her expression for a clue as to the outcome of her confrontation with Michael.

"I just don't get it," she began.

Vince looked at her with direct eye contact as he listened.

"How can someone be so callous and uncaring? My own brother sets me up to suffer the most humiliating and demeaning thing a woman can experience and offers no explanation or apology."

"It obviously didn't go well."

"He denied it and tried to make up a lie. I know you don't know this, but I have saved his ass so many times, not just from being in trouble but from dying. He has overdosed multiple times. I learned how to do emergency treatments to detox him. He's alive because of me, and I would have been raped, and maybe killed, because of him. The irony is disgusting."

Vince tilted his head and frowned.

"How can someone you think you know turn out to be so different? My own brother, whom I would never suspect would do me any harm, betrays me. I just can't get over it."

"He's got a lot of drug problems."

"Yeah he does, but that's no excuse for betraying a member of his own family."

"You're right. It's no excuse but it is a reason. Without the drugs, I don't think he would have ever done this to you. I'm not defending his actions, but he was trying to solve his problem, not deliberately hurt you."

Julie drew in a long breath, absorbing the perspective of Vince's statement.

"I can't stand the falseness of who he is."

"What do you mean?"

She looked at Vince and turned her gaze to the ceiling. "I'm an honest person. I say what I believe and I am who I am. I thought my brother was that way as well. Now I know he's a liar. He's not who he appears to be. He's untrustworthy and I just can't have such a disingenuous person that close to me."

Wearing a silk robe, standing in a luxury apartment, falling in love with this beautiful woman, it suddenly felt so deceptive. Appearing as Vince while concealing David Diegert made her words sting. It forced him to realize he was doing something just as bad as Michael.

"So what are you going to do?" asked Vince.

"He's out of my life. I'm out of his. I told him the next time he overdoses, I won't be there to help him. If he dies, he dies. He's on his own."

"That's a pretty tough stance. I like it."

Julie removed her gloves as she walked into the kitchen, got a glass from the cupboard and filled it with cold water from the fridge. "You want some water?"

"No thanks, I'm good."

Crossing to the couch, she sat down, took off her combat boots and curled her legs under her. Vince sat on the other end of the couch. She took a long drink of water before setting the glass on the end table.

Sighing, Julie said, "I'm filled with anger toward him. I don't like the negative energy of hate, but I can't just let his betrayal ... and his ... sins go unaddressed."

"He really hurt you and now it's like he's going to get away with it."

"Exactly. There is no one else to hold him accountable. If I treat him as I always have, what kind of a chump am I?"

"I sense you're not totally comfortable with the idea of him being out of your life."

"How can he be? The next family event, which is a fundraiser this weekend, I will have to appear with him. But now I have to also think of how endangered my life may be because of him."

Gazing at the fabric of the couch, Julie had a look of consternation that kept her from smiling and deepened the furrows on her brow. Vince loved her pretty face with its gorgeous smile. Now though he was seeing the true person behind the beauty. She was as complex and troubled as anyone. She had difficult emotions to deal with and challenging situations that were not going to be solved for her just because she was beautiful. She had to look inside to find strength and resolve.

"You know you don't owe him anything," said Vince. "You've helped him all along, but you don't have to. It's okay for you to let him be on his own for a while. Do you think you were enabling him?"

She turned her head to look over the back of the couch. With her eyes averted she reluctantly replied, "Yeah I guess I was." Turning to Vince she said, "I just kept hoping he would change. Learn from his mistakes and get his life on track. He could be so much more."

"But then?"

"But then he would make promises. He would swear he was going to stop drinking, stop taking drugs, and of course before the end of the day he would renege on all that and get blitzed again." She shook her head, put her forehead in her palm. "I could see he was headed for trouble, but I thought I could help him. I never thought he would deliberately hurt me."

"This is getting a bit circular. I think you've got your thoughts figured out. You just have to learn to live with the emotions."

She looked up at Vince as a kind smile emerged on her lips. She held her gaze upon him as her face became more contemplative. "You know I never said thank you for saving my life."

Vince's words stumbled a bit as he replied, "Oh... that's all right. I think you showed me how you felt."

"Maybe, but I still want to tell you that I'm very grateful you came for me. You could've sat outside waiting, but you followed me in even though I knew you didn't want to be there."

Vince, filled with humility, looked away and circled his gaze back to her.

Julie continued, "You showed a lot of bravery in there.

You showed me your true self. Since actions speak louder than words, you shouted out, I am a brave man who will defend my friends."

Her smile broadened, but tears were filling her eyes. "I can't find the words to tell you how scared I was in that room with those creeps. When you came bursting through that window I was so relieved. And then when you kicked ass on those guys I was amazed."

She wiped her tears with her hands. "You are the guy I've always wanted to meet. A guy who is kind, gentle, loving, but who realizes the world can be a tough place and is able to be tough right back."

Leaning forward, stretching out her hands to his she said, "I really, really like you. I know we haven't known each other that long, but it's been intense. I don't want to scare you off, but I really want to share my life with you."

Vince felt her words and message in his Diegert brain. *You showed me your true self.* Had he? Was his true self a combination of kind Vince and violent David? *Bravery.* The Ojibwa meaning for bravery was to realize that you are not good enough and that you fear others will find out. An Ojibwa develops bravery by looking inward to face the fear of not being good enough with personal integrity. Diegert always felt not good enough. Perhaps facing that fear and overcoming that sense of inadequacy was the mission of Vince. As Vince, did he feel good enough? Wasn't Julie, right now, telling him she thinks he's good enough? If he proved to her she was right to see bravery in him, wouldn't he be fulfilling the spirit of the Ojibwa belief? He realized he was ill-equipped to respond to her. He did not know how to tell her how he felt. He struggled as he realized her statement required a reply, which either deepened the relationship or turned it off. A neutral response was a mistake that would kill her feelings. He needed to be brave right now and tell her he loved her. For a moment, Diegert thought he'd rather face a room filled with four armed creeps. Looking inward he forced himself to think and feel like Vince. He looked at her lovely face and thought of her integrity and strength. He loved how he felt with her and hoped to make her happy. These feelings, as unusual and foreign as they were for Diegert, were becoming genuine for Vince. Holding her hands, he let his feelings do the talking with the voice of the new person Vince allowed him to be.

"Julie, it's true we haven't known each other long, but I already feel like I know you better than I've ever known another woman. You are such an incredible person. You have strength, integrity and perseverance. You are kind, thoughtful and loving with a tremendous commitment to your family. I feel so fortunate to have met you and I'm grateful to have the opportunity to share my life with you. I really, really like you too and I don't want to scare you, but I hope to be with you forever."

Julie's tears streamed down her face as she reached across the couch and hugged Vince. The silk robe made it easy for him to slide down onto the couch cushions. She lay on top of him, joyfully crying. Vince felt great; this was going to be the beginning of an awesome relationship. Diegert was terrified; this risked total exposure and was extremely dangerous.

CHAPTER 30

JAPANESE NOH THEATER WAS THE oldest continuing performance of Japanese cultural expression. Performances consisted of three dramatic plays with humorous stories portrayed during the breaks between dramas. The three plays depicted ancient traditional stories that were usually already well known to audiences. The plays contained little dialogue and instead their messages were conveyed through movement, dance and costumes.

Although there were many themes portrayed in Noh Theater, a typical three-play performance would feature a Kami play in which a sacred story of a Shinto shrine was depicted. A Shura Mono, or fighting play, centered on tales of warriors, samurais and ninjas. Kinjo Mono was a play in which the protagonist experienced intense grief following the loss of a lover or the death of a child. These forms and others were combined into portrayals in which the story was told to preserve culture, share values and convey that humans experience the same losses and victories throughout generations.

Some theater companies sought to infuse modern theatrical production techniques, while other troupes avoided any modern methods, preferring to maintain tradition by limiting itself to only that which was available when the stories were first created. The most traditional forms of Noh never left the islands of Japan, while more modern productions were finding audiences around the world who were interested in these exciting theatrical versions of ancient Japanese stories.

In spite of not having a long-term committed relationship with a woman, Avery Forsythe did maintain close friendships with several attractive women in London. Sakura Yakugi was an account manager for the Mizuho Global Investment Bank office in London. The Mizuho Bank was instrumental in converting Japanese investment from Yen to Digival. Avery and Sakura met at a party, celebrating the Mizuho Bank's switch to Digival. Her personal net worth, as well as the bank's, doubled after three weeks and had since tripled again. The early adopters of Digival were the ones reaping profits on investment like no one has ever earned before.

Having bought the tickets three weeks before, Avery was excited to invite Sakura to join him for an evening of Noh Theater. On the phone she replied, "I'd rather go to the Yes Theater. What do you mean by No Theater?"

After a brief lesson on Japanese history, of which she was completely unaware, she agreed to go. Avery liked going out with Sakura because she liked to walk. Her apartment wasn't too far from LPU, and the theater wasn't too much farther. Being London, Avery made sure to bring his umbrella.

To really get the feel of the story and truly see the expressions of the actors, Avery believed you had to sit close. This being his first time with Noh Theater he wanted to experience the micro expressions of the actors to truly feel these ancient stories. Sakura would have preferred a seat a little farther back, but she did not want to dampen his enthusiasm. The theater was about three quarters full, mostly people of Asian descent, but that wasn't bad for an eight week production which was only in its second week.

The first play was an ancient tale of conflict and cooperation between the God of the Earth, Haniyasu-hiko and Susanowo, the God of the Ocean. During a particular fierce storm scene, those sitting close could feel a fine mist emerging from the stage as Susanowo sent waves crashing against the chest of Haniyasu-hiko. As the story progressed, earth and water realized they needed each other and peace was found on a quiet shoreline.

Following the high drama of earth and ocean in an epic battle a Kyogen, which is a humorous skit, was performed. In this short, light story, a young man seeks a bride. An old man tells him he'd be better off with a donkey. The young man expresses his desire for love; the old man tells him a donkey will be much more faithful, obedient and useful. The young man asks, but what of children? The old man with an exaggerated flourish, tells the young man he'd be better off with a herd of donkeys!

The Shura Mono was next. The story opened with a great general marshalling his army to attack a rival village. The general had a thousand men on horseback ready to storm the other village and plunder everything they own. It was through decimating conquest that this general had amassed such great power. The village had only 100 men and they had only farm tools to use in their defense. One young man, who had been studying the way of the Ronin, set forth on a mission to kill the general, hoping that the powerful man's death would prevent the invasion of his village. Dressed in black and armed with a sacred sword given to him by a village elder, the young man silently stole through the dark of night, evading the general's guards and entered the tyrant's sleeping chamber.

As the actor with the Katana approached the general's bed, he raised his sword, let out a primal scream and leapt off the stage, swinging his blade right at Avery's head. With lightning reflexes, Avery rolled to the side, pushing Sakura out of her seat and down to the floor. The ninja's blade cleaved the back of Avery's seat, embedding it deep into the plastic, foam and fabric. From below his seat, Avery grabbed his umbrella. With his hand on the handle, he pressed a button, releasing a 24-inch blade from within the shaft of the umbrella. Standing defiantly over Sakura, Avery grasped the hilt with both hands, projecting the blade forward. The ninja yanked his sword from the back of the seat and leapt to the aisle. Avery moved forward, exiting the row and squaring his enemy.

The audience was in stunned panic as they stampeded the exits. What at first seemed like a part of the show was now creating pandemonium amongst the patrons. Screams rang out as slow people were being pushed out of the way by faster ones. The unarmed security guards were unable to enter the theater as the entire gallery of attendees rushed the exits.

The ninja's movements appeared to Avery to be more cautious. He seemed to think killing Avery was going to be as easy as murdering the sleeping general. Seeing Avery armed with a blade seemed to have surprised the black clad swordsman. Avery capitalized on the element of surprise as he moved with practiced katas to threaten the defensive ninja. Blades clashed as strike met parry, move was greeted by countermove, and they each realized that the other was skilled and determined. The ninja charged with his blade raised high. As he approached, he slung the sword sideways, hoping to slice open Avery's abdomen. Avery moved his blade vertically, deflecting the strike as he rolled his shoulder, keeping the ninja's blade away from him. Upon release, Avery rotated his body, bringing his blade back towards the ninja's throat. An instantaneous duck spared the ninja from having his neck slit like an envelope. Each man returned to a defensive stance, eyes scanning for vulnerability. The ninja said, "The one who sent me said you must die."

"Do you know his name?"

"He said he was no longer under your control, but he needed your death to be truly free."

"As a Ronin, the only way out of this is your death or mine," pronounced Avery.

The ninja took one step and leapt into the air, kicking out at the hand in which Avery held his sword, deflecting the blade. Simultaneously, he swung downward, striking Avery on the collarbone and slicing a gash across his chest. Blood streamed into Avery's white cotton dress shirt as the ninja nimbly landed in front of the third row of seats.

Avery spun to face his tormentor, as blood cascaded down his shirt, over his pants, and onto the floor. The ninja stood. He seemed to be assessing Avery's injury, calculating the rate of blood loss and the time until he bled out. Avery knew it wouldn't be long, but he also was not yet out of the fight. Despite hemorrhaging, he two-handed his hilt and moved forward with his sword held like a baseball bat. With measured steps, he let the ninja know he was still in it 'til death.

Avery flinched his blade, setting up a distraction that kept the ninja's eyes focused far to the left. Emerging low from the third row was Sakura Yakugi, with her hand bag. The leather bag had metal cornices and a set of strong chain handles. As she stepped into the aisle, Avery said to the ninja, "I'm not too worried about this cut. See I forgot to take my Coumadin this morning."

The slight cocking of his masked head indicated the ninja's confusion, but his head was suddenly cocked even farther as Sakura swung her bag into the ninja's temple, snapping his neck, sending him flying into the third row of the right wing of the theater.

Avery moved quickly, unclipping the chain handles from the handbag and using them to bind the wrists of the unconscious ninja.

Getting to his phone, Avery ordered the LPU ambulance to meet him at the stage dock of the theater. With lights and sirens blazing, the vehicle arrived in two minutes. As he was placed in the ambulance, Avery ordered the attendants to retrieve the bound ninja. Sakura sat next to Avery as his laceration was bandaged.

"Are we going to the hospital?" Sakura asked.

"No," replied Avery, "We're taking you home and I will get the medical treatment I need at LPU."

"Not at a hospital? Who's going to treat you at the university, a med student?"

Smiling, Avery said, "Don't you worry. I know what I need and I know where I can get it. But first we're going to get you home safely, Slugger."

Sakura cracked a devilish smile.

"I'm not kidding; you hit that guy so hard, he's lucky to be alive."

They both looked at the unconscious ninja.

"Who do you think he is?" she asked.

"I don't know, but I'm sure going to find out."

CHAPTER 31

JULIE HAD TO GO TO PARIS TO VISIT some friends and attend the opening of an art exhibit at the Louvre. She and Vince would next see each other in four days when they were scheduled to have lunch with her father, Dean.

Vince went back to his quarters in the underground labyrinth of LPU. Scrolling through his phone, clearing it out, he deleted all the irrelevant messages until he came upon one from Carolyn Fuller. Although it seemed like a bit of a rant, the message contained a picture of a rather droll looking fellow with the all caps statement underneath, "I HATE RICHARD RAMSEY!!!"

Looking at the picture Diegert got an idea about how he, and only he, could help her.

Later that night, Diegert approached the bar Etcetera, wearing a black ball cap, dark glasses, black jeans and boots along with a gray Henley and a short black leather jacket. Looking tough came easy and Diegert was bringing it in with him as he climbed the stairs to pass through the door.

Having figured out a disguise uniquely suited for this mission, Diegert had gone through the transamination process so his face now had the perfect appearance for doing what he had planned and making a clean getaway.

Richard Ramsey loved Etcetera, especially on

Thursday night. Drink specials for the ladies brought out fun loving girls. Ramsey was right there having himself a good time, even if he was ruining the evening of the women for whom he couldn't keep his eyes and hands off.

"Where do you work, you lovely young thing," Ramsey asked a buxom girl with half her head shaved and the other half covered in long blonde curls.

"Harrod's," she said with a sense of challenge. "You're American aren't you?"

"Shh, that's top secret."

"You Yanks. Ya come over here and you all think you're James fucking Bond."

"The three letter agency for which I work, under penalty of death, is not to be named"

"The CIA. You work for the fucking CIA. Anyone with one good eye can see that."

Ramsey's exaggerated facial reaction and frantic gestures made him look like Harry Potter hearing the name of Valdermort. The bold buxom girl and her two friends laughed at Ramsey who replied, "Now you've done it, but I can commute your death sentence if you'll have a drink with me."

"Drink or die? Well to look at ya, death might be preferred, but if you're buying for all three of us?" She gestured to her friends, one of whom sported a rod through her nostril, the other wore bright red frames around thick magnifying lenses. "We'll have a drink with ya."

From a back corner of the bar, Diegert nursed a beer, while doing nothing more than occasionally nodding at anyone who happened to look at him. He looked like a quiet loner, observing social interactions but not participating. Watching Ramsey with the three young ladies, who seemed to want to move on after one drink, was an ordeal to endure. Ramsey kept jabbering and buying them more booze, even though their eyes were all over the bar, he just kept trying to get one of them to give him a kiss.

After nearly an hour of steady drinking, all that fluid had its effect. Ramsey made the girl with the half-shaved head promise not to leave as he hurried off to the men's room. Diegert's time to act had finally arrived as he followed Ramsey into the loo.

The device, shaped like a solid figure eight, was two squat cylinders, one nested into a cut out within the other. The cylinders separated. One was a full circle, and the other had the cut out indentation. The full circle had a button in its center. Between the two pieces existed a strong polymer filament, the length of which retracted into the full circle like a measuring tape. Exceptionally thin but extremely strong, the line was capable of withstanding tremendous pressure. Its profile was elliptical with razor sharp edges. Super fine and almost translucent, the line's unique cross sectional design made it practically invisible. Depressing the center button released the line. Grasping both of the short cylinders and pulling taut, the garrote became a lethal weapon. The line's sharp cutting edges gave this modern version of an ancient tool, the ability to slice through human flesh like fishing line through cheesecake.

Diegert pulled the cylinders apart, twisting a single loop into the line. Stepping behind Richard Ramsey as he pissed in the urinal, Diegert flipped the looped line over the agent's head. He drove his knee into Ramsey's back as he simultaneously pulled back on the garrote. The sharp filament made a surgical incision through the skin. Blood pooled at the edge of the slit as the garrote traveled inward to the trachea. With steady force, the razor line glanced off the tracheal cartilage and cut into the collagen fibers of the windpipe. Ramsey gasped, as the line effortlessly sliced its way across the open passage of his breathing tube. Diegert's force never let up and the line cut through muscles, nerves and blood vessels across the entire neck. As the circumference diminished, the noose tightened around the vertebral column. Encountering the tough ligaments surrounding the cervical vertebrae required Diegert to exert maximal force. The line sliced through the ligaments, entered the intervertebral space severing the spinal cord and vertebral arteries while exiting by way of the spinous processes. This final stricture completely separated Ramsey's head from his neck. The head tilted to the left toppling to the floor where it rolled like a bleeding bowling ball. Blood fountained up from the open neck wound, splashing against the wall, cascading over the porcelain into the urinal. Ramsey's knees buckled as the body fell to the left spraying an arc of blood across the bathroom wall.

Diegert stepped to the sink, rinsed the razor filament and retracted the line. He stowed the deadly figure eight in his pocket and left the bathroom. His black clothing was speckled with blood, but it was hard to see in the bar's dim light. Crossing the bar, he pulled off his ball cap and dark glasses. He purposefully looked up at the surveillance camera as he headed for the exit. The girl with the half-shaved head did a double take as Diegert passed by. She shouted after him but her attention, and that of the entire bar, was suddenly drawn to a guy emerging from the men's room shouting for the police.

Outside, the ball cap and dark glasses went right back on. Diegert walked a block, turned the first corner he came to, and the next, and the next until he was a kilometer and a half away from the scene. He slowed his pace as he heard the rise of the sirens that were converging on Etcetera. He thought of his act, but he did not choke on the violence. Instead he allowed the emotions to flow through him. The attack was so quick, so decisive, that only now could he do as Avery had instructed him and open himself to the experience. As he continued to walk into the dark night, he sought to become the empty self. Not searching for meaning, but accepting the act and the death as a necessary component in a complex web of fulfilling his life's mission.

CHAPTER 32

AVERY CLOSED THE DOORS BEHIND HIM as he looked through the plate glass window into the large white tiled room. It was in this room, deep in the recesses of the LPU labyrinth, that battles to the death were conducted for the purpose of selecting operators capable of fulfilling the requirements of Cerberus. Avery's elite squad of assassins were the best of the paramilitary force, which he oversaw and kept ready to serve Crepusculous. The young Asian man, unmasked as the ninja at the Noh Theater, had been placed in the tile room about an hour previous. Still dressed in his black pajama outfit, his face bore bruises from the handbag that had knocked him unconscious in the theater. Through the loudspeaker, Avery addressed the young man. "As a purveyor of violence, you will appreciate the purposes of the confines you now occupy. I will just dispense with the whole process of questioning, since I believe a man like you would never reveal that it was Jarod Masoni who orchestrated your dramatic attack at the theater. Instead you will be given the opportunity to demonstrate your ability to fight, or die trying."

"I want a lawyer," shouted the young man.

Avery smiled as he chuckled. "Oh, I'm sorry; you do not seem to grasp the consequences of your actions. The only trial you'll face is that of survival."

Pressing a button opened the single door on the opposite wall from the plate glass window. Into the room stepped Tiberius Dupre'. The tall black man wore combat boots, dark canvas pants, and a black under-armor shirt under a Kevlar vest. He also wore tactical gloves and leather forearm gauntlets. Crossing the room, he moved to the opposite side and faced the young man. The moment of mutual observation was interrupted by the clang of the Gough Knife tossed into the room, coming to rest by the center floor drain. Tiberius flexed his head, crackling his vertebrae.

The young Asian man shouted, "What the hell is this? I don't want to fight. I want a lawyer."

Avery's voice projected into the tile room, "The way of the ninja is one of honor and personal fortitude. When you took on the role, you committed yourself to a lifestyle defined by your ability to fight. Your willingness to attack, using stealth, speed, strength and lethal violence. All of this is now necessary for you to prove your commitment to your chosen way. This is not a court of law, but a proving ground for your commitment to the ways of the ninja."

"Holy shit!" said the young man as he rose to his feet.

Tiberius stepped forward and the smaller, lighter man quickly moved to the left, evading him. Tiberius assumed a pugilistic stance and pursued his opponent. The Asian man continued to move left, scampering away, seeking to avoid any contact with his big, determined opponent. Tiberius began chasing the man, who moved even faster, running in an evasive circle. After three laps around the room, Tiberius suddenly stopped, reversed and caught the Asian before he could counter his momentum. The punches dislocated the smaller man's jaw, cracked his ribs and bloodied his nose. Tiberius struggled to hold him up to try to hit him again. The smaller, thinner man fell unconscious, his body turning into a rag doll as Tiberius dragged him over to the sidewall and sat him against it. "I can't kill this guy," said Tiberius.

"I know," came Avery's reply over the loudspeaker. "You're free to go, Tiberius, thank you."

Moments later Avery entered the tile room. Picking up the Gough Knife, he stepped over to the beaten man with the grip in hand and the blade turned away. Loudly snapping his fingers, Avery said, "Hey wake up. Come on get with it." The young man opened his eyes, blinked several times struggling to focus. Tapping the hardened steel blade against the tile, a metallic echo bounced through the room. Widening his eyes, the ninja focused on Avery.

"It is the way of the Ronin that your life must end in battle," began the mystical black man. "If you are defeated, your final act is to take your own life." Avery placed the knife in the ninja's hand and gently tapped him on the shoulder. The young man's injured jaw made it impossible for him to speak. Avery gently placed his hands on the damaged face and snapped the temporomandibular joint into place, restoring the function of the jaw.

Wincing in pain, the young man opened and closed his mouth several times before spurting, "She was my girlfriend."

"What?" said Avery.

"Ayuti was my girlfriend. Masoni got her hooked on drugs and tricked her into pornography. She was an actress in our troupe, but she is now addicted and working for Masoni's men making porno movies."

With eyelids barely wide enough to see through, Avery asked, "Why did you attack me?"

"Masoni said he would let her go if I killed you. He

said he knew you would go to the Noh Theater. He tracked your tickets and told me what night you would be there. He sent your picture and said when you were dead, Ayuti would be freed."

"So you are fulfilling the role of the ninja as an honorable warrior."

Nodding, the young man said, "I play a ninja in a stage show. I've read about them for the role, but I haven't actually killed anyone."

"Would you kill Jarod Masoni if you had the chance?"

Holding a direct stare, the young man said, "I would kill him to get my Ayuti back."

"What is your name?"

"Takeda Shingen."

"Well Takeda, if you are willing to fulfill your role as a true ninja, I will be able to help you."

"What do you want me to do? I'm not really a ninja."

"You will stay in this facility and train with my soldiers, like the man you met moments ago. You must improve your fighting skills. You will not only act as a ninja, but you must prove to me that you are truly worthy of the title and capable of serving in my forces."

With a doubtful grimace Takeda said, "I don't know if I can do that."

"Why such doubts?"

Shaking his head, Takeda said, "There are no real ninjas. On stage I can wear the black pajamas and twirl a sword around, but in real life that won't work."

"Yet you were willing to attack me in the theater."

"It was the only chance I had to free Ayuti. I couldn't not do it."

"You couldn't do it either," Avery smirked.

"Knocked out by a handbag," observed the young man

as the hint of a smile made him shudder in pain. Regaining his voice he said, "I will train with you, but I want a gun, not a sword, Kevlar, not cotton pajamas, night vision goggles, GPS, and good boots, not bare feet. That ninja stuff is bullshit; I want to be a modern operator, like Call of Duty."

Eyeing him as if selecting a puppy from a litter, Avery said, "The equipment will be modern, but the expectation of principled, disciplined behavior is just as it was in ancient Japan. Training in my army will require your absolute commitment. Failure will result in death. You will know you failed when your life is bleeding out in front of you."

The young man's eyes widened, and his jaw fell open, triggering a yelp of pain. "What is the alternative?"

"I call Tiberius back in and I do not relent to his suggestion of mercy."

Turning his face away, Takeda gazed at the floor. "When do I get to rescue Ayuti?"

"When you've convinced me you're ready to kill Jarod Masoni."

Lifting his eyes to meet Avery's, Takeda said, "You're giving me a chance to save my girl, while sparing my life. Like in the ninja story, I guess I now owe my life to you."

Avery's smile grew slowly but soon stretched across his angular face as he stood, reached out his hand to Takeda and pulled him up, steadying him before they walked out of the tile room.

CHAPTER 33

WITH DAVID GONE, CAROLYN KNEW she needed someone new inside Crepusculous. The CIA sleuthed out Vince Kronig's cell phone number. Carolyn was pleasantly surprised when Vince agreed to meet her two days hence for coffee.

Wanting to get to the appointment before her, Vince parked his silver gray Porsche 918 Spyder in an on street spot about twenty meters from the outdoor café she had selected. He was seated at a table for two in the corner of the chained off sidewalk close to the coffee shop's wall of glass windows.

The sidewalk was busy with passersby and he enjoyed people watching as he relaxed in the unseasonably warm weather. Curiosity was eating him. He was eager to find out what Carolyn wanted. As David, he had enough history with her that he could easily guess her request. As Vince, he was surprised to be asked to this meeting. He immediately agreed not only to satisfy his need to know, but because he still had a spot in his heart for her. She didn't realize it, but she helped him find meaning in his life when he was at his lowest. She saved him from a likely execution, helping him return to Europe. She did it to stop the multi-bomb attack Crepusculous had planned for America. So far, that attack hadn't happened, and as far as he could tell, the plan had been abandoned. The bombs, however, were unaccounted for, thus they continued to present a significant threat. He guessed she probably wanted to talk about the bombs.

Carolyn approached from the west, dressed in a mid-shin length skirt with thin black and white horizontal stripes. Her gait was altered by her pregnancy and she walked slower than the people around her. She wore a white top, which stretched over her abdomen. On top of that she wore a peach jacket which could no longer be done up if she'd tried. He stood up, pulling out the chair for her. Before she sat down, they shook hands.

"Thank you," she said.

"My pleasure."

Returning to his seat, he leaned forward, gazing at her pretty face. She did have a glow about her, although the medical professionals would call it gestational hypercapillarization.

"How are you doing?" he asked her.

"I am well, in spite of, or perhaps because of, my condition," she said with a quizzical smirk.

"I think it's fabulous that you are with child. I hope the pregnancy has been a good one."

"Yes, thank you, it has. I'm due in two weeks," she said as she gently stroked her protruding belly.

"Oh that's coming soon. You and your hus- I mean, partner must be excited," stammered Vince.

"I'm looking forward to the delivery. It's a good thing pregnancy is not a permanent state," chuckled Carolyn.

"I also understand there's been a change in your job as well."

Carolyn lost her smile and her stony expression demanded more information.

"I know it was tragic, but you are now the senior CIA Officer in the UK."

"Where did you read about this? I saw no report in the news."

"You know, the world is at our fingertips. It was covered in the U.S. news. Is progress being made in solving the crime?"

Lost in thought, Carolyn was silent for a moment. She seemed to have a hard time shifting gears from one topic to the other.

"No… no progress has been made. The evidence in Ramsey's murder is rather strange."

"How so?" asked Vince with a rising eyebrow.

"It's really puzzling, but the security camera inside the bar captured the prime suspect as he left the men's room."

Vince shrugged. "That sounds good."

"Yeah, but the guy took off his hat and glasses and looked right at the camera as he passed by."

Wrinkling his brow Vince said, "That still sounds good. You got a shot of the guy's face."

With a frown and a shake of her head, Carolyn said, "The guy was Richard Ramsey."

Pausing, while looking at Carolyn askance, Vince said, "The killer is the guy who was killed?"

Bringing her hand to her chin, lowering her eyes and shaking her head, Carolyn said, "You can't make this shit up. It's just unbelievable."

"What about witnesses? It was a crowded place. Somebody must have seen something more?"

"Yeah, the police are interviewing everyone who was there," she said dismissively.

"Was he a good colleague? Did you enjoy working with him?"

A blank expression crossed her face as she hesitated to answer. Vince quietly waited.

"Everybody has quirks. Some of his, I won't miss."

"I see."

"Vince, the reason I asked you for this meeting is to share something with you that is highly classified. I know you don't have clearance but without taking a risk we will not progress. I'm going to have to trust you."

Slowly nodding his head like a bobble toy he said, "You can trust me."

"I have no reason to believe that, but I'm in a tough spot. Did you ever meet David Diegert?"

Shaking his head Vince said, "No."

"The coincidence that you and he are half-brothers is something with which I still struggle."

"Is David Diegert classified information?"

"No, but a terrorist attack upon the United States set up by Crepusculous to wreak economic ruin was something for which David had credible intelligence. The classified part is that he was working undercover to determine the locations of several thermobaric bombs pre-planted in the U.S."

"Whoa."

"Yeah, it's a serious situation. We want to locate the bombs and disable them without Crepusculous knowing."

"I heard David Diegert was a violent assassin. He killed a lot of people."

"Yes, he was, and did."

"Then why would you trust someone like that?"

"I did not work with him because of his predilection for violence but because, like you, he had access to information within Crepusculous that could lead us to identifying the locations of the bombs."

"How did you meet David Diegert? What was he like? I'm curious about having a half-brother I'll never get to know."

"Look I can only tell you so much. I only knew him for a short period of time. He was a tough guy that's for sure, but he was also thoughtful and very concerned about stopping Crepusculous from attacking America. He saw the greater good and was trying to help."

"Then what about him blowing up the apartment building in White Chapel?"

"I can't explain everything and I have no idea why he was involved in that. But if you saw that video then you know how much damage a thermobaric bomb can do. There are twelve of them secretly located in the U.S. We need to find them and secure them. Will you help me?"

"You want me to spy on Crepusculous."

"Yes. We can provide you with some intelligence and point you in the right direction, but we'd be trusting you to keep this confidential and report back to me with what you find. Your new found father has sides he hasn't shown you yet."

"Look I don't want people to be blown up, but I just joined the family and I'm not yet all that familiar with the company and I sure haven't gotten any access to Crepusculous. I can see why you'd think I could be helpful, but I think you're expecting too much."

"Does that mean you won't help?"

"It means I have to think about it."

"OK, I already sent you a text under the name Sarah Marsden. We can communicate through that."

Vince checked his phone to see the text under the false name. He nodded at Carolyn.

While looking at her phone Carolyn sarcastically exclaimed, "Great!"

"What's wrong?"

"Oh nothing, it's just that my parents arrive tomorrow." Carolyn went on, speaking to herself as if to commit it to memory, "Delta airlines, from New York, 4:00 pm arrival."

"That's nice, they're coming to visit."

With a sardonic smile she said, "I hope it's going to be nice."

"Will they get to meet the father and stay for the delivery?"

Vince knew this was a difficult question for her, but the stress on her face was much more than he expected. She was struggling with her reply. As her face softened into a thousand mile stare, she absent-mindedly said, "They don't even know I'm pregnant."

Vince remained quiet. He watched as she came back to the present moment.

"I'm sorry to mention my personal problems. It was nice meeting you Vince. If you will excuse me I need to use the lady's room before I go."

Rising out of his seat Vince extended his hand, "I wish you all the best with the birth of your child. Do you know if it's a boy or a girl?"

She shook his hand with a firm, practiced grip. "I do not. I guess I'm old fashioned about it, but I do not know."

"Well then, you will enjoy the surprise."

"Thank you," she said as she slipped her phone in her pocket before entering the coffee shop in search of the lady's room.

Vince walked to the edge of the chained off seating area. He looked in the direction of his car, then gazed up the street in the opposite direction. When he did so a familiar face caught his eye, but the sight was fleeting. The man had turned away and Vince could now only see that the man wore black cargo pants and a black jacket with what looked like padded panels. His pants were tucked into sturdy black tactical boots. The attire was not that unusual, but the recollections started flooding his brain. Was he being followed by someone from Crepusculous?

He turned to walk to his car, all the while wanting to spin around to observe the man, but he knew not to give away such an obvious tell. Arriving at the Spyder he took the top down, placing the roof pieces in the forward stowage compartment under the hood. Sitting in the driver's seat, he watched the front door of the coffee shop and saw Carolyn Fuller exit the building. She walked down the sidewalk in the opposite direction from him, towards the suspicious man. As she approached the first intersection, Vince saw the man in black step out of a doorway and fall in behind her. At the curb, a white van came to a halt on the crossroad in front of her. The side panel door opened and the man in black pushed Carolyn into the van. He climbed in behind her without looking back. The van's door closed automatically sealing tightly enough that Vince could not hear Carolyn screaming.

The van turned left, passing by Vince. His hybrid Porsche violently lurched from its parking spot, did an immediate U turn, and sped up to the van. An exotic silver sports car did not make an inconspicuous chase vehicle. The van seemed to realize it was being followed as it turned several corners, attempting to evade the tail.

Inside the van, there were no seats in the back, just a wide-open cargo space with a metal floor interrupted by two interior wheel well fenders. The man in black from the street forced Carolyn's hands behind her back, binding them with flexicuffs. Over her mouth, he placed a length of duct tape before moving forward to the passenger seat.

Each time the van made a fast turn, Carolyn was thrown into the walls of the van. With her hands behind her back, the impacts of her collisions clanged off the metal walls.

The van careened through the streets as it made its way to the M4, accelerating up the entrance ramp and speeding into the right lane. On the highway, Vince was able to catch up to the van and pull up beside its front quarter panel. In spite of being a much smaller vehicle, Vince drove the side of his car into the front corner of the van forcing it out of its lane and onto the shoulder. The van's driver struggled to keep the vehicle stable. He was forced to slow down on the rough surface of the shoulder. As both vehicles continued forward, the driver of the van turned into the Porsche, its greater bulk forcing the two seater sideways as the van sought to regain the pavement. Vince felt his car pivot on the corner of the van, his tires screeching as they slid across the asphalt. The van kept pushing the Porsche. Vince realized he was going to crash into the back of a large lorry. As the big truck's solid metal bumper loomed in front of him, Vince turned the wheels of the Porsche, releasing it from the van while slamming on the brakes. The van, suddenly without the strain of plowing the Porsche forward, accelerated into the rear corner of the lorry, smashing its front quarter panel against the heavy metal bumper. Glass and plastic flew from the dented metal in a widening stream of debris as the van's driver pulled back into the right lane accelerating his damaged vehicle.

The force of the impact sent Carolyn forward into the console between the two seats. Her head collided with the heavy plastic, bruising her forehead. The man in black grew angry with the driver.

"God damn it, keep this fucking van on the road and get us to LPU."

Vince's car had gauges, scrapes and an indented passenger door, but the mechanics remained intact. He down shifted to accelerate and was right back on the tail of the van.

"What is this fucker doing chasing us?" exclaimed the black clad passenger.

This time Vince approached the rear quarter panel of the van. He recalled seeing a video where a cop car stopped a fleeing suspect by angling the nose of his car into the rear of the offending vehicle, sending it into a tailspin. Vince's problem was that the back of the van was higher than the hood of his Porsche. If it was going to work he would have to apply force to the rear wheels.

Glancing at the overhead sign, he saw an exit to the Heston Service Area coming up in a kilometer. Pulling his car close, he set his wheel next to that of the van. His car was lighter, but it had a powerful engine located behind the seats over the rear axle. Turning the steering wheel hard, he forced his left front wheel and fender up against the van's right rear wheel. The van's larger wheels crushed the front fender of the Porsche tearing the body part off the vehicle. Vince was nearly decapitated when the front fender skin flew over his head as it sailed into the highway. Contact between the two spinning tires produced a noxious cloud of acrid smoke as the van's wheels resisted the lateral force. Vince could see they were fast approaching the exit for the Service Area. Torquing the steering wheel as he leaned to the left, Vince gunned the car's supercharged engine. His rear wheels screeched as additional power flowed to the road through his extra wide tires. The little car had the strength of a truck and used it to skid the van's rear end as the pavement for the exit widened in front of them. The driver of the van had no choice but to exit as the stench of burning rubber and thick smoke trailed behind them.

Vince braked hard, separating his car from the van, which regained control and began to turn towards the gas pumps of the service area. Quickly accelerating, Vince bashed the van, lurching it forward so it missed the turn for the area servicing regular cars. The van's only choice was to turn into a vast, empty parking lot reserved for large lorries and extra-long trucks. As the van crossed the lot heading for the exit on the far side. Vince spun the wheel, gunning the Porsche, setting it perpendicular to the van and rocketing into the right front wheel. The front bumper cladding shattered as the low profile of the sports car drove into the van's front tire, lifting it on to the Porsche's hood, tilting the van to the left. The van plunged forward, rolling over the Porsche before colliding head on with a lamppost. As the airbags deployed, the van's driver and front seat passenger were both smacked hard in the face.

Carolyn banged into the left side wall when the van's right side went skyward. Blood oozed from a laceration on her head she received through hard contact with an internal door hinge. Smearing blood on her hand from her lacerated head, Carolyn's pregnant belly made it nearly impossible to regain her balance.

Vince could see that the right front tire of the van was shredded; this vehicle was going nowhere. Reaching into the long stowage compartment of the door, Vince extracted a Brooks Brothers umbrella. The driver of the van, a bit dazed by the punch in the face from the airbag, struggled to stand as he exited the vehicle. Vince strode up, striking him across the face with the curved handle of the umbrella. As the driver stumbled, Vince grabbed his collar and pressed him up against the side of the van. Spinning the umbrella, he placed the metal ferrule against the stunned driver's throat. Vince popped the end of the umbrella handle as hard he could, driving the metal shaft through the skin and into the trachea. Blood poured where only air belongs through the impaled windpipe. The driver instinctively clutched at his throat as he slid to the ground. Vince withdrew the brolly as the man choked on his dying breaths. Stepping to the side, Vince flung the sliding door open. In the van's interior, the man he saw on the street held Carolyn in a headlock with a pistol pointing at her head.

Vince recognized the man--Pierre LeBeau. He was an operator for Crepusculous. Vince first met Pierre when David Diegert was at the headquarters training facility in Romania. Pierre was the only guy there to show Diegert any friendship. That friendship though was sorely betrayed when Pierre appeared in the elevator that served the penthouse at the Ambassador Hotel. Diegert possessed the single source device for detonating a dozen thermobaric bombs within the United States and was escaping with his mother. The sight of his only friend caused Diegert to hesitate, allowing Pierre to fire a taser, electrocuting Diegert, and taking him and his mother hostage. Pierre's betrayal enraged Diegert, and now the traitor was kidnapping Carolyn. Pierre and Vince had never met, but the operator recognized Panzer's newfound son.

In his French accent, Pierre shouted, "What the fuck are you doing? You are way out of line. We are carrying out orders. If you were anyone else," he raised his pistol pointing it at Vince, "you'd be a dead man."

Carolyn let out an astonished groan as, from under her skirt, an unexpectedly large volume of fluid fell to the floor. Pierre looked down in disgust. Vince swung the umbrella, knocking the gun out of the Frenchman's hand. The pistol hit the floor, sliding under the driver's seat. As

Vince stepped into the van, he shoved Carolyn to the side thrusting her into the console between the seats. The amniotic fluid was surprisingly viscous causing both men's feet to slide on the slippery steel. Pierre swung a fist, destabilizing himself and falling to the floor. Vince bent his right knee and dropped it into Pierre's abdomen. From his kneeling position, Vince punched Pierre viciously, bloodying his nose and gashing an eyebrow. Pierre scissor kicked his legs, raising his left up to strike Vince in the face with the heel of his boot. Taking the strike on the chin, Vince fell back, into the puddle of amniotic fluid. Pierre looked to see the emergency jack strapped to the side of the van. Above the jack, held by a pressure clip, was an 18-inch tire iron. Snatching it, he instantly swung it at Vince who lifted his head just in time to see the iron coming. Raising his umbrella, he deflected the blow, entangling the iron in the black fabric. Pierre drew back, ripping the umbrella from Vince's hand. Vince rolled as Pierre cleared the umbrella fabric and swung back through with the iron. The metal truncheon dented the sidewall of the van as it narrowly missed Vince.

Carolyn saw the pressure clip from which Pierre had taken the tire iron. It was a thin, rigid piece of metal firmly adhered perpendicularly to the wall. She backed over to the clip and placed the flexicuffs upon the metal edge, exerting as much force as she could. The binds tightened around her wrists, but she ignored the pain as she continued to pull on the cuffs. She slid the plastic strictures back and forth, feeling them weaken. As the men continued fighting, she struggled to get her hands free. Abrading the plastic on the metal edge produced enough fatigue to snap the cuffs. Carolyn pulled her hands in front of her as her binds broke. Ripping the duct tape off her mouth hurt like hell, but breathing deep felt so good. She reached under the driver's seat.

Pierre gathered himself as he rose to his feet. Vince scooched across the floor but not fast enough to stop Pierre from using the iron to bash him in the knee. Pouncing on Vince, Pierre straddled his body, choking him across the throat with the tire iron. Vince struggled to get out from under the bar while Pierre put all his weight on the shaft of steel. Unable to breathe, Vince kicked his legs as he tried to roll and struggled to press the bar off his throat. Each effort was less effective as his strength began to seep away. With his hands falling involuntarily to his sides, more and more molecules of carbon dioxide poisoned his system.

"Get off of him," shouted Carolyn pointing the pistol at Pierre. With a snarl Pierre only pressed down harder.

"I'll shoot you," threatened Carolyn.

Pierre said nothing as he held her gaze and continued to choke out the life of Vince Kronig.

Carolyn's eyes shifted to look at Vince. Pierre seized the moment, swinging his left hand, knocking the gun out of her grasp and onto the pavement outside the van.

His return swing slapped her across the face. "You stupid bitch," he shouted, "You're too weak to shoot anybody."

The reduction of pressure was all Vince needed to draw a breath. He swung his fist as he rolled his body. The punch caught Pierre in the ear with a painful sting. Vince's second strike hit Pierre's jaw hard, torquing his head as his teeth clashed. Pierre jabbed the tapered end of the iron into Vince's abdomen nearly piercing the skin. He then swung the hardened steel bar clobbering Vince in the temple. The strike sent Vince's right side into an acute neurologic paralysis. He fell to the floor with half of his body in a spastic state.

Carolyn squirmed over to the van's open side door and dropped outside on to the ground.

Pierre, his face contorted and his ear ringing, looked down on the disoriented man who had lost control of half his body. He knelt next to him and raised the tire iron over his head. Vince lifted his left arm in an anemic attempt to protect himself.

Explosions amplified in the steel walled interior of the van, as one, two, three gunshots sent bullets into Pierre's torso. The propulsive force knocked Pierre off Vince, plastering him against the closed door of the opposite side of the van. Blood splattered and Pierre groaned as air sucked into his thorax through the wounds.

Vince, with his right side still in acute paralysis, crawled over to the duplicitous Frenchman. "You betrayed me in the Ambassador Hotel."

Pierre's face broke into a look of shocked surprise. He questioned this confusing message as his life exsanguinated from his chest.

"You injected me with a sedative. You see me now with a different face, but you know who I am."

"Diegert?" croaked Pierre.

With his left hand, Vince clutched Pierre's throat with crushing force. He squeezed on the windpipe hastening the inevitable for the fatally wounded man. As he watched the light leave Pierre's eyes he said, "My name is the last word you will ever speak." All the tension drained from Pierre's body as Vince loosened his grip letting the lifeless corpse crumple to the floor.

Looking through the open side door of the van, Vince saw Carolyn gasping. She still held the gun and looked at Vince with the strangest expression. He realized she overheard the exchange with Pierre and she probably wanted an explanation, but right now, she was in labor.

With only half his body at full strength, Vince struggled to lift the driver's body into the van. Both dead bodies lay in the cargo space as Vince closed the doors. While his extremities regained function, Vince put Carolyn in the passenger seat of his heavily damaged, but still operating Porsche. Back on the M4, they sped toward the West Middlesex University Hospital.

"Who are you?" demanded Carolyn.

"I'm the guy who just saved your life and you're the girl who just shot a man to death. I'd say that makes us two sides of equal."

"You knew that man, how? What did you mean when you said, you're seeing me with a different face, but you know who I am?"

"I wanted him to remember me."

"He called you Diegert. Are you David Diegert?"

The problem with being honest and trustworthy as Vince, was telling the truth.

"How could you change your face?" she asked.

He sighed, took in another breath realizing that an honest answer to her question would change everything. She however was someone who helped him recognize the good within himself. She was special to him and he owed her an honest answer. She was also carrying his child. He sighed a second time. "Wireless nanocytes."

"So Vince Kronig is David Diegert."

He nodded his head.

"What about the guy who got blown up?"

"Nanocytes changed that guy's face to mine and then they blew him up for everybody to see."

"So now, anybody's face can be changed?"

"Crepusculous is keeping a very tight lid on this technology. But if they want you to have a new face then you will."

"All that discussion we just had about David Diegert, was rather facetious since you are him."

Shrugging his shoulders, he said, "Yeah, I guess so."

Carolyn's face suddenly became even more tense as she clutched her abdomen.

"Are you okay?" he asked.

"It's a contraction, not too bad, but this baby… your baby, is coming out."

"You said it wasn't mine."

"Did you believe me?"

"No."

"Do you want this baby? Are you ready to be a good father?"

The questions were basic, the kind to which one should have given preemptive thought, and been ready to answer, but Diegert had not done that. He swerved the car around a slow moving van and pulled back into the lane.

"I don't want this child to grow up without his father like I did."

"Wanting to prevent your child from growing up as a bastard is not the same as taking the responsibility to be a good parent."

She used the word bastard. He hated that word and he hated being that word. He did not want his child to be a bastard. He cast a stern glance at her.

"Aah-yeeh!" screeched Carolyn as a much more powerful contraction gripped her uterus. She threw her head back, clutched the armrest of the door with her left hand, as her right grabbed Vince's arm. The car swerved to the left. Vince had to fight the strength in her arm to keep the car in the lane. The exit for the hospital was two kilometers away. It looked to Vince like the baby was going to come out and fall into the wheel well. A few moments later Carolyn's breathing slowed, she released his arm, looked at him and said, "Hurry."

"Hang tough, we're almost there."

"This is really not the way I wanted to start a family. You've screwed up my whole life, and this baby will remind me of that every day."

Vince took the exit, squealing his tires as he accelerated through the streets to the hospital's emergency entrance.

Bounding from the car, Vince shouted, "Help, Help, this woman's in labor."

People in blue scrubs pushed through the double doors, quickly loading Carolyn onto a gurney.

As she was rolled away she yelled, "You did this to me."

Vince stood outside slowly shaking his head. Before he could be asked questions by the hospital staff, he returned to his car and sped away.

CHAPTER 34

IT WAS ALMOST NOON. VINCE WAS beat up, speckled with blood and was definitely going to be late for lunch with Julie and Dean Kellerman. He needed new clothes. It seemed almost too American, but just ahead was a shopping plaza with a TJ Maxx. In the store, he washed up in the men's room, found a pair of khaki pants and a navy blue polo shirt. He changed in the fitting room. As he exited, he was met by a security guard.

"Excuse me, sir," said the muscular young man in a light blue uniform. The badge on his chest read: TJ Maxx Security, Jacob. "You were reported to be covered in blood."

"Yes, there was a traffic accident, with injuries. I'm an EMT, off duty, so I stopped and helped. Now I'm late for a date and I have to get going."

The young man looked at him, seemingly assessing his story for authenticity.

Vince continued, "I don't believe I've violated store policy."

"No... no sir you haven't. I just wanted to make sure you were okay."

"Thank you. Yes, I'm fine."

He paid for his new clothes, stuffed his old clothes in a plastic shopping bag and headed out to his car. As he approached the battered Porsche, he pulled out his phone to call Julie.

"Hey, where are you?" she asked.

"Sorry, I'm going to be late. I was in a car accident."

"What? Are you okay?"

"Yeah, yeah, I'm fine, but my car is really beat up. A van pulled into my lane, chewed up the front end and bashed in the passenger door. The guy said he didn't see me as he changed lanes."

"But you're okay? Do you have to go to the hospital or see a doctor?"

"No... no I'm fine, just running a little late. Is your father there?"

"Yes. We're here. How long will it take you?"

"About fifteen minutes."

"Oh... okay, then we'll see you soon."

"Yes. Thanks, I'm looking forward to it."

This lunch was especially important to Julie. She wanted her father to meet Vince in a place where they could get to know each other without interruption. She knew her father harbored some suspicion about Klaus Panzer suddenly having two sons. To then have his daughter dating one was unsettling. Julie felt if her father got to know Vince, he would like him. She also wanted to discuss her concerns about Michael. She wanted Vince to be there. She needed his support and wanted him to corroborate her story. Dean Kellerman turned a blind eye and deaf ear to Michael's drug problems. She would need resolve to hold her convictions with him. Vince knew he had to be there for her.

The Petersham Restaurant was within the hotel of the same name. Tucked in a sylvan enclave on Nightingale Lane, the establishment's long and distinguished history of serving London's most well to do patrons made it a favorite place for Dean Kellerman to enjoy lunch. The dining room offered a charmingly bucolic view of the River Thames, despite its convenient location in Richmond. Cars were parked by a crew of valets. Vince smiled when he saw the look of trepidation on the young man who approached his car. Tossing the keys as he stepped out, Vince said, "I don't want any scratches on this car." Vince held a deadpan look as long as he could before cracking a smile as he turned and walked into the building.

His smile broadened, in spite of the split on his lower lip, as he entered the dining room to see Julie sitting with her dad. Crossing the room toward them, he was surprised when Julie jumped out of her seat and scampered over to him. Dean was also taken aback by her abrupt move.

Julie rushed to embrace him, kissing him fully on the lips. The sudden public display of affection attracted several pairs of dining room eyes. Vince eagerly received the kiss but winced as the pressure mounted.

"Hey, you said you were okay," blurted Julie as she pulled back, inspecting his injuries. "Look at your head and your lip." Grabbing his arms she continued, "Where else are you hurt?"

"Stop it," said Vince with a smile. "I just banged my head as the car was jostled about. I'm fine."

He took her hand as they approached the table.

Dean Kellerman rose from his seat as the couple drew near. His full head of silver gray hair was parted from the right and combed into a classic wave of Anglo handsomeness. At just six feet tall, Mr. Kellerman projected good health even if his athletic days were well in the past. His tailored suit was impressive as it fell into place on his upright frame. He extended his hand to Vince, who had to relinquish holding Julie's in order to accept the meeting of the palms.

"It's a pleasure to see you again," said Kellerman. "We didn't get much of a chance to talk at your party."

"The pleasure is mine, sir, and I appreciate the opportunity to have lunch with you."

All three sat down. Julie wasted no time returning to her inquiry about the car accident. "What highway were you on?"

"The M4."

"The guy just turned into your lane?" she asked incredulously.

"My car is small and low, but it sure surprised me when he just kept coming over and pretty soon his wheels were knocking the hell out of my car. I beeped the horn and he finally realized, but not before significant damage was done."

"He did stop though?"

"Yeah. We had to wait for the cops to get it all sorted out. His insurance will have to look at the car to assess the damage. The damn thing still runs. The valet was sure surprised when I tossed him the keys," said Vince with a chuckle. Smiles, all around the table.

"You're okay though? You're not hurt?"

"Yes, I'm fine," insisted Vince as he reached over, placing his hand on Julie's forearm. She immediately put her hand over his as she gazed into his eyes. Dean Kellerman's eyebrows raised at the gushing emotions of his daughter. It was easy to see that she was head over heels about this guy.

"Do you think the car can be repaired?" asked the elder member of the group.

Turning from Julie, Vince looked at Dean replying, "No, in spite of the fact it's still running, I think they'll total it."

"Your father may be upset. I understand he is quite particular about his collection."

"Yes, you're right, but this Porsche was not one of his true exotics."

Leaning forward, Kellerman said, "Forgive my forwardness, but how does it feel to learn that your long lost father is in fact one of the world's wealthiest men?"

Vince sat quietly as he let his response percolate. Julie and Dean remained quiet while the answer was assembled.

"The wealth and money are the least of my concerns. Growing up, the whole concept of a father was foreign to me. Some of the other kids I knew didn't have fathers. Their parents had divorced and dad didn't come around much, but he still existed. One kid lost his dad in an auto accident, but I just didn't have one. Never did and had no idea who he was."

"Your mother didn't tell you anything?"

"That's right. She was an extremely self-possessed woman. If she didn't want to talk about something, then no words would be said."

The waiter arrived to take their orders. Julie chose the cobb salad. Dean selected the filet mignon, a cut of beef described in the menu as, the world's most tender and delicious piece of meat. Vince ordered the beef as well.

As the waiter left, Kellerman continued his inquiry. "So how did we get here?"

"When my mother died, the lawyer she hired to be the executor of the will informed me that within the document was the identity of my father. My mother had placed his name in the will to be revealed to me upon her death."

Both of the Kellermans focused intently.

"When the name was revealed, I had no idea who he was. As you know, he keeps himself out of the spotlight.

Even having studied all the economics I had, he was never mentioned or put forth as a case study."

"Why did you choose to study economics?" asked Dean.

"My mom was always elusive about money. As a physician, she had a good income. We lived comfortably, not extravagantly, but we never went without. I just found the power of money fascinating. Seeing some of my classmates whose parents really struggled, showed me how different life is with insufficient funds. I could see its power and influence in the choices they had to make. Studying economics in high school gave me a name for my observations and taught me that the topic was much bigger than the struggles of my friends."

Julie interjected, "It's a fascinating topic."

"Yeah, one that most of us don't bother to understand."

"True," said Dean. "Most people confuse economics with finance and think it's only about money."

Smiling Vince jumped back in. "You're so right. Economics is as much about power as it is money. Money carries power, but it's limited. Economics seeks to understand the power that exists between people and amongst people as we all seek to insure access to vital resources. Money is not the only way to acquire what we need."

Folding his hands in front of him and closing his eyes, Dean sought his way to saying, "You see I find it quite curious that one who has such a perspective on power and money is now the son of one of the wealthiest men the world has ever known."

Vince and Julie looked to Kellerman seeking clarity in his statement.

"What do you mean, Dad?" asked Julie.

Kellerman shifted in his seat as he attempted clarification. "I... I mean out of all the possible areas of specialty one could develop, you, Vince, are an economist. While your new found father seeks to control the economy of the entire world."

Both of the young people sat quietly letting the gravity of Dean's words settle on the table.

As responses were being developed, lunch was served. The waiter set the meals in front of each diner. Julie's Cobb salad came in a huge bowl. It looked like enough salad to serve ten. Vince caught the wide-eyed reaction of his girlfriend.

The beef for each of the men's meals was served on a wooden cutting board, which accompanied their dinner plate. Nested in a cut out on the board was a steak knife with a six inch serrated blade fixed to a rigid wooden handle. The knife was honed to a fine point and razor sharp, the perfect tool to slice through beef as if it were butter.

"This looks lovely," said Dean, lightening the mood.

Vince picked up the knife, effortlessly slicing a piece of beef. Placing the morsel in his mouth, he enjoyed the most delicious and tender meat he had ever eaten.

The three diners were quiet for a few moments while they all enjoyed their food.

Dean restarted the conversation, "I don't mean to be accusatory or question your choice to study economics, it's just that I'm old enough to be suspicious of coincidences."

"Suspicious are you now?" replied Vince.

As he placed another piece of beef in his mouth Dean said, "Convince me it's just a coincidence."

Julie's attention turned to Vince. Her curiosity for Vince's explanation was as high as her father's. She was excited to hear more of Vince's life story.

David Diegert remained immersed in the role of Vince so the untrue story he was going to tell didn't feel like the lie that it was.

"My mother said to me, you learn money and you will understand power. She didn't realize how deeply that statement affected me. It was the unintended motivation to become an economist. The question my mother never did answer was, who is my father? She would say when the time is right you'll find out. It pissed me off that she knew and wouldn't tell me. At times, it would drive us apart but I always came back. She knew I would. I could not hold a grudge and she knew there was no one else who could fulfill her role. I'd get angry and distance myself for a while. She stayed just as busy as ever and waited until I returned, the disagreement never being mentioned." Addressing Dean, Vince asked, "What do you mean when you say my father wants to take over the economy of the world?"

Dean swallowed his beef, took a sip of water and said, "Digival is your father's idea. He wants a global corporate currency in spite of the tremendous risk. I do not fully agree with the actions he has taken. But by owning all the currency, he can control the economy. His plan is rather benevolent at first. He's lulling the masses into complacency, but I know your father very well. He will turn that money into pure power and the world's economy will be at the control of Crepusculous."

"But Dad, they're giving people more buying power, while also funding schools, daycare centers and old age homes." Julie's fork lifted lettuce, three types of fruit and tangy dressing into her eager mouth.

"That's deceptive charity," said Dean. "What they're

doing is getting people dependent on Digival. Getting them used to buying stuff with it. So that dollars, euros and yen all fade in their memory."

"What about paying the taxes?" asked Julie in spite of not yet swallowing.

"That's the same thing, only worse because it gives the currency credibility while undermining the government's own money."

Vince spoke into the void as Dean focused on slicing more beef. "It's really quite brilliant and exceptionally bold. Using the value and influence of Omnisphere to change the way the world uses money is unprecedented. I'm thrilled to be part of it and all my money is now Digival. How about you, Dean?"

Placing a fork full of meat back on the table, Dean said, "I am not all in."

Surprised, Vince said, "A board member and you're not committed?"

With a sense of resentment Kellerman replied, "Because I'm a board member I'm not putting everything into one basket. If this plan fails we'll be left with nothing."

"Except all the assets," quipped Vince.

"Yes, we will still have the assets, but we will not have the capitol to make the assets work," said Dean as he popped a piece of beef in his mouth.

"So you're holding on to pounds in case their worth returns. That seems hopeful?"

Chewing with force and hurrying to swallow, Dean looked like a hungry dog gobbling down a treat.

"Dad, did you tell the other members of the board about your hesitancy?" asked Julie.

Needing two swallows to down his mouthful, Dean recovered to say, "I am entitled to my own opinion in spite of what the board decides. I was the single dissenting vote, so the board is aware of my position. I have kept sums of money in current denominations. If they become worthless, it will not matter, but if Digival becomes worthless, I will be able to recover with this money. Can you see the economic sense in that Mr. Kronig?"

Smiling slowly, Vince nodded as he too sliced more beef.

Seeing an opportunity to change the subject Julie said, "Dad, I have something to tell you about Michael."

"Something good I hope," said the exasperated Kellerman.

Frowning, Julie continued, "Dad, Michael put me in danger." Seeing the doubtful reaction on her father's face, she continued. "He literally set me up so a group of men could have their way with me to pay off drug debts." Dean set his utensils down as he absorbed what his beautiful, intelligent daughter was saying. "I walked into a trap and those men would have hurt me if it weren't for Vince." She turned her gaze upon him, as did the elder Kellerman.

Vince nodded as he chewed.

Tears welled up in her eyes and ran down her cheeks. She dabbed them with a napkin.

"He betrayed me, Dad." Her words came out as an accusation mixed with a stifled sob. "He cannot be trusted. He only cares about drugs. He will use people so he can keep getting drugs." She wiped fresh tears with the napkin. "I'm sorry."

"That's okay, darling," said Dean. "Were you hurt by these men?"

Nodding her head she said, "Yes, but it would have been way worse except Vince was there."

"How many men?"

"Four," said Julie as she extended the fingers of her right hand.

"You were rescued from four attackers by an economist?"

"Vince has some mad skills."

"What is the status of these men now?"

She answered, "Severely damaged and deceased."

Spinning his head to look at Vince, Dean asked, "You killed them?"

Swallowing, Vince responded, "Three. One was left to take the blame."

Dean leaned back in his chair as he fixed his gaze on the young man. It was as if he was taking in a broader view of an expanding vista. There was a lot more to this guy than just economics.

"Who were these men?" asked Dean, now much more curious about details.

Vince and Julie looked at each other. Julie took the lead. "They were scumbags. Drug dealers preying on the addicted. Assholes who were willing to accept as payment a woman to be raped."

Vince shifted his eyes to Dean. "They were armed, experienced and unwilling to negotiate."

"Vince took them out like a badass," complimented Julie. "He was ferocious."

With both of them looking at him, Vince shrugged. "I don't like to see innocent people getting hurt."

Gazing beyond the Kellermans, Vince noticed a black man at the hostess podium. The man was fashionably dressed in a black and gray sashed tunic. Over his lower body he wore draping panels of dark cloth front and back. Avery Forsythe spoke to the hostess as he scanned the room. Within seconds, he had found them. Vince picked up on his reaction. Avery was surprised to see him dining with Dean and Julie Kellerman.

Julie inhaled deeply, straightened her spine and said, "I have told Michael, in no uncertain terms, that I will not have anything more to do with him. I want him out of my life."

Dean's mouth fell open as he absorbed the words. He was visibly struggling to find a response. "I... I'm so sorry you had this terrible experience, but I can't have my family fall apart."

"Dad, I'm sorry but he can't be trusted. I have to be careful because he's dangerous. He's already demonstrated that he's willing to hurt me and I can't let myself get in that situation again."

"Of course my dear, your safety is paramount, but can't we remain a family?"

At the hostess podium, Avery was now flanked by Tiberius Dupre' and Fiera Zeidler. Tiberius towered above Avery while Fiera searched the room with her eyes, spotting Vince on her first pass.

"I don't know, Dad. Time will tell if that guy can change. I've spent years trying to help him overcome his addiction and what did it get me? Pimped out like a whore to be raped by his dealers. Repairing this relationship is his job, not mine."

With the eyes of Cerberus upon him, Vince saw Avery lean over and speak to Tiberius.

Shaking his head Dean said, "You know he doesn't have the capacity to fix things."

"Yes I do, that's why I'm done with him. If he doesn't acknowledge what he did and make amends for the absolute disregard with which he treated me, then fuck him. I don't want anything to do with him."

Such angry language disturbed the paternal Kellerman, but he recognized Julie was right. Michael never acknowledged any of the damage in his wake. The many times he had embarrassed everyone and insulted people, he never apologized in the sober morning. He was oblivious to other people's feelings and blind to the consequences of his outrageous behavior. Julie had every right to hold him accountable and Dean knew that meant this issue would never be properly resolved. Set up to be raped! He truly had no scruples.

Avery leaned over with words for Fiera's ears as well. Both of Avery's operators exited the lobby as Avery stepped back from the podium into the shadows of the atrium.

"Darling, you know he and I already have a strained relationship. Without you, he will have no one from the family to care for him."

"I do know that, Dad. And that's why I'm letting you know because the next time he's in trouble he will be on his own. I do not believe he will survive."

Dean snapped. "Will not survive?"

"You may not have noticed, but Michael overdoses on a regular basis. I have reversed his toxicity so many times. He would have been dead years ago if I hadn't learned how to do an emergency detox."

Looking down at his plate and placing his forehead in his hands Dean gasped, "My God."

"I want you to know that we will soon be rid of Michael as a result of his own actions."

Vince peered around the dining room and gazed out the windows. Outside the entrance, he could see Tiberius, dressed in combat black, standing as a sentinel.

Dean Kellerman looked distraught. He was unable to

say anything more and Vince felt like the man was missing his wife right now. It was the type of moment when one feels the loss of those whose deaths occurred far too early.

As the waiter came to clear the plates, Vince placed the steak knife in his lap and wrapped it up in the black cloth napkin. He clandestinely slipped the blade into his pocket.

"Would anyone care for dessert?" asked the waiter.

Julie shook her head.

"No thank you," said Vince.

"We'll take the check now please," said Dean before turning to Vince with a smile. "It was a pleasure to dine with you, young man. Knowing your father as I do, I dare say there is quite a bit of him in you. I can see that you and my daughter are quite fond of each other and I hope your friendship grows." The elder man's smile faded as he continued, "We've had a difficult conversation at the table today, but I'm grateful you were able to spare Julie from harm. I hope that I can trust that you are not the sort of man who gossips the gory details of family tragedies."

"I am not," said Vince.

The waiter returned with the check. Dean did not read the small document, nor produce a credit card, nor calculate a gratuity. He just scrawled his signature. The waiter bowed and walked away.

"Thank you," said Dean. "I look forward to seeing you in the company of Julie again." Addressing his daughter he said, "Are you coming with me darling?"

Julie looked at Vince, who said, "You better go with him. I have to deal with my car, and it may be a while. I'll call you tonight."

"Tonight?"

Shrugging, Vince said, "Yeah, I'm sorry. I just don't know how long it will take to straighten out the mess."

Pulling out his phone he said, "I have to make a call before I go."

"Okay."

She leaned over and convincingly kissed Vince on the lips. Dean Kellerman stood impatiently, watching.

Julie rose from the table, took her father's arm and said, "Let's go, Dad."

As they exited the dining area, Vince placed a call to the parking valet. "Yes, this is Vince Kronig, I would like my vehicle brought to the front entrance please... Yes, that's the one. The heavily damaged Porsche. Thank you."

Hanging up, Vince wanted to make sure Julie and her father were not being harassed by Avery and his operators. He was confident that Panzer's Director of Clandestine Operations would not take action against Dean Kellerman. His concerns, however, did not disappear until, through the lobby, he saw Kellerman's Rolls Royce pull away with Julie comfortably in the back seat.

Entering the lobby, Vince felt the movement from the left as Fiera fell in behind him, placing the barrel of a pistol into the small of his back. Before she could speak, Vince said, "Fiera, I so enjoyed target practice with you when you told me that sexual seduction was your best weapon."

Vince spun to the right, grabbing her gun and disarming her with expertly placed torque upon her wrist. He continued spinning, striking her in the jaw with the heel of his left palm. The force snapped her neck, disorienting her. He pushed her into the coatroom where he encircled her neck in the elbow of his right arm, collapsing her airway. With his hand on the back of her head, he forcefully flexed her neck as he knelt to the floor. The maneuver compressed the pons of her midbrain, depressing her respiration, producing a rapid loss of consciousness.

The sleeper hold had done its job and Fiera lay on the floor an inert, but living mass. Vince pocketed her pistol.

Stepping outside the restaurant door, Vince approached Tiberius. "Hey, it's good to see the Nigerian Prince again." The statement distracted the big man long enough for Vince to sweep his left arm in a forward arc, catching both arms of his adversary and turning the Cerberus operator's torso to the left. Extracting the steak knife from his pocket, still wrapped in the napkin, Vince raised his right hand and plunged the knife into Tiberius's left shoulder. The blade entered the muscle above and behind the collarbone. Releasing the handle, Vince struck it with enough force to drive the blade through the scapula, fracturing the shoulder blade. Stepping back to avoid the blood as it sprayed a fan of crimson on the hotel's granite exterior, Vince struck Tiberius with three powerful punches to the head, dropping him in a heap onto the old stone walkway.

Hotel guests, restaurant patrons and the young men of the valet staff gasped at the violence. Vince looked to his left into the calm, soulful eyes of Avery Forsythe, as he slowly and deliberately emerged from the shadows. His facial features and childlike eyes of wonder belied the ruthlessness of the man. Vince knew this, but looking into the man's eyes produced a calming, soothing sensation no matter the circumstances.

"Where is Carolyn Fuller?" asked Avery.

"You know I'm not going to tell you."

"It is my mission to find her."

"I don't care. I'm not helping you." Patting his left pocket Vince said, "I have Fiera's weapon. Don't make me shoot you."

Avery could see the outline of the pistol and the end of the grip at the opening of the pocket.

As the two stared each other down, the valet delivered Vince's beat up Porsche.

Stepping to his roadway menace, Vince said, "You can tell Klaus that there is no fucking way I'm letting him hurt her." Vince gave the valet a ten-pound note. Pulling the pistol from his pocket, he placed it on the passenger's seat. Gunning the engine and lurching up onto the walkway, Vince stopped the vehicle inches from Avery's feet. "You tell my father she is off limits. If he has a problem with that, he is to speak directly to me." Vince let a sardonic smile cross his face as he said, "Tell him he's experiencing the love of his son."

In spite of its dilapidated condition, the Porsche left a patch of rubber as it peeled off the walkway, accelerating down Nightingale Lane.

Avery gathered Tiberius and Fiera as he departed the restaurant.

Vince sped to the M4. It was a little before 2:00 p.m. and he needed to get to Heathrow before 4:00 p.m. From Richmond to Heathrow was about forty miles, but with London traffic the trip would take over two hours. Even with a Porsche 918 Spyder, this highway provided no options for a faster, shorter trip. At 3:54 p.m., Vince left his car in a long-term lot and made his way to Delta arrivals. At the service counter, he borrowed the handheld whiteboard, placing the honorifics and name, **Dr. & Mrs. Fuller** in big bold black letters. Standing by the exit of the gate, he looked for a couple who appeared bewildered, anxious and confused. It surprised him how many people looked that way before a well-dressed, gray-haired couple approached him.

"Hello there, we're the Fullers." The man offered his hand. "I'm Dr. Marty Fuller and this is my wife Laurie."

"It is a pleasure to meet you," said Vince as he shook hands with both of them. Smiles were also exchanged but soon faded when the obvious became unavoidable. Vince said, "Carolyn was involved in an accident and is in the hospital."

Her parents gasped. Laurie clutched Marty, who struggled to support her.

"She's all right," said Vince. "She's stable and being watched and I will take you to her now. Please sit here."

Vince directed them to a large upholstered bench against the wall.

With all three of them seated, it appeared to Vince that Laurie was especially hard hit by the news. She asked, "Is she all right? What happened to her? What kind of an accident?" Marty's look pleaded for answers to his wife's questions.

"I can't answer all your questions, but I can tell you, she was in an automobile accident on the motorway. Her injuries have been stabilized and she's no longer in the ICU. We'll get more information as soon as we get to the hospital."

"Injuries! What type of injuries? How badly is she hurt?" insisted Laurie. "I've been trying to reach her since before we got on our flight. It's unusual for her not to respond. She knew we were coming. How long has she been hospitalized?"

"The accident happened earlier today. With the time change, it would explain her lack of communication."

Laurie was growing distraught and getting angry. Marty tried to calm her, but Vince knew they had to get going.

"I'm very sorry that you've landed here and received this bad news, but I suggest we collect your luggage and get on the tube as we have a bit of a journey to the hospital."

It was difficult for them to concentrate on practical matters, but Vince's words made sense. He reassured them. "I will escort you all the way to the hospital."

They collected their luggage and wheeled the bags over to the tube station to board the train to London. Vince explained that the surface roads were the slowest of all choices while the train was not only faster but also cheaper. He told them he had met Carolyn in a pub on beginner's darts night. They had a lovely conversation about American politics and she told him she was working as a publicist for an American computer-consulting firm called Datathink.

Vince could see Laurie and Marty smiling wanly as they realized their daughter lied to people about her job with the CIA.

"Does she have a nice apartment?" asked Laurie.

"I… I don't know," said Vince. "I've never been there. It's a good address. It's in a nice neighborhood, but I've never visited."

Laurie looked at him admiringly. He was so handsome, but she was also suspicious. She strained to make sense of things. It was difficult to piece together her daughter's life from the information this young man was providing. Marty had grown sullen, enduring the train ride in silence, obviously anxious to get to his daughter.

Vince sought to ease their concerns. "It won't be too much longer. We have to make one exchange and then we'll take a bus that stops at her hospital."

They both nodded, no longer interested in conversation.

AVERY RETURNED TO THE LPU UNDERGROUND. Tiberius

went to medical--his wounded shoulder needed immediate attention. In spite of the blood loss, Avery was relieved that Diegert spared the actual shoulder joint and drove his blade above the collarbone rather than below it, where it would have severed major arteries. It was the GPS in the Porsche Vince had been driving that allowed Avery to locate him. Checking the signal now identified the car in a garage at Heathrow airport. Recovered from Vince's chokehold, Fiera hacked into the CCTV of Heathrow and searched the backlog of video.

Avery was deep in thought, contemplating where Diegert would want to go. To where would he be flying? Fiera scanned video of gates for departing flights. Without a clue as to a possible destination, it was slow going. Men Diegert's size and build were plentiful Realizing he would have had enough time to change his face, Avery recognized they might never find him.

Growing bored with the fruitless search, Fiera asked, "What if it's just a ruse and he parked his car there to throw us off?"

"He could have taken a cab or a train back to the city," thought Avery aloud.

"I'm on it. I'll review videos of the tube entrances and the cab stations."

VINCE TOLD THE FULLERS THEY'D BE exchanging at the next stop. He stood holding the handle of the largest rolling bag. When the train came to a stop and the doors opened, he and Dr. and Mrs. Fuller exited. They crossed the platform. Vince reviewed the map posted on a kiosk, confirming that the M train would get them to the West Middlesex University Hospital.

"The M train will be here in four minutes. It will take us to the Boston Manor station, which is close to the hospital. It's just a short bus ride from there," explained Vince.

Laurie looked up at him, nodded her understanding before asking, "Are you Carolyn's boyfriend?"

Chuckling, Vince awkwardly replied, "No... not exactly. Not in the traditional romantic sense. We're friends and I'm quite fond of her, but boyfriend/girlfriend would not accurately describe our status."

"Young people these days make everything so complicated," she said looking from Vince to her husband.

Dr. Fuller was intently listening to the conversation before adding, "Well we greatly appreciate you meeting us and helping us navigate the tube."

Laurie looked on, but the suspicious nature of her gaze only grew more intense.

When the M train arrived, they boarded with their luggage and found seats.

"I THINK I GOT SOMETHING," SAID FIERA.

Avery peered over her shoulder at the video image. Fiera zoomed in and they both recognized the face of Vince Kronig.

"That's him," acknowledged Avery. "But wait. Is he toting a rolling bag?"

Fiera played the video in which Vince was pulling a large rolling luggage bag. He stopped at the train's door to usher in an older couple before entering behind them. Was he just being polite or did he meet this couple at the airport?

Avery and Fiera looked at each other. The mystic

mentor spoke. "He met those people at the airport."

Giving voice to her thoughts Fiera said, "Who are they and where would they be going?"

"Where does the train go?"

Fiera rolled her eyes. "The train from Heathrow goes to Piccadilly, but it can connect with other trains along the way and goes everywhere."

"Review Diegert's GPS from the car, look for locations where the signal was stable. Perhaps he is returning someplace," ordered Avery.

ARRIVING IN BOSTON MANOR STATION, Vince and the Fullers exited the train and ascended to the street. They hopped on a London Bus for the short remaining portion of the trip "West Middlesex University Hospital is just a few blocks away," said Vince. Marty and Laurie looked around as the bus moved through traffic. It was fifteen years ago that they were last in London. They had never visited this part of the city. It was not a tourist area. At the moment tourism was not on their minds. Seeing their daughter and being assured she was okay was their only concern.

The bus dropped them right in front of the hospital. Entering the lobby, the trio approached the front desk. Vince did not need to represent them. Laurie stepped right up to the counter. "We're here to see our daughter who was admitted through the emergency department. She was involved in an auto accident."

"Certainly, ma'am, I can help you. What is her name?" asked the pleasant, polite and plump receptionist with her Indian influenced British accent.

"Carolyn Fuller."

Tapping on her keyboard, the receptionist focused on her screen. "Okay," she said, "Carolyn is on the third floor, room 3157 in the obstetrics department. Please show me some identification."

Laurie and Marty each produced their passports. While the young lady examined the booklets, Laurie sought clarification. "Did you say the obstetrics department?"

"Yes," said the dark-eyed young lady, smiling as she returned the passports. "Take the elevators just down the hall. Her room is on the west side of the building."

Laurie stepped back, looked at Marty and then glared at Vince. She turned back to the lady at the desk. "Thank you," she said.

Vince swallowed hard as he grabbed the luggage handle and made his way to the elevator. Inside the cabin, on the way to the third floor, Laurie said to Marty, "Do you think it's because of overcrowding that they would put a trauma patient in obstetrics?" Marty just frowned and shrugged.

At the door to room 3157, Vince gathered the luggage and stood to the side. He was going to remain in the hallway, allowing the Fullers an unencumbered family reunion.

AFTER REVIEWING RECENT HISTORY OF DIEGERT'S GPS, Fiera told Avery, "There are two stable locations before the restaurant. The first is the service area off the M4 where the van was found, the second is West Middlesex University Hospital."

"What train will take you to the hospital?"

Switching her screen to a map of the tube system, Fiera deduced that from Heathrow, the M train to Boston Manor station was just a short bus ride from the hospital.

"The M train would get you there." She immediately

began searching the CCTV from the Boston Manor station. Avery followed her actions on the screens. "There they are," she exclaimed. "This was only about fifteen minutes ago."

Avery's face looked even more contemplative than it usually did. "Excellent work, Fiera. I've got to put together some tactical gear, gather some additional personnel and we are then going to the hospital."

LAURIE AND MARTY FULLER ENTERED ROOM 3157 to see their daughter Carolyn standing by the window of the room. Carolyn looked out over a courtyard that was within the hospital's grounds. Picnic tables, benches and manicured shrubbery made it a comfortable and quiet place to enjoy the outdoors.

"Honey," said Laurie Fuller.

Carolyn, hearing her mother's voice, turned from the window creating a profile, which displayed an extremely protruding abdomen. Her eyes grew as big as CD's and they all saw the shock in one another.

Laurie gasped, drawing her hand to her mouth as she fell back into Marty's unstable frame. The parental couple quavered as Carolyn stood by the window, motionless and temporarily speechless.

After several convulsive breaths and silence well beyond awkward, Carolyn broke. "I can see you are surprised, but so am I that you are here."

Laurie squeaked, "You knew we were coming."

"Yes, Mom, I knew you were coming, but I just didn't expect to see you here."

Marty blurted, "You never told us you were pregnant."

"I know… I know, it's awkward and complicated--"

Her words cut short by a contraction clutching her uterus. Carolyn stepped to the bed and sat on the edge as the pressure on her womb increased. The pain halted the conversation and Laurie moved to Carolyn's side, her maternal instincts overpowering her shock and dismay. Laurie lifted Carolyn's legs and set the pillows so she was now lying on the bed. The contraction lasted about forty-five seconds. Carolyn said, "They're getting longer and more frequent."

Her mother tried her best, but the tears fell from her eyes as she laid her head on her daughter's forearm and wept. Marty moved behind his wife placing a hand on her shoulder. He looked at his little girl, now lying in labor, about to give birth to a child he had no idea was even on its way. What had happened to so egregiously break down basic family communication?

The strain and bewilderment on her father's usually kind, warm face made Carolyn feel ashamed. She was embarrassed and forlorn. She was confused and so greatly disappointed in herself. She and her parents were going to have to work through this and hopefully come out as a proud parent and happy grandparents, but right now that seemed a long way off.

Laurie gathered herself, stood up and wiped her face with a tissue as she straightened her spine. "Young lady, you've got a lot of explaining to do and I have a lot of questions, but right now I have to get something off my chest." Gesturing to Marty she went on, "For your father and me, I must say we are shocked and disappointed that you did not tell us you were pregnant. We would have been much better prepared had we known." Laurie paused to let that sink in. Carolyn looked right at her just as she had been taught when being admonished as a naughty child. Laurie let Carolyn dangle on the line as she towered above her. "The other thing that I must ask is, who is the father?"

Now Carolyn really hated Diegert and the position in which he placed her. How could she tell her parents that the father was an assassin who killed the president and then died while carrying out one of the worst acts on terrorism in the modern age, only to come back to life with a different face? No, she could not tell them that. Her back up plan would have to work. Richard Ramsey was dead. He was a jerk and a lout, the perfect kind of guy to have an illegitimate child.

Laurie walked to the door and dragged in Vince. Pointing at him, she asked, "Is this the father?"

Carolyn's eyes went to CD size again. She immediately knew how it was that her parents were there. A sense of gratitude for him meeting them at the airport quickly vanished as she realized the potential impact of answering her mother's question.

Looking at Vince, then to her mother and turning her gaze upon her father, Carolyn realized she could not delay her reply. She said, "No. No, he is not the father. Vince is a friend I met when I first came to London. He's a great guy and I'm very glad he helped me out by picking you up at the airport. Our friendship is not the kind that leads to pregnancy." Realizing how awkwardly she had concluded her statement, Carolyn closed her eyes and shook her head, but she was not going to bother restating anything.

Carolyn then said, "Vince, if you've got to go, I understand. Thanks so much for all your help."

Vince, realizing he was being dismissed, also recognized that he was being shut out of his child's life. Carolyn's statement forced him to be an outsider. A friend, but not a member of the family. He would one day have to overcome this lie if he was to fulfill the role of father to his child. Right now though, he was being dispatched with gratitude, but undoubtedly excluded from the arrival of his first-born child.

"Oh yeah, right, I gotta go. It was a pleasure to meet both of you," said Vince as he shook hands with Marty and Laurie. The suspicion in Carolyn's mother's eyes never left. She held his gaze as she clutched his hand longer than was customary.

At Carolyn's bedside he said, "I wish you all the best and I hope the delivery goes well."

She looked up at him with a tepid smile, which turned into a painful frown as, yet another contraction seized her abdomen. Stepping back to allow Laurie to be by her daughter's side, Vince headed for the door. At the threshold, he looked back. "Send me a text with the good news. I can't wait to hear if it's a boy or a girl."

CHAPTER 35

AVERY, FIERA AND THREE BEEFY members of an Omnisphere security team drove to West Middlesex University Hospital. Fiera parked the vehicle across the street. Watching people exiting the building, Avery realized if Diegert had changed his face, he could walk right by them. All eyes were eager to spot their quarry.

After ten minutes, Fiera exclaimed, "There he is," as she observed Vince exiting the hospital. He crossed the street in front of them, heading toward the bus station.

"Do we go get him boss?" asked the guy with the blond crew cut.

"No," said Avery holding up his hand. "Our mission lies within the hospital."

Vince skipped the bus, walking briskly to the Boston Manor station. On the tube, he called Julie. "Hey, how ya doing?"

The lady with the overstuffed shopping bag sitting across from him could only hear Vince's side of the brief conversation.

"Yeah, I'm fine. Are you at your apartment?"

"Great, I'll be there in about twenty minutes."

"Yeah, see you then."

As the train took him to Julie, Diegert thought about the dual roles he was playing. Not only spy and assassin, he was now torn between his new found feelings for Julie and the respect, admiration and affection he felt for Carolyn, the mother of his child. It hurt when she denied him to her parents. He understood the difficult position she was in, being an agent of the CIA, but that child needed a father, and he was going to be that man. He kind of wished the train ride could last forever and he wouldn't have to get off and choose. There was no way he wanted to relinquish either role and be just one person, with an exclusive life. He shook his head to clear his mind of crazy thoughts. The train came to a stop in Kensington station. Vince knew that Julie waited for him, in her home on the third floor of the Kellerman building.

The Omnisphere guard with the beard, Fiera and Avery all changed into royal blue medical scrubs. Fiera's hack of the hospital database informed them of Carolyn's location. Before exiting the van, Avery placed a call to the LPU ambulance directing them to arrive at the patient discharge area of the West Middlesex University Hospital. "We'll meet you there in ten minutes," he told the driver.

Looking like medical professionals, the three Crepusculous operators entered the hospital and took the elevator to the third floor. The bearded man went in search of a gurney. Avery and Fiera went to room 3157. From the pockets of their scrubs, they both produced small plastic pistols, loaded with hypodermic darts filled with a tranquilizing agent. The pistols used spring action to fire the darts. As they entered the room, Laurie Fuller turned to Avery to say, "Doctor, my daughter needs--" her words cut short by the drugs injected from the dart Fiera fired into her. Marty Fuller, shocked to see his wife fall, had been shot by Avery and it was only seconds before he joined her on the floor. Fiera moved to Carolyn's bedside, stifling her scream with a strong hand over her mouth. Avery injected a sedative in her IV line and, after a brief struggle, Fiera released Carolyn. The unconscious pregnant woman breathed rhythmically. The man with the beard arrived with a gurney. While he and Avery transferred Carolyn, Fiera went down the hall seeking the right room. She was looking for a woman whose labor was progressing and who was ready to deliver. In room 3132, she found a young Asian woman with a panicked expression. Her mother sat in a chair with traditional herbs and prayer flags. Fiera surveyed the scene, smiled politely, and pulled the code call button on the wall. Every nurse on the floor moved directly to room 3132. Avery, with Carolyn under a pale blue blanket, directed the gurney to the elevator. Fiera joined them as they waited. When the doors slid open, several doctors stepped out and hurried down the hall. Carolyn was rolled in and, during the descent, Avery received confirmation that the LPU ambulance was in place. On the ground floor, they rolled the patient to the discharge area. The door guard, anticipating the discharge paperwork, looked up from his desk with his hand outstretched. Avery smiled as he took the man's hand and held it tight. He pulled out his pistol and fired the dart down the man's short sleeve, impaling it in his armpit. The man's quizzical look faded as he slumped forward with the dart conveniently concealed in his axilla.

ARRIVING AT THE KELLERMAN BUILDING, Vince took the elevator to the third floor. Julie, dressed in black leggings and a baggy gray V neck t-shirt, stood by the door watching the lighted numbers progress. When the doors opened, she leaped upon Vince, hugging him and kissing him as if he had been away for a year. Vince, laughing and smiling, wrapped his arms around her, rejoicing in the love he had found.

"I'm so glad you're here," said Julie.

"Believe me I am so glad to be here with you," replied Vince.

Ignoring hunger, ignoring thirst, they indulged in erotic kisses, gradually shedding their clothes as they made their way through the apartment. On the giant bed, they made love with lustful abandon, deepening their bond and strengthening their love for one another.

ONCE CAROLYN WAS SECURELY LOADED, the ambulance pulled out from the hospital, entering traffic on its way to LPU.

Avery, spoke with Klaus Panzer on his phone. "Mission success, we are on route to LPU."

"Excellent," came Panzer's reply. "Please let me know when I can come see my grandso… I mean grandchild."

THE END

Thank you for Reading

Please post a review on Amazon, or the site of your choice. Your review will let the world know how you enjoyed this story.

A review needn't be long.
A sentence of two is sufficient.

I appreciate your time, effort and energy spent sharing your opinion with other readers.

Thank you.

Bill Brewer

ABOUT THE AUTHOR

Bill Brewer writes to engage his readers. Using imagination and research, he creates compelling characters whom he thrusts into dangerous situations. To thrill his readers, Bill sets a blistering pace and keeps the action coming as the plot explodes across the pages. The story reveals its secrets as the characters experience triumph, betrayal, victory, and loss. While you're reading, look for passages filled with anatomical details that this University Professor of Human Anatomy & Physiology uses to bring realism into his story.

When not teaching or writing, Bill can be found seeking adventure, peace and camaraderie, hiking, biking and paddling near his home in Rochester NY.

SOCIAL MEDIA

Please visit my website and subscribe for e-mail updates.

billbrewerbooks.com

Also, please follow me on

- Facebook: Bill Brewer Books
- Twitter: @Brewer Books
- Instagram: billbrewer434

THRILLEX Publishing

CPSIA information can be obtained
at www.ICGtesting.com
Printed in the USA
FSHW010510081220
76702FS

9 781734 507737